𝒜𝓊𝒹𝓇𝑒

AUL

Aul, Kelly
Audrey's sunrise

8/7/2018

D0283747

Audrey's Sunrise

Kelly Aul

Scripture quotations are from the King James Version of the Bible

Printed in the United States of America

ISBN   978-0615655437

Dress made by Matti's Millinery & Costumes

Making Your Costume Dreams Come True!

www.mattionline.com

BOOKS *by* KELLY AUL

NEVER FORSAKEN

1. Audrey's Sunrise
2. In the Midst of Darkness (Coming Soon!)

Special thanks to:

- ❖ My family, who answered my silly questions, and so patiently listened to me and all of my ideas. For always being supportive of everything I've done.

- ❖ To my mom, Maggie Aul, sister, Natalie Aul, and Hope Winrod, thank you so much for all your amazing help with editing and your endless advice.

- ❖ To my mom, thank you for writing the Salvation message at the end of this book. Your passion for preaching the good news is something I will never forget.

- ❖ To Natalie, for all those late night talks and for inspiring me to write in the first place.

- ❖ To my dad, Tom Aul, thank you for answering all my historical questions. I'm still in awe of how much you know!

- ❖ To Hannah and Matti Burkhardsmeier, thank you for graciously sharing your God-given talent on the cover. Your beautiful historical costumes and designs are breathtaking.

Also, thanks to:

- ❖ My two special editors, my brother, John Aul and Jacob Hagen who toiled with me day and night.

- ❖ To Leah Drexler and Sydney Martens, for all the support, and for never saying anything critical about the beginnings of this book.

I couldn't have done it without any of you. Most importantly, I give all the glory to my Heavenly Father.

I dedicate this book to my Heavenly Father.
Lord, You are my everything, my life and my length of days.
I give You all the glory and my heart's desire is that whoever
reads this, will see You.

O Lord, thou hast searched me, and known me. Thou knowest my downsitting and mine uprising, thou understandest my thought afar off. Thou compassest my path and my lying down, and art acquainted with all my ways. For there is not a word in my tongue, but, lo, O LORD, thou knowest it altogether. Thou hast beset me behind and before, and laid thine hand upon me...

Whither shall I go from thy spirit? or whither shall I flee from thy presence? If I ascend up into heaven, thou art there. If I take the wings of the morning, and dwell in the uttermost parts of the sea; Even there shall thy hand lead me, and thy right hand shall hold me.

Psalms 139:1-10

PROLOGUE

August 1820

One stormy night, several miles off the misty shores of Ireland, swells crashed against the sides of a large packet ship that rolled heavily over the fierce waves.

"Throw them overboard!" The Captain shouted through the thick salty wind.

"No...please! Me wife, she's in the family way. Leave her alone an' take me instead...wait, take this!" Evan Fintan earnestly replied. His pleading gaze was hardly noticed in the heavy rain that seemed to fall in sheets upon the deck. He then slowly opened his drenched jacket and pulled out a beautiful shell. Even in the darkness it shone like the sun when it became wet.

"No Evan...not that!" Rose, Evan's wife, cut in. Evan was about to surrender the shell to the heartless Captain when Rose threw herself between them to grab it. Unfortunately, she only made the shell slip from Evan's hands instead, and it shattered as it hit the sodden deck.

"No!" She cried, as her husband stood watching in horror at what had just taken place. Rose quickly dropped to her knees to pick up the broken pieces before a wave could wash them away.

"Lay, I said throw them overboard!" The commander ordered once again. A few of the able crewmen grabbed the couple and were about to throw them into the black depths when Evan started to struggle and cried out.

"God, save us...please save me wife!" The Captain didn't know what to think of the plea, but suddenly felt a small pang of something he'd never felt before.

"Sir! There's a ship a few miles west of us," the first mate called. "Though, they're not flying any colors...Captain?" He called again because he didn't think he had heard him through the wind.

"We'll give the woman to them," he finally sneered in return.

"But Sir, it would be impossible in this storm!" It was then that he sighed in frustration at the persistent sailor.

"Put her on a lifeboat, if she makes it to the other ship, fine, but if not, it's what they deserve. I will not have stowaways on my ship."

"Aye Captain," the man replied and left to heed his orders.

"Evan!" Rose screamed as she was torn from her husband and dragged to the small boat. She was then slowly lowered over the side of the ship. Evan tried to go after her, but two other men held him back. Through tear filled eyes, he suddenly noticed that he still held the scarlet red scarf Rose had been wearing. His grasp tightened the scarf until his knuckles were white as he fearfully watched his beloved wife being tossed by the violent waves, hoping against hope, she would make it safely to the other ship. When he couldn't see Rose through the tempest any longer, he was left with horrible questions that he was convinced would never be answered. Would his wife make it to the other vessel? Would he ever see her again or meet his unborn child?

CHAPTER ONE

March 1839

*D*ear Diary, today is my 18th birthday. I can scarcely believe it! Of all the birthdays I can recall, I received the most wonderful gifts this year. My grandparents gave me a black leather Bible. It's so small that I won't have to carry about the large family Bible anymore. And my mother gave me a beautiful bracelet made out of some sort of shell pieces the color of the sunset.

Rupert Gordon has asked me to accompany him to his family's spring ball next month. I hope Mother won't force me into going; I can hardly stand the Gordon's. They have a vast dislike toward anyone not of the same social standing. And Rupert's so very insufferable. I know it's wrong of me to say that, but I can't help it.

Audrianna Wesley, whom friends and family called Audrey, was sitting in her favorite spot in the large garden. It was located just behind Primrose, her grandparent's England home. Audrey loved to spend time there praying, reading the Bible, and writing in her diary.

"Miss! Your mum wants to see you," Lanna Ryan, Rose and Audrey's ladies maid called in her heavy Irish accent.

"Did she say why she needs me?" Audrey asked sounding disgusted.

"Well…." Lanna didn't have to finish, for Audrey could tell by the look on her face.

"I suppose she's going to make me attend Rupert's ball," she sighed.

"Why, I'm sure she just wants you to be happy." Lanna smiled and once again thought Audrey was particularly beautiful when she was angry. Her dainty nose would slightly wrinkle and her face took on a scarlet glow.

"Besides, Rupert is quite wealthy!" She continued sarcastically. Lanna and Audrey's relationship was far different from other ladies and their maids. But ever since Lanna had come to work for them nearly five years ago, they'd grown very close, although Audrey was three years her senior.

"Well, I better find out what my mother wants. At least if she has me go to the ball, you would most likely be my chaperon."

"But what about Claire? Surely Miss Rose would want her to do it. She's much older than I." Lanna suggested Primrose's housekeeper.

"Yes, but Claire hasn't been feeling well lately. Poor thing," Audrey then stood up from the shaded area amongst the many sweet smelling golden rods and lilac bushes. After arranging her skirts, Audrey kissed Lanna's cheek, gathered her things and walked up the stone walkway that led to the back door of the house.

"Mother, you wished to see me?" Audrey asked Rose, who was sitting at her small desk in the hall writing a letter.

"Yes, we need to pick a color and fabric to have a dress made."

"For what occasion?" Audrey asked then held her breath.

"For Rupert Gordon's ball of course. All of your evening gowns are going out of fashion. Of course, Lanna will need one as well if she's to be your chaperon. I was thinking we might raise the hem of one of your gowns for her to wear for she's nearly a foot shorter than you. I do wish we had someone more suitable, but Lanna will have to do. We don't have the necessary means to get both a new gown and a chaperone of proper decorum. And as you well know, we can't have Claire attend because she's been having those intolerable spells of late."

"Mother," Audrey finally stated. "I wish to please you, but I…I just can't bear to go. You know how I feel about that single minded man and his family."

"Come, come Audrey, why are you so determined to think ill of Rupert? He's very amiable."

"We have nothing in common. Why, he's not even a Christian."

"Utter nonsense," Rose laughed. "Where do you get such notions? Rupert and his family have always attended church. In fact, his father is a deacon and very highly esteemed." When Rose stood, she noticed Audrey's flushed face. "Oh, you must stop spending so much time in that filthy garden. You're getting far too much sun and it's bad for your complexion!"

"But mother, I love it there. That is where I read and pray," Audrey exclaimed and met her mother's gaze.

"Well, it doesn't really matter what you do out there, we need to make a decision on your dress," Rose declared triumphantly. If Audrey wasn't frustrated enough already, her mother continued, "Also, you're a woman now, so you must start wearing your hair up."

"If you wish it," Audrey finally replied and sighed heavily as she watched Rose open the top drawer of the desk to put her stationery in it. She then walked toward the parlor.

CHAPTER TWO

One month later, it was finally the day of Rupert Gordon's long awaited ball and the preparations for attending had begun quite early.

"Were you able to get it?" Audrey hastily asked when Lanna snuck back into her room.

"Aye, an' I'm pretty sure no one saw me," Lanna breathlessly replied as she set down the sewing basket on the dresser. Since the ladies maid had been spared of her daily duties to prepare, her and Audrey had spent most of the day trying on their gowns and experimenting on new hair styles. However, when they put on their dresses and decided to practice their dancing, Lanna accidentally stepped on some of the delicate lace on Audrey's new gown and ripped it.

"Oh, do you think you'll be able to mend it?" Audrey held up the torn lace and looked at Lanna nervously. Rose had paid quite a bit for the satin evening gown and would be more than a little angry if anything happened to it. So instead of telling her, the young ladies decided to try and repair it themselves.

"Now, don't you worry. It will be as good as new before you know it," Lanna reassured and began to carefully sew the lace back onto the hem.

About fifteen minutes later, Lanna stood up from where she'd been kneeling and sighed, "I'm done." She then slowly backed away and gazed up at Audrey in her dusty rose colored gown which had puffed sleeves and a sheer fabric that draped over the full skirt with small beaded flowers delicately sewn on it.

"Jaykers! You look grand," she exclaimed.

"Thank you. You did a fine job indeed. I have to admit that Mother does have extraordinary taste when it comes to clothing. If

I were going anywhere else tonight, I would fancy wearing it far more. Lanna, you look beautiful as well," Audrey said in awe and stepped down from the small stool she stood on.

The ladies maid's bright red hair looked divine with her jade green gown with its dainty lace neckline and small ruffles over the bodice. Audrey could hardly believe the dress had been hers before Lanna had added the lace on the neckline and shortened the hem a bit.

"I'm so glad you'll be with me tonight!"

"Indeed, I am too."

"How much time do we have?" Audrey asked. Lanna then looked at the clock on the mantle over the small fireplace.

"Ah, the time has flown by. It's nearly time to leave. Rupert will arrive in nearly half an hour," Lanna gasped.

"We had better decide what to do with our hair then," Audrey quickly suggested.

"If you can possibly do anythin' with me unruly mass," Lanna sighed and touched one of many curls that had fallen into her face.

"What? It's beautiful and I already have a wonderful idea of what I'm going to do. Then you can fix mine. Sound alright?" Audrey reassured and saw Lanna nod in agreement.

When they were all ready, Lanna picked up the sewing things and left Audrey's room to put it away before anyone noticed it was missing.

Once alone, Audrey walked over to her vanity to take one last look in the mirror. After securing a stray hair, her thoughts moved to her mother once again

"Lord, how will I ever make mother see that she needs to stop being so consumed with such dismal things? How do I make her understand that I'll only be truly happy serving You, Father. Please help me to say the right things when the time comes. Thank You for Your wisdom, in Jesus Name, amen." Audrey stood up, walked over to her night stand, and picked up her small Bible when there was a knock at door.

"Come in," She called. Harold opened the door. "Oh Anna!

You look beautiful."

"Thank you," Audrey smiled. She loved the nickname her grandfather used for her. In fact, she couldn't recall him ever calling her any different. Harold was also very doting toward his only Granddaughter. She could do no wrong in his eyes.

"Rupert's carriage is here and Lanna is waiting for you downstairs…you don't look very pleased," Harold stated. Audrey only sighed in return. "To tell you the truth," he said, a smile slowly crept onto his face, "I've never really cared for the Gordon's, and I presume I know why you don't either."

"We'll just have to pray for them I guess," Audrey quietly replied.

"You're certainly kindhearted," he declared.

"It's not me. It's Christ in me."

"Well, anyway. Try to have a good evening." Harold swiftly changed the subject, then kissed Audrey's forehead and left.

Once he had shut the door behind him, Audrey sighed heavily. *When will my family take my faith to heart?* "Lord, help me to be patient tonight," She glanced up at the ceiling and prayed.

After putting on their capes, Audrey and Lanna were on their way to the carriage, but when they came to the drawing room, Audrey stopped to say goodbye to Rose and her grandmother Victoria, who were working on some embroidery in front of the large glowing fireplace.

"You look very nice dear."

"Thank you Grandmother." Audrey then glanced at Rose, who was working on her needlepoint a bit more intently than usual. But she never looked up.

"Don't talk too much and remember to act becoming…as a genuine lady," Audrey's mother charged.

"Have a good time," Victoria added cheerfully.

"Goodbye," Audrey quietly replied and tried to smile.

Audrey and Lanna stepped into the carriage and were surprised, but at the same time relieved that Rupert wasn't there to greet them. However, there was a beautiful bouquet of pink roses on the empty seat.

"How charming." Lanna exclaimed sarcastically. When they sat down, Audrey slowly opened a small note that was on top of the flowers.

My Dear Audrianna,

I'm so pleased that you've consented to be my hostess for this evening. I'm sorry that I wasn't able to accompany you, but I had to prepare. This will be a night you will always remember. The Gordon's have a way with parties you know.

All my love.
Rupert Gordon the Third.

"Now, maybe yer man isn't such a doss after all," Lanna couldn't help but laugh.

"This is certainly going to be a long night," Audrey sighed.

The Gordon Estate was the largest and most breathtaking home in Augustine and the surrounding towns. The girls felt like royalty as they approached the wide gate with two butlers standing on both sides of it.

While the carriage came to a stop to wait for the gate to be opened, Audrey glanced out of the window and noticed a homely man, standing beside the hedges that grew just outside of the stone wall. He was leering right at her!

Why is he staring at me so strangely? A cold shiver went through her, for he wouldn't take his eyes off her for a second.

"Who is that?" Audrey pointed at the man.

"I don't know. He's probably a skinned toe rag." Lanna reassured as Audrey turned to her in confusion.

"Lanna…you and your queer phrases," Audrey momentarily forgot about the frightening man and chuckled at Lanna's Irish vernacular for a moneyless scoundrel. Lanna often used unusual words that no one understood. Although she tried not to use any when Rose was present because she loathed them, Audrey thought they were very amusing.

When the carriage finally arrived at the main entrance, she had completely forgotten about the man. A butler opened the door and they were greeted by none other than Rupert's mother Beatrice, a pale, matronly looking woman.

"Hello dear. You look lovely," she smiled and unexpectedly welcomed Audrey with open arms.

I've never seen her so pleasant before, Audrey thought. However when Lanna stepped out of the carriage, Beatrice's warm smile quickly faded. Then, before Audrey could say anything, Rupert's Mother pulled her aside.

"Is she your chaperon?" She whispered and gazed rudely at Lanna, who suddenly felt very self-conscious from the scrutiny.

"Yes," Audrey replied, wondering what she meant by the obvious question.

"Well, she's not at all suitable. You can take one of mine," She ordered and turned to one of her maids that were standing behind her. "Go get Margarete."

"Wait!" Audrey boldly interrupted, "You are very generous, but Lanna is to be my chaperon." Beatrice just stood there blinking at Audrey and tried to figure out why in the world she would prefer this plain Irish girl over her more qualified attendants. The Lady of the house also wasn't used to being turned down for anything. In fact, she prided herself for her constant meddling.

"Very well," She finally replied, sounding exasperated as if Audrey would give and change her mind all of a sudden.
After a few moments of awkward silence, Beatrice finally told her other maids to escort Lanna and Audrey to a large guestroom to freshen up a bit.

Audrey sat on the large bed covered in gold silk linens.
This is a guestroom? She looked around the large room that was almost bigger than all of the bedrooms at Primrose combined. Lanna then wandered over to the white marble fireplace and glanced up at a life size portrait of what appeared to be Beatrice in

her younger years.

"Why do we need nearly two hours to freshen up?" She asked Lanna, who was now looking out one of the magnificent windows.

"Aye, it doesn't make much sense to me either." The young ladies browsed around the spacious room for several more minutes until Audrey couldn't stand it any longer. They then decided to leave the grand room and explore a bit or at least help with some of the preparations.

Audrey had just opened the door when she saw Rupert coming down the long hall.

Oh bother! I wish we would have stayed inside. Oh well, I have to talk to him sooner or later, Audrey sighed and tried to push aside her poor attitude as he approached.

"Oh, there you are darling," He greeted emphatically. "You look radiant!"

"Thank you. You look well also," Audrey politely replied. She had to say something nice in return although there wasn't anything good looking about the immature little man.

His oily countenance made her cringe as he grinned smugly. But that wasn't the worst. The hardest thing to overlook was his mustache which seemed to curl up at the ends. Regardless of what she thought, nearly every young lady that planned to attend the ball was coming mainly to gain his attention. Rupert was a very eligible wealthy man, but the problem was, he knew it.

"I know...I do look well don't I? My mother advised me to lie down for a while because I felt a headache coming on earlier." Audrey quickly glanced at Lanna, who was covering her mouth to try and keep from laughing. She then had to lower her gaze to the floor to stop herself from giggling as well, and hoped Rupert hadn't noticed.

"The guests should be arriving in about an hour or so," Rupert said, as he took Audrey's arm and escorted her to the large staircase.

Several hours later, Audrey found herself on the dance floor in the lovely ballroom amidst a few hundred people dancing to The Viennese Waltz. She once again gazed up at the arched ceiling that had beautiful angelic paintings and the largest chandelier she had ever seen.

Although she was enjoying herself considerably, she was getting tired of dancing with only one man. There were other gentlemen who had asked her, but Rupert would somehow cut in every time. Audrey was also getting tired of the glares from at least ten other young ladies because of all the attention Rupert was giving to her.

If only they knew how happy I would be if Rupert sought one of them instead, she thought as she tried to avoid several scowls on her way to get some punch. And that's where she found Lanna, who was helping serve. Audrey couldn't help but notice a couple of men's eyes wandering over to the mysterious red head.

"Well, I see you're finally takin' a break from dancing," Lanna greeted and handed Audrey a glass of punch.

"Yes, it's beginning to get warm," She sighed. Suddenly another woman approached.

"Hello Audrianna."

"Marian," Audrey nodded, "How are you?"

"I'm fine." Marian sighed and slightly raised her chin as if she remembered to act smug.

"I've noticed that you've been dancing with Mr. Gordon quite a bit."

"Yes…I guess I have." Then, as if on cue, Rupert sauntered over to them.

"There you are Audrianna."

"Rupert! I haven't had a chance to talk with you all night." Marian cut in and quickly moved between him and Audrey.

"Oh, yes. I suppose I've just been so busy. How have you been my dear?" Rupert asked Marian, who clutched his arm, but his gaze remained on Audrey. However, before she could reply, Rupert pulled away from her grasp and moved closer to Audrey.

"Actually, I came over to ask if you would like to walk with me on the terrace for a while."

"That would be lovely." Audrey surprised Lanna by quickly replying. Just to get out of the crowded room was music to her ears. Not to mention, she would be able to get away from the now pouting Marian.

So, after finishing their punch Audrey, Lanna, and Rupert strolled out into the heavenly fresh air.

What once sounded like a grand idea was now making Audrey swiftly regret agreeing to walk with Rupert. They had walked in silence for a bit, but then he began telling them about all of the people he was smarter than. The young women looked at each other miserably.

Oh bother, I would rather be in the stuffy room than listen to his endless bragging! Audrey sighed as she pretended to be interested in what Rupert was telling her and Lanna.

If only I could think of something to say to make him stop. But alas, she was at a loss.

Unbeknown to Audrey, her ladies maid was trying to do the very same thing. After several more minutes had passed, Lanna finally came up with a brilliant idea of suggesting they all go back inside to get some refreshments. However, when she voiced her idea, Rupert quickly agreed.

"What a wonderful idea! You get us some and we'll stay here." Audrey looked horrified!

"But…that's not what I…." Lanna tried to interrupt but it was no use, Rupert insisted. As he started walking again, Rupert realized that Audrey was still behind him so he turned to look at her and found she was standing in the same spot, staring in the distance. He didn't notice her worried expression.

"I've wanted to tell you something for quite some time now," he stated as he slowly sauntered back to Audrey, whose gaze was still fixed on something by the hedges. An eerie feeling washed over her for she had spotted the same mysterious man outside the gate glaring intently at her once again.

"And I have a feeling that you'll be most honored," Rupert continued and apparently didn't care if she was looking at him or not.

"Oh, Audrey…." His voice lowered, "You're so beautiful!"

Without warning, he grabbed hold of Audrey's arms, quickly pulled her to him, and pressed his lips against hers. Audrey was so shocked and outraged that she slapped him with all her might, and ran as fast as she could back to the house.

When Lanna came back to the terrace holding the punch several minutes later, she stumbled upon Mr. Gordon sitting on the ground, holding his jaw. He didn't appear to be very pleased.

"Where did Audrey go?"

"She went inside. Could you give me one of those?" Rupert replied calmly and pointed to the fruit punch.

"What did you do to her?"

"Nothing! Now give me a glass, you Irish snippet. I have a terrible headache," he shouted and pounded his fist on the ground.

"How dare you speak to me that way," she quickly set the drinks on the ground just out of Rupert's reach and went to search for poor Audrey.

A few moments later, Lanna found Audrey in the powder room sitting on the floor in the corner. Grateful that they were alone in the small room, Lanna rushed over to her. "Audrey, what happened?"

"Oh Lanna, we have to get out of here…I must go home!" Audrey sobbed and buried her face in her hands. When Lanna sat down next to her, Audrey wiped her eyes and told her the whole story. Lanna was so angry that she could have gone to Rupert and slapped him again!

"How could he do such a thing? What if someone saw us?" Suddenly they heard two ladies walk in, but thankfully, they were entirely oblivious of the upset young ladies still in the corner.

"Did you see that?" the shorter woman asked as she adjusted the brown mink fur that was draped around her shoulders.

"Can you believe that Audrianna Wesley would kiss a man she barely knows?" the other woman huffed and then began to powder her nose much more than necessary.

"Well, earlier this evening, Beatrice informed me that Rupert was planning to ask for her hand tonight." Upon hearing this,

Audrey and Lanna slowly turned to each other in surprise.

First he kissed me. He was probably going to ask me to marry him next! Audrey thought. *Mother would be thrilled if she knew.*

"He was going to ask that dull girl?" the taller of the two gasped.

"Apparently, Audrianna doesn't consider herself to be dull. I heard she thought she was far superior than the likes of Rupert Gordon."

"Superior?" she huffed once again, "I'm shocked that Mr. and Mrs. Gordon would even allow their son to pursue a Wesley. It's scandalous really. You knew Audrianna was an illegitimate child, didn't you?" she asked the shorter woman, who had now moved to fluffing the feather in her hair.

"What? So it's true Rose Wesley was never married?"

"Yes. Why else would Audrianna and her mother both bear her maiden name?" With that, both women left, leaving Audrey and Lanna to their troubled thoughts. If Audrey had been surprised before, she was completely confused now.

"I wish this night would end," she whispered, trying to sort out all of her questions and concerns. *Illegitimate? It can't be...I just can't be...but then again, Mother has never spoken of it.*

"Don't heed any of their ceaseless blarney. That's all it is," Lanna comforted when she realized how upset Audrey was.

As they finally did come down the grand staircase, Audrey and Lanna couldn't believe the mess all of the guests had left behind, that several maids were now cleaning up. When the butler, who stood by the front entryway, saw the young ladies, he approached them.

"I have a carriage waiting for you, Miss. Mr. Gordon wanted me to inform you that he isn't feeling well and you will be riding home alone."

CHAPTER THREE

$\mathcal{T}$he morning after the dreadful ball, Audrey was sitting in the garden writing in her diary. When she finished, she glanced down at the small brook with a heavy sigh. Audrey couldn't get her mind off of the horrible things the two busybodies had said in the powder room. She wanted to ask her mother if what they said was true.

But I will never be able to, Audrey hopelessly thought as she recalled how cold her mother had been when her and Lanna had returned from the party the night before.

"Oh! You're home. Did you enjoy yourself?" Victoria greeted as Audrey and Lanna silently walked into the drawing room.

"Yes, it was alright...." Audrey quietly replied and took off her cape then handed it to Lanna.

"Who did you dance with?" Audrey and Lanna suddenly realized that Rose stood at the top of the stairs in her silk robe and her dark hair was in a long braid that reached her slim waist.

"With Rupert mostly."

"Did he dance with anyone else?" Rose pressed.

"That I don't know."

"Did he take interest in you?"

"I'm not sure." With that, Rose stiffly walked back to her bedroom without another word.

"Goodnight dear." Victoria then took her leave as well.

"Well, I better go to my room." Lanna grasped Audrey's arm. "Don't fret. Everythin' 'ill be alright," Lanna smiled reassuringly before they went their separate ways.

Audrey then picked up her Bible, turned to Jeremiah the twenty ninth chapter and verse eleven, and read aloud.

"'For I know the thoughts that I think toward you, saith the

Lord, thoughts of peace, and not of evil, to give you an expected end. Then shall ye call upon me, and ye shall go and pray unto me, and I will hearken unto you. And ye shall seek me, and find me, when ye shall search for me with all your heart.'" After taking a deep breath, she looked up at the brilliant blue sky.

"Heavenly Father, so much has happened. I don't know what to do. I just want to run away from this horrible place, where everyone is completely ignorant of You. What am I to do? This scripture says that You want to give me a future and a hope, of peace and not of evil. Help me to keep trusting in You, in Jesus' Name, Amen." As Audrey stood up, picked up her things, and started walking toward the house, she saw her grandfather coming toward her holding a small envelope.

"Anna, a messenger delivered this, and it's for you. I presume it's from the Gordon's," Harold called.

Audrey, who thought that her heart had just stopped, slowly took the paper and opened the note. She tried to stay calm because Harold didn't go back to the house, but now stood before her.

Dearest Audrianna,

I must beg your pardon for not escorting you home last evening. I will be coming to Primrose shortly to ask a question of some importance.

All my love,

Rupert Gordon.

Audrey was so alarmed by the note that she felt her knees start to buckle. She also knew she was doing a horrible job of concealing her worry from her grandfather, who was still looking right at her.

"What's wrong?" he asked anxiously and grasped her arm because she looked like she was about to faint.

"Oh, it's nothing, I hope. Please excuse me, I have to find Lanna," her voice quivered.

"What is it?" Harold called after her, but it was too late. Audrey was already halfway to the house.

"I'm sorry, but I can't explain now!" She quickly turned back and shouted.

After he watched her go inside, Harold suddenly caught a glimpse of a strange man standing just down the road a bit.

That's odd. Who could that be so far from town? Harold knew there was a small fish market close by, but that was still nearly fifteen miles away! As he kept watching the mysterious man, he then noticed that he was scanning the nearby land very intently, as if memorizing it.

Maybe he's lost, he guessed and decided to approach him. However, when he took a few steps, the man quickly left as soon as he realized Harold had seen him.

Very odd...very odd indeed. Harold finally turned back toward the house and made his way back inside. If he would have watched the man any longer, he would have seen the stranger rush into the woods, beside the dirt road.

"Lanna, Lanna!" Audrey shouted as she rushed through the back door and down the hall.

"Stop that howling! It's not at all ladylike," Rose snapped from her place at her desk.

"I'm sorry Mother. Do you know where Lanna is?" Audrey meekly asked in embarrassment.

"Well, I presume she's upstairs cleaning," Rose sighed as if annoyed and moved her gaze back to the papers she was working on.

Audrey, trying to ignore her mother's foul mood, silently made her way up the stairs.

"What am I going to do with that silly girl?" Rose quietly asked herself after her daughter left.

Audrey finally found the ladies maid right where Rose had guessed. Once inside the room, she found Lanna tiding up.

"There you are."

"What is it?" Lanna jumped in surprise. When she told her of Rupert's note, Audrey sat down on the edge of her bed and sighed.

"Rupert mustn't come here! If mother finds out about his

proposal, it will be the end of me."

"Aye, what a blarney eejit," Lanna sat down beside Audrey when she motioned for her to sit.

"Lanna," Audrey reproached, for she knew what that Irish word meant, and it wasn't good.

"Sorry. I'm just so angry with that daft paddy," stated Lanna, "First the wretch steals a kiss, then he expects you to pretend that it didn't happen. I could hardly sleep last night because I kept thinking of what I would've done if I had been there. I probably would have slapped him like you did, but I would've thrown dirt in his face as well!" Lanna exclaimed as Audrey tried to hide her amusement.

"But I feel like it's all me fault." Her tone swiftly changed from anger to regret.

"What?" Audrey asked.

"If I wouldn't have left to get the punch, you might not be in this mess."

"You couldn't have known." Audrey embraced her warmly.

"I'm so glad we're cronies," she smiled.

"Oh Lanna, you have no idea how glad I am as well."

"So what are we going to do?" Lanna took Audrey's hand.

"Well, I'll just have to face him and be straightforward as I convey my refusal."

"Aye, you tell him that you wouldn't marry him if he was the last paddy on earth, and you never want to see or speak to him again!"

"I should just let you handle it I see," Audrey burst out laughing at her ladies maid's Irish temper.

After talking it over, they finally decided to go to the Gordon's estate as soon as possible. Audrey merely informed her mother that she and Lanna were going for a carriage ride, then they were off. However, as they climbed into the carriage, Audrey had a strange feeling that they shouldn't go.

What's wrong with me? She asked herself. *Oh, I'm probably just nervous about facing Rupert. I wish I didn't have to, but it might be the only way to get rid of the disgusting man!*

"Is there somethin' wrong?" Lanna asked when she caught a glimpse of her worried expression.

"I'm fine, a bit nervous perhaps."

The closer they got to the Gordon's Estate, the worse she felt. *Maybe we should turn around,* she reasoned with herself. But before Audrey, Lanna, or David the driver could say or do anything, the front left wheel cracked and quickly broke off its axle, which spooked the horses. Without warning, the whole carriage turned over! The poor driver was thrown, and everything inside the carriage, including Audrey and Lanna, were tossed everywhere.

The deadly silence was almost deafening after the horses had gotten away and the dust finally settled. Audrey slowly came to and found herself in the midst of confusion. Her head pounded in pain as she looked around the damaged carriage. When she slowly touched her face, Audrey felt a gash on her cheek from hitting the door handle. Blood was slowly dripping from it.

"God, please let everyone be all right," she cried, when she saw the small ladies maid lifelessly lying face down on one of the seats.

Every bone in Audrey's body ached as she gradually crawled over to see if she was breathing. Once there, she noticed a large cut on Lanna's arm.

We have to get help quickly! Oh, I wonder how David is, Audrey fearfully thought. Thankfully the carriage door was on the top of them now, so she slowly stood up. However, when she took a step, she winced in pain. Her knee must have struck something hard, because it hurt terribly. As Audrey looked down at Lanna again, a strong determination rose up inside of her. She then valiantly climbed out. Once she carefully slid down the side of the carriage and onto the ground, she surveyed the wooded area. Immediately she saw the poor driver, lying deathly still several feet from the crash. She rushed to his side and found that he was breathing and had several scrapes on his face and arms.

Thank God he's alright. It's a miracle! Audrey silently prayed and discretely pulled up her skirt to look at her throbbing knee. Sure enough, her stocking was ripped and stained with blood. She carefully pulled it off and found a large scrape, but it wasn't too severe.

"Where are we?" she whispered to herself. In the distance, Audrey spotted a small vine covered cottage.

Oh good. Perhaps whoever lives there can help us, although it will be painful to get there. Audrey began limping but gasped and clutched her leg as tears stung her eyes in pain.

"Dear Lord," she breathlessly cried, "I pray that this throbbing will stop." She continued, though it was painful at first, but with every step she took it lessened. Audrey had almost reached the cottage when she was startled by a man who seemed to appear from nowhere. He had a strange smirk on his face.

"Oh, thank God. Could you help us? Our carriage has crashed." As she was talking, Audrey realized he looked very familiar.

I know I've seen him before, but...wait...he's the queer man who stood outside the gate last night! She gasped and started to scream, when another man came up from behind and quickly covered her mouth. Forgetting her pain, Audrey struggled with all of her might to free herself.

Inside the overturned carriage, Lanna was awakened by a shrill scream. She sat up quickly and winced as pain shot through her right arm.

"Help, someone!" she groaned as she slowly stood up and reached for the opened door. When Lanna looked up, she jumped in surprise at the sight of David, their driver, who had just climbed up to help them.

"Where's Miss Audrey?"

"She's not in here?" Fear washed over David as she slowly shook her head.

"It must have been her...," they both stated in a whisper.

Lanna couldn't help but notice David was holding his side as he helped her out of the carriage. She was about to ask if he was alright, but he beat her to it while he tore a piece of his shirt and tied it around her swollen arm.

"Are you hurt anywhere else?"

"Aye, don't fuss over me, Audrey needs help!" Lanna replied.

While Audrey was being dragged toward an old wagon, she started to weaken from struggling and was about to lose hope. She was then roughly set in the back, but the man, who held her kept his dirty hand over her mouth.

"Is she the one he wants?"

Who would want me, and for what reason? Audrey thought.

"What did he say again?" The man holding her asked.

"You fool…he's told us time and time again. Said we had to find a...." All of a sudden there was a loud thud.

"Charlie?" Audrey's captor called. Then Audrey saw him! David, who had just hit the other bloke over the head with a branch, was now coming up behind the bearded man. She tightly shut her eyes when she saw David pull the branch back to swing.

"Are you alright?" he finally asked Audrey, who still had her eyes closed. "Miss Audrey?" he asked again. When she slowly opened them, Audrey gazed down at the two unconscious kidnappers. The one who grabbed her from behind was short, stalky, and had a black scraggly beard, while the older man had a long scar along his jaw. He was indeed the one who she'd seen at the Gordon's.

"Are you hurt?" David finally broke into her musings. He wasn't prepared when Audrey jumped down from the wagon and embraced him.

"Oh thank you, David. I was so frightened!" her voice quivered in fear. However, when a sharp gasp escaped his lips, she quickly backed away.

"We should leave before they come to," David tried to hide his painful expression and gently grasped Audrey's elbow.

"I'm sorry…are you alright?" she slightly blushed.

"I think it's my ribs, but I'll be fine. What about you?"

"My knee is a bit sore, but it could have been far worse. Wait…where's Lanna. Is she alright?"

"Her arm is the only thing that's hurt, but I don't think it's too serious."

"Thank God," Audrey sighed with relief.

They were walking back to the carriage, when Audrey glanced up at the tall stable hand, who continued to clutch his side.

David Lawrence had worked at Primrose since he was about fifteen. His duties included taking care of the horses, carriages, and small stable. He then moved his dark eyes in her direction as well.

"Do you have any idea what those men wanted?" he asked.

"I'm not sure. They were about to say, but then you came and rescued me."

When they reached the carriage, Lanna was standing beside it holding her wounded arm.

"What happened? Oh Audrey…your face!" she gasped and rushed to Audrey's side to look at her cheek.

"The kidnappers were probably common thieves that thought they could get some kind of ransom money. As soon as we return to Primrose, perhaps Mr. Wesley shall accompany me to speak with the Constable," David informed.

"What? Someone tried to kidnap you?" Lanna's grip tightened on Audrey's arm as fear quickly washed over her.

"There were only two. One of them was the same frightening man at the Ball."

"The bloke you saw just outside the gate?" Lanna's eyes widened, "Jaykers!"

Audrey turned to David and caught his gaze.

"Please don't tell grandfather. I wouldn't want to worry him." When David opened his mouth to disagree, she continued, "Besides, you did say they were just common thieves."

"Yes," he sighed, "But don't you think he'll want to know about them?"

"Alright, I suppose you're right, but could I tell him?" Audrey finally gave in.

"As you wish. Well, we had better start walking back to Primrose. The horses have run off and I don't think we'll find them anytime soon. Will you both be well enough?" He asked the young ladies.

"I hope so, how far away are we?" Lanna asked.

"Probably a few miles, but someone might come along."

Thank you Lord, for protecting us. I'm sorry I didn't heed Your warnings earlier. Help my family not to worry. Audrey silently prayed.

CHAPTER FOUR

$\mathcal{B}$y the time Audrey, Lanna, and David finally reached Primrose, it was almost dark. They were approaching the door, when Harold suddenly came out.

"Anna, where have you been? It's nearly eight o'clock!" Then he saw Audrey's face, Lanna's bleeding arm, and David's scratches.

"Good Lord, what's happened?" Victoria was the next to step out of the house as Harold embraced his granddaughter. Everyone's attention swiftly moved to the lady of the house, who gasped loudly when she saw their disheveled clothes and hair.

"Harold, bring the poor dears in out of the cold night air!" She exclaimed, "We must send for a Doctor."

Once they went inside and the Doctor tended to their wounds, everyone retired to the drawing room and Audrey began to tell her grandparents what had taken place.

"I still can't believe the three of you only had minor injuries. Especially with David being thrown from the carriage," Victoria said.

"God protected us." Audrey simply replied, but her grandmother only stared at her. "Where is Mother?" She asked to change the subject because the silence was beginning to get uncomfortable. She had actually been wondering where Rose was ever since they had returned home.

"She must still be in her room. It seems like she's been there ever since we finished our tea and you still hadn't returned. She's been quite worried...we all have."

Mother, worried about me? Audrey asked herself. Victoria quickly stood up.

"Oh dear, I completely forgot to tell her of your return. Although, she must have seen you since her bedroom window overlooks the entrance. I'll go and get her." She was about to leave when Audrey also stood.

"Thank you, grandmother, but I'll go to her," she turned to David and Lanna, who were still sipping their tea.

"Please excuse me, everyone. David, thank you again for everything."

"You're welcome, I'm just glad you're alright." He politely got to his feet along with Harold, and smiled.

After seeing her daughter limp down the road toward the house with David and Lanna, Rose began to weep with relief. She couldn't remember ever being so worried about Audrey. Because she didn't want anyone to see her at her present state, Rose was determined she would not leave her room until she regained her composure. She knew it was selfish of her, especially for Audrey's sake. She despised herself because her sadness and regret had always implied she somehow resented her daughter.

If she only knew how much I really love her. But how can I go to her now? She thinks I'm heartless...and perhaps I am. Ever since the fateful day so long ago, Rose became more and more withdrawn from everyone she loved, including God. There were countless times she tried to free herself from the ensnare of her depression, and would seek Audrey out. But once in her company, Audrey would start talking about her close relationship with her Heavenly Father. Rose would get so jealous of her only daughter's happiness, that she couldn't bear to be with her any longer. And her sadness would wash over her again, but far worse. Rose began to wipe her eyes.

How did I become this person who despises her own flesh and blood, but is also worried sick about her at the same time? It was then she heard a knock at the door.

"Who is it?"

"It's Audrey." Rose quickly got up, and rushed to the mirror to make sure there were no signs of tears or worry on her flushed face.

"Come in," she finally called.

Audrey slowly opened the door, peered inside the dim room, and found her mother stiffly glaring at her.

"Mother, are you all right?" she meekly asked.

"I'm fine. Where have you been?" Rose sounded much calmer than she really felt. For when she saw the cut on her daughter's face, her emotions nearly got the best of her.

Audrey began to explain the ordeal. However, when she finished, Audrey was surprised to see fear in her mother's eyes. Something she'd never witnessed before. Rose, didn't know what to say. All the fear that haunted her from her past came over her again in one dreadful moment. She could hardly breathe as she relived the dark night.

"Mother, what's wrong?" Audrey cried as Rose sat down at the window seat. She breathed heavily in attempt to calm herself, or at least keep from fainting.

"Do you have any idea what the horrid men wanted?" her mother finally choked, but feared Audrey might already know.

"No. Mother you're scaring me!"

"Where's the bracelet I gave you?"

"I'm wearing it, but what does this matter?" Audrey innocently held up her wrist with the small adornment hanging from it. Seeing it, Rose sighed in relief.

"What is it?" Audrey asked again.

"Nothing."

"There's something you're not telling me. What are you hiding?" she boldly questioned.

"I said nothing, now just leave me alone."

"I'm sorry, but I'm not leaving until you tell me what's frightening you so."

"You wouldn't understand." Rose turned from her daughter and looked out the window.

"Yes I would." Audrey moved closer and lowered herself on the same window seat beside her. "I know…I know you never married…and that I'm…." She felt her face grow warm, but she couldn't finish. Rose then met her gaze with piercing eyes, but at the same time, they were filled with agony.

"You can't understand."

"Well then, will you tell me?" When her mother remained silent, Audrey heard herself recklessly continue. "Why are you so distant towards me? I'm no longer a child. You can tell me! Please stop avoiding me and let me in," she pleadingly cried, but Rose only walked to the other side of the room.

"At least let God into your life. He can help. He'll forgive you if you'll just ask Him. He's merely waiting for you." *Now I'm certain I've gone too far. Lord, please forgive my disrespect.* Audrey had longed to tell her mother those words for some time. However, she couldn't help but wonder if she'd made a horrible mistake.

"God help me? Help *me*?" Rose suddenly shouted and made Audrey jump in surprise. "You're so naive! God had His chance to help me, but He didn't. He let your father die along with a part of me," she fumed as she marched up to her daughter and firmly grasped her shoulders. "Audrey, the sooner you realize this, the better off you'll be. There isn't a God...if there is, He doesn't care about us. And I'll be hanged if I allow you to serve an uncaring God any longer!"

Audrey was completely taken back by her mother's last callous statement.

"Why can't you see that I'm right? Don't you remember what has just happened? You were in a carriage accident and almost abducted. Where was your God in all of that?" Rose continued.

"No, He tried to warn me, but I didn't listen. It was my fault...all my fault," Audrey choked.

"How could you possibly have known what would happen?" She finally released Audrey and scowled.

"The Bible says God warns His children of things to co—" Audrey abruptly stopped when Rose let out a disgusted sigh.

"You sound just like your father. Always quoting scripture to me as if I were a child. 'Be not overcome of evil, but overcome evil with good,'" Rose mocked in a high pitched voice.

Why did I ever come here? It would have been better if mother had remained distant towards me. Audrey realized there tears were now streaming down her face. Thankfully, Rose was now sitting at the edge of her bed, gazing at the floor. When Audrey couldn't take it anymore, she rushed to the door but slowed when Rose spoke quietly.

"For your safety, I think it would be wise if you didn't leave the house for a while." All Audrey could do was nod in return. She then ran to her bedroom, threw herself on the bed, and cried herself to sleep.

Lanna, who was on her way to her room in the attic, accidentally overheard the whole quarrel. She had never heard Rose speak to her daughter that way before.

Audrey must be heartbroken.

"Lord," she prayed, "Please help Audrey an' Rose work out their differences." Lanna wasn't sure what else she could do besides pray for them, but she felt very sorry for them both.

CHAPTER FIVE

O ne week after the horrible dispute, everyone at Primrose started to sense a feeling of contention. No one really knew what is was or where it had come from, but it seemed to follow Rose and Audrey wherever they went. Although Audrey tried to be cheerful, anyone who looked at her immediately saw sadness in her eyes.

Lanna prayed and prayed for a way to tell Audrey she heard the horrible fight. Then one morning, she finally decided to approach her about it. However, on her way to Audrey's bedroom, she started to get nervous.

"Aye, I'm just going to tell 'er. We're cronies...surely she'll understan'," she whispered to herself, but quickly stopped when Claire walked by.

"Top of the morning," Lanna greeted the other maid and felt herself blush.

"Good morning," Claire eyed her curiously. Thankfully, she continued down the hall. The ladies maid then took a deep breath and knocked on the door.

"Come in."

Lanna smiled at Audrey who was sitting on her bed with an open Bible on her lap.

"How does your arm feel?" Audrey asked.

"Much better I'd say. How are you?"

"I'm well, although I'm a bit weary from not being outside. I miss the garden."

"Why, it must be safe by now," Lanna stated, "It's been nearly a week and I've gone to the market three times since the carriage accident and I haven't seen any quare men...at least not starin' at me," she casually sat down at the edge of the bed.

"Has Rupert tried to contact you yet?"

"No," Audrey laughed, but it sounded strained. It was as if she was trying to free herself from the dark cloud of grief that lingered over Primrose.

"I'm fairly certain he won't be coming to call anytime soon. The letter I sent Mr. Gordon clearly explained everything." Soon after the accident, Audrey had sent Rupert a long letter so he wouldn't suddenly come to Primrose. They giggled for a few moments but then Lanna caught a glimpse of her trouble expression.

I can't bear seeing her like this, but Lord, what should I do? Suddenly, Lanna got an idea. "If ya like, I could speak to Miss Rose when she returns, an' ask if we could go outside for a while?" After a moment of silence, Audrey got to her feet, wandered over to the window, and buried her face in her hands. Quiet sobs immediately followed.

"Jaykers!" Lanna rushed to her side, "I must tell you somethin', lass," she said quietly and sat Audrey down on the window seat. "The night of the carriage accident, I overheard you an' your mum talking." Audrey turned to look at Lanna, tears still brimming in her eyes. Lanna had never felt so ashamed.

"Aye, I heard everythin'. I'm so sorry."

"Oh Lanna," Audrey embraced the small maid. "Don't be sorry. I'm glad you know. It doesn't seem so bad now." Lanna sighed with relief and Audrey stood up and started to pace.

"I'm so confused…I don't know who I am. And now my relationship with mother is far worse than ever before! I'll never be able to ask her about my father now. It's all my fault. What should I do?" she cried.

"Don't cry Audrey, God knows. His word says He chose you before the foundation of the warrld. He'll never leave you nor forsake you," Lanna comforted, "Cum, let's go outside. Miss Rose won't mind if we just go to the garden. At least until she an' your relations return from the luncheon." Audrey wiped her eyes and smiled.

"Thank you Lanna, I love you so much."

When they opened the door and walked down the stone walkway, Audrey immediately started to feel better. With the combination of the singing birds and fresh air, she wondered how Heaven could be much sweeter. She couldn't help but reach for Lanna's hand and run to her favorite place under the willow tree beside a small brook that trickled through the garden and into the wooded area behind the modest estate.

As the girls made themselves comfortable, they thanked God for the day and read Audrey's small Bible for a while. They then decided to have a picnic.

"You stay put. I'll fetch everythin'," The ladies maid told her and cheerfully made her way to the house. While she waited, Audrey spread her shawl out on the warm grass and lied down on it with a sigh. She couldn't seem to rid herself of the nagging feeling that was disobeying her mother by leaving the house.

Perhaps I should go inside, she thought. *Yet, mother didn't fully understand when she bid me to stay in the house. She's never understood me.* Audrey decided to push her troubles aside for now, so as not to ruin such a lovely day, thanks to Lanna.

"Father," she gazed up at the sky, "Thank you for Lanna. She's dearer than a sister. As for mother, please show me what do to. Advise me, help me to leave it in Your hands." Once she finished praying, the troubling feeling came back for a moment, but it quickly passed when she heard Lanna return.

"Lanna?" Audrey asked. But instead of hearing her soft accent, she heard a low husky voice!

"Sorry missy, I ain't Lanna." Audrey sat up quickly. Before she could even scream the scraggly man from the accident, grabbed her arm and roughly jerked her from the ground.

David, who was in the stable, had just finished cleaning one of the stalls when he heard a strange noise coming from the garden. He went to see what it was, but could hardly believe what he found. A man was slowly dragging Audrey into the woods! David quickly reached for the first thing he could get his hands on and went after them rather slowly for his ribs were still considerably sore.

Lanna made her way back to the garden, holding the heavy basket. She glanced over to where Audrey had been sitting, but no one was there.

Where did she run off to? she looked around the garden.

"Audrey?" There was no answer. She was about to call again when someone covered her mouth and lunged behind a tree.

"David! What are you doing an' why are you holdin' a pitchfork?" she asked once he pulled his hand away from her face.

"Shh! It's Miss Audrey. She's been attacked! Now stay here no matter what," he whispered. After Lanna promised to stay put, she fearfully watched David try to run, toward the woods, as well as could be expected. It was only then that the ladies maid saw Audrey being held by a large man. However, when he realized that David approached, he stopped and threw Audrey to the ground.

"God, please help them!" Lanna gasped, as she watched Audrey scramble behind a tree while the horrible man turned to her rescuer.

"You'd better turn around and leave us be." Henry bellowed. "Let her go."

"Come and stop me," the bearded man provoked while his accomplice slowly snuck up behind David, holding a pistol.

Lanna had to cover her mouth to keep from screaming. David didn't waste any time as he leaped toward him with the pitchfork. They struggled for a while, but when David took a blow to his side, he fell to the ground. The pain from his previous wounds was too much for him. However, Henry wasn't finished. The next thing David knew was the bearded man took a hold of his collar and lifted him up roughly which made the pain intensify. So much so, that David could hardly breathe. Suddenly he heard someone standing behind him begin to laugh.

"David, watch out!" Audrey shrieked, but it was too late. He was struck on the back of his head with the pistol. Lanna couldn't hold in her uncontrollable cries any longer as David fell to the ground and Audrey swiftly got to her feet to run for her life.

Unfortunately the men easily caught up with her, and once they had her, they headed deeper into the woods.

Lanna didn't know what to do, so she waited until they were out of sight before she rushed over to the lifeless stable hand.

"David!" she cried. When he finally came to, he touched the back of his bleeding head.

"Leave me and follow her! Don't lose her," he groaned.

"What about you?"

"Go…she needs you, Lanna."

"But what can I do?"

"Just follow them so we know where they're taking her. Don't let them see you…I'll get help," David tried to sit up, but he feared he would pass out again.

"You nade help David."

"Go!" he insisted. Lanna finally got up and glanced up at the wood in determination.

"God, please help me find her!"

CHAPTER SIX

udrey had never been so terrified in all her life! She had to stop resisting her captors for she didn't have any strength left. But she continued to silently pray after being set in the back of the old wagon, hiding in the woods. Audrey was held the same as nearly a week earlier, but this time it was the older man who had his callous hand over her mouth.

What do they want with me? She thought as her mind reeled with plans to escape. However, even if she were able to free herself from the tight hold, Audrey hadn't the slightest idea where she would run for she had no idea where they were anymore.

God, please let someone see me. They must have driven several miles, at least it felt like it to Audrey. Suddenly, they came to a stop.

"What's wrong?" Charlie asked his accomplice who held the reigns.

"I thought I heard something, but it must lust be the waves."

"Then we're gettin' close."

Waves! We're by the shore? Audrey thought in alarm and began to struggle again, but to no avail.

"Hey, hey! Quiet down, lass," her captor growled and tightened his hold.

What if I never see my family again? The horrible assumption crossed her mind, which caused tears to sting her eyes. Audrey's stomach felt awful as a sense of hopelessness washed over her. They drove a bit further until a small fish market slowly came into view.

"Wait…what's this?" Charlie broke the silence, "We can't drive through here."

"Well, what do you want me to do then?" Henry huffed.

"You bloody fool! Why would you go this way? If we drive

past the people, someone is bound to recognize the girl."

Oh please...please let someone see me! Audrey hoped as she watched several fishermen mending their nets at the edge of the market.

"There's no other way to get back to the ship. We have to go through here," Henry nearly shouted in return.

The ship? Where are they taking me? She wished the kidnappers would continue to argue so someone would hear their angry voices.

"Well then, we'll have to wait until they all leave," Charlie replied. Henry snapped the reigns and steered the wagon behind some thick pine trees for cover.

"We might as well get something to eat while we wait," Henry whined.

"And what do you suggest we do with her?"

"We'll just tie her up and gag her mouth."

"Go ahead then...this is your blasted idea." The driver jumped down from the seat, tied the horse to a tree, then approached the back of the wagon. Charlie, who held Audrey, looked down at her.

"I'm going to let go of your mouth and if so much as a peep comes out of you...so help me!" He abruptly stopped talking when he saw her flinch and slowly took his hand off. She just stared at him while Henry began tying her hands behind her back. But she couldn't remain silent any longer.

"What is it you want with me?" she whispered.

"Hush!"

"Please tell me," Audrey pleaded. "You can have anything, just release me."

"I told you to keep quiet," Charlie shouted and struck her across the face. He then roughly gagged her mouth and jumped down. When both men made sure she was tied securely, and the wagon was hidden, they made their way toward the fish market. Audrey's wrists burned as she tried to loosen the tight bonds.

At first Lanna had a hard time tracking Audrey and her captors, but when she finally found the wagon tracks it was fairly simple. However, after following them for nearly three hours, her feet began to ache terribly. It was then Lanna wished she would have taken one of the few horses at Primrose.

Where could they be taking Audrey? the ladies maid sighed and kept walking. She couldn't help but imagine what the horrible men might want with Audrey or what was happening to her right at that moment. The mere thought made Lanna shiver. Suddenly she realized what she was doing.

This kind of thinking won't help me one bit, she scolded herself for her useless worrying. How many times had she and Audrey read in the Bible that worrying couldn't add a cubit to their stature or a day to their life?

Lord, please protect her and help me find her.

Lanna's gaze shot upward. *What was that noise? It sounds like people's voices.* She swiftly looked around until she saw a fish market through the trees. But the wagon tracks didn't lead toward the market.

"Where's Audrey?" she whispered to herself and intently searched for a sign.

They couldn't have driven right through without being seen.

Nearly an hour after the men left, Audrey finally gave up trying to free herself. She couldn't feel her wrists anymore from pulling against the ropes so vigorously.

Oh God, what should I do? If only I could make some kind of noise to gain someone's attention. Audrey gazed through the thick trees and watched all the people going about their business.

They're so close! What can I do? When she couldn't stop her tears from falling any longer, she suddenly caught a glimpse of something out of the corner of her eye. She turned to see what it was, and found her ladies maid gazing at the ground in confusion. At first, Audrey was almost too shocked to move. Thankfully, her senses quickly returned. She began to make as much noise as she possibly could by kicking the side of the wagon. After a few moments, Lanna heard the commotion and immediately began to cry as she rushed to the wagon.

"You poor wee thing!" She exclaimed and quickly removed the gag then started to untie Audrey's hands.

"Oh Lanna, I'm so glad you're here! We have to hurry, they'll be back at any moment."

"Aye, I'm trying, but your hands are shakin'," Lanna replied.

"Sorry, I'm just so frightened," Audrey whispered in return.

"There...." They jumped off the wagon, but hesitated.

"Which way shud we go?" Lanna gasped, "Into the woods or to the market?" Audrey didn't answer as she started to run into the woods. Lanna had never seen Audrey like this before. But who could blame her?

When they could go no further, the fearful girls dropped to the ground behind a large tree to catch their breath.

"Do you think we've lost them?" Audrey asked with obvious anxiety in her voice.

"They don't even nu you're gone yet," Lanna stated and hoped what she said was true.

"I can't stop trembling," Audrey cried, so Lanna crawled over and put an arm around her.

"We must be a sight." She faintly smiled trying to lessen the tension. Their hair was in terrible array and their dresses were dirty and torn. With Lanna's bandaged arm and the scratches on both of their faces from running through the brush during the escape, they did look pretty tattered.

"We'd better get started again." Audrey got up, took Lanna's hand then met her gaze.

"Thank you for coming after me," she whispered.

"There she is!" Without warning, both young ladies were startled by the shout. Their captors, now driving the wagon directly toward them. Audrey and Lanna began to run, but they knew they couldn't outrun the horrible men. However, this time Audrey was determined not to be taken without a fight! When the wagon reached her, Charlie put the reigns in one hand and took hold of her arm to try and lift her up to him, but she viciously scratched his face. He then quickly released her and winced in pain as Audrey fell to the ground.

"Leave her alone!" Lanna screamed. Henry took that opportunity to jump down from the other side of the moving wagon and ran over to Audrey, who frantically picked up a nearby jagged rock.

"Charlie, I could use some help over here!" As soon as the driver heard him, he stopped the wagon, reached under the seat, and pulled out a pistol and two sacks. He then marched over to Lanna, who had fallen to the ground after tripping over her skirt. But when she saw Charlie approaching, the ladies maid scanned the grass for something to defend herself as Audrey had done.

"Lanna, run," Audrey cried and watched her dear friend reach for a piece of wood. Audrey's attention swiftly moved back to Henry as he also moved closer. She scrambled to her feet. He was about to take her hand when Audrey quickly hit his arm with the stone. She was going to rap him again when a loud gunshot pierced the sky and echoed throughout the thick woods. Audrey quickly shut her eyes and hoped against hope that it wasn't Lanna.

For a few moments, all was quiet.

"Alright, that's enough," Charlie broke the silence, "Henry, don't just stand there. Fetch her!" After begrudgingly mumbling something under his breath, the bearded man heeded Charlie and stepped up to Audrey. He reached out and squeezed her upper arm tightly. Although she couldn't bear the thought of finding Lanna wounded or dead, Audrey had to know for sure if she was alright or not. She slowly opened her eyes and glanced over to where the ladies maid had been.

"Get up and go over to the wagon now!" Tears of relief immediately came to her eyes when she found Charlie pointing his gun at Lanna, commanding her to her feet through clenched teeth. Lanna walked to the wagon as Audrey was led to it. Charlie continued to point the gun at them.

"Tie her hands," he nodded to Henry once again. When he finished, both young ladies eyes widened as Charlie lifted up the sacks in his other hand and smiled.

"I don't know what you want, but you're making a horrible mistake." Audrey pleaded one last time, but was completely ignored as Charlie roughly slid the sack over her head, then did the same to Lanna. Once they couldn't see any longer, there was no way they could escape. All Audrey and Lanna could do now was blindly let both men lift them into the wagon.

"Finally," Henry sighed as they climbed back onto the wagon seat.

"Who knew women were so hard to capture."

"Well, I told you we shouldn't have left her"

"Let's just get to the ship," Henry grumbled in return.

CHAPTER SEVEN

$\mathcal{B}$y the time they reached the fish market again, all the people had gone home.

"See? I told you we'd be able to drive this way," Henry laughed patronizingly and turned to Charlie. But all he did was sigh.

"What do you think he wants with her anyway?" Henry broke the silence once again a few minutes later.

"Well, we'll soon find out." Even though Audrey couldn't see anything with the smelly potato sack over her head, she still listened intently to the men's conversation.

Audrey and Lanna felt the jolt of the wagon coming to a stop, then they were lifted out and set in the back of a small boat that had been hidden at the very edge of the rocky harbor.

"Audrey," Lanna whispered and nudged her arm, "Are you all right?"

"Where do you think we are?" she replied.

"I think we're in a boat."

"Quiet back there!" One of the men shouted. Everyone remained silent for the remainder of the ride toward a large vessel that was anchored about a mile out.

They finally reached the ship and the young ladies were carried onto the deck and roughly set on some rigging. By now the young ladies were both so frightened and disorientated, all they could do was cling to each other.

"I'll go find him," Charlie stated and made his way to the quarter deck.

"Captain," he called as he walked up to a large man looking through his looking glass. "We've got the lass you've been searching for." However, the only reply Charlie was given was an awkward silence.

"I'm sure about it this time." He then gulped.

"Oh really," the man pulled away the glass from his eye and slowly turned to face him. "As I recall, you said the exact same thing only a few days ago," The tall Captain sneered and looked intently at the old sailor. "What happened to your face?" he continued, as Charlie glanced down in embarrassment. He didn't say more and finally sauntered over to the young ladies, who still sat atop the rigging with the brown sacks over their heads. Once several of the crewmen saw them, they couldn't move their gaze from the sight. However, when the Captain approached, they swiftly went back to their duties.

"I see you brought *two* maidens this time, just to be certain you didn't fail me again," he chuckled sarcastically and turned back to look at Charlie, who followed close behind. He then quickly pulled the sack off Lanna's head. At first, the ladies maid had to shield her eyes, but once her sight was restored, she glanced up at the men standing around them, gawking.

"A maid?" Audrey and Lanna both jumped in fear at the sound of his deep intimidating voice. The ladies maid's plain uniform instantly gave her status away.

"Well…you see. It's the other lass…." Charlie started to sweat, trying to think of how to reply. That was when Henry boldly stepped forward.

"We had to take the maid as well, cause she kept trying to free the other one," he rushed over to Audrey and pulled the sack off of her.

"Why didn't you just get rid of her?" Henry and Charlie glanced at each other nervously.

"Aye Sir—we hadn't thought of that."

"Of course you didn't." The Captain moved his gaze to Audrey. After blinking several times, Audrey was able to make out the tall man, whose voice made her tremble.

"What do you want with me?" She whispered, but he ignored her question as he turned around and faced the other men.

"Bring them to my quarters," he demanded and walked away without another word.

Audrey and Lanna were led into a fair sized room toward the back of the ship, directly under the quarter deck. Once inside, they were untied and seated on two very elegant chairs that faced a large desk. Behind were several tall windows that overlooked the stern.

"Lanna, I'm so frightened. What's to become of us?" Audrey rubbed her sore wrists after the men had left and locked the door behind them.

"Why, everythin' 'ill be all right as long as we stay together." Suddenly the door opened and the fearful man stepped in. He walked to his desk with maps piled all over, and sat down. He then looked at them and smiled.

"I am Captain John McNeil. And you are?" He politely asked until he saw it! The item he'd been longing for, searching for ever since he first laid eyes on it so long ago.

What luck! Those two worthless dogs actually found her. Captain McNeil still hadn't managed to take his eyes from it as the young ladies introduced themselves.

"I'm Adrianna Wesley and this is Lanna Ryan. Now if you would be so kind as to tell what it is you want with us, we can be on our way. I'm quite certain there's been a horrible misunderstanding," Audrey boldly stated, but McNeil wouldn't reply. He seemed mesmerized by something.

What is he staring at? She thought and followed his gaze down to her shell bracelet on her wrist.

"Where...where did you get that trinket?" he stammered, trying to hide his delight.

"This?" Audrey slowly lifted her arm. "It was a gift from my mother. I dare say, she purchased it from a traveling merchant."

"And what is her name...your mother I mean?"
Lanna caught a glimpse of Audrey's expression and found it matched her own bewilderment.

"If I tell you, will you release us?"

"Of course my dear," McNeil finally looked up from the jewelry.

"My mother's name is Rose Wesley. There, you have it. Now if you would be so kind, promptly take us back to shore." Audrey swiftly stood and took Lanna's hand. McNeil only leaned back in his chair and laughed.

"You don't know do you?"

"Know what?" The young ladies asked in unison.

The Captain came to his feet, walked around his desk, and moved closer to Audrey. It was then she noticed he had a strange limp when he walked.

"Well," his voice lowered, "You obviously don't know who I am and how valuable your bracelet is to me," McNeil sneered and touched the end of Audrey's dark auburn hair that had fallen loose.

"Don't touch 'er!" Lanna shouted and pushed away his lingering touch. Audrey backed away in fear as McNeil shoved the ladies maid back in her chair. He then roughly took Audrey's wrist, ripped the bracelet off, and stormed out of the room.

"No!" She cried and helplessly dropped into the chair next to Lanna.

"Did you find it?" William Scotts, the ship's second in command, turned from his place at the helm when the Captain climbed the stairs to the quarter deck.

"I finally have what I need," McNeil held up the bracelet, "Now we can get rid of them." he picked up his glass and peered through it. After handing the steering wheel over to the second mate, William called to the men who had captured Audrey and Lanna.

"Henry! Charlie! Bring the maidens out here."

"Sir, Henry is rigging the head pump," Charlie informed once he arrived.

"Fetch someone below deck then."

"Hey Irish, you gotta help me."

"With what?" said the man, whom everyone called Irish because of his thick accent and slightly graying red hair.

"I need help with the women."

"What women?" he finally moved his gaze from the net he'd

been mending and asked in confusion. Irish never saw Audrey and Lanna brought on board because he'd been working in the hull.

"Just come on... Captain's orders."

"Alright," Irish got to his feet and noticed Charlie's scratch. "Aye, what happened to your face?" The sailor only gave him silence in return as he led the way back to the room where the young ladies were being held. When they walked into the Captain's quarters, they found Audrey sitting in the chair with her face buried in her hands, and Lanna sitting beside her trying to be of comfort. Charlie coldly walked over to them, but Irish stopped and stared at the frightened women.

"Come on you two. The Captain wants ya." Audrey looked up with a tear streaked face. Irish, who was still standing by the door, was cut to the heart.

What does McNeil want with these young girls? he thought, *The Captain's done some pretty underhanded things in the past, but not like this.* Audrey and Lanna slowly got up and silently followed the sailors.

As they made their way toward McNeil, most of the crewmen stopped their work and stared at them. It made both ladies felt quite uncomfortable. When they finally stopped in front of McNeil, Audrey's discomfort deepened the moment he laid eyes on her. He was smiling, but had a wicked glint in his eye as well.

"Why do you look so frightened? Aren't you enjoying your stay aboard this grand ship with its grand Captain? Now that I have what I've been searching for," he stepped closer to Audrey and held up the shell bracelet. If anyone would have noticed Irish at that moment, they would have thought he'd just spotted the ghost of Davy Jones himself! Everyone was much too consumed with the maidens to consider his pale face. His gaze was fixed on the piece of jewelry.

"You'll take us to shore." Audrey boldly ended the Captain's sentence. McNeil glared at her angrily. He wasn't used to people speaking up to him, especially a woman. Before he could even think of a reply, a young sailor stepped forward amidst the small crowd that had quietly formed.

"I'll take them to shore, Sir," he offered. McNeil bellowed, although no one really knew what he found so humorous.

"No need." Suddenly, the Captain realized everyone was gawking at Audrey and Lanna. "Everyone get back to work! You too, Joseph," he pointed at the man who'd volunteered. The crew reluctantly made their way back to their duties as McNeil returned his gaze to Audrey.

"Don't worry Lass. You'll soon return to shore. Charlie, Irish! Throw these two overboard," he calmly ordered and turned to his sailors. Audrey and Lanna quickly glanced at each other in panic.

"No please!" They both cried. As soon as the crew heard it, they all started shouting at once.

"Aw Captain! Let 'em stay awhile!"

Henry, who had finished with his previous task, ran halfway up the quarter deck stairs.

"Please Captain, couldn't they stay awhile?" he whispered. "It's not very often we get two ladies aboard. Can't us sailors have a little fun once in a while?"

"Quit your squalling, dog!" McNeil shouted and pushed Henry back. He then began to stroke his beard as he looked out to the horizon. Several silent minutes had passed before he finally turned to face everyone's pleading looks.

"All right…we can have a little fun with them first. Then I'll do what I like with 'em." Hearing this Audrey nearly fainted. She would rather be drowned than spend a night on board with countless barbaric sailors.

Lord, please keep Lanna and I from harm, she silently prayed.

"Show them to the brig... for now," the Captain smugly ordered. Henry happily turned and walked passed Irish, who was still standing there gazing into the distance. As he made his way back to his work, Henry wondered why Irish looked so sullen.

We're finally gonna have something to look forward to on this dull ship.

Audrey and Lanna were led down two flights of very steep stairs into the hull. They were immediately met with a thick stench of sweat and years of rotting wood and cargo. Audrey covered her mouth and nose to keep the horrible smell out and waited for her eyes to adjust to the darkness.

How could anyone live in these conditions? She thought as she looked at the sailor's meager belongings amongst piles of dirty rope, barrels, and stagnant water.

"This way," The tall man, who had volunteered to take them to shore earlier, spoke up. He led them through an even darker hall.

We must be at the back of the ship by now. Audrey's thoughts began to reel again. When they came to a small room that looked like a jail cell, Audrey and Lanna looked at each other and slowly stepped through the barred door. There was some straw on the plank floor, two crates in the corner, and a small port hole overlooking the water. Without another word, the man left. Audrey walked over to one of the crates and let out a hopeless sigh as she sat down.

"How could this happen to us? It's a complete nightmare," she cried as Lanna knelt beside her.

"Somehow…." Lanna hesitated, "Somehow we'll get out of this kip. I'm sure of it."

"If only I had my Bible," Audrey said. However, she didn't notice the ladies maid's warm smile that slowly crept onto her face. She pulled out the small leather Bible from the front pocket of her apron, while Audrey sauntered over to the port hole.

"Jaykers, I nearly forgot!" she exclaimed and Audrey quickly turned around. She rushed over to Lanna and held her beloved book against her chest.

"You're such a dear, but how did you manage it?"

"I saw it lying on the grass in the garden so I picked it up before I started my search for you." Audrey sat down on the crate and opened the precious book.

"A few days ago I was reading about when Paul and Silas were beaten and thrown into prison. Do you know what they did?" Audrey asked the wide eyed ladies maid. "They didn't sit there, feeling sorry for themselves and their misfortune. They prayed and worshiped God. Then, later that night, an angel appeared and rescued them!" Lanna jumped up and took Audrey's hands.

"Aye, let's do that right now."

"It can't be…it's not possible," Irish told himself for what seemed like the hundredth time. He was leaning against the rail of the forecastle consumed with his thoughts. Ever since he saw the shell bracelet his mind couldn't stop reeling.

How did McNeil do it? How did he find it? It just can't be. Irish turned around and gazed over the bows and taffrail to the beautiful sunset. He'd often thought about what might have happened that night so long ago, but lately he'd finally managed to forget the painful memories.

I wish I had enough courage to go down to the brig and ask the young lass who she is and where she got that bracelet. She is very beautiful. I wonder if…no, she can't be.

"Hey Irish! What are ya doin' over there?" Jake Harper called and walked over to him. "Aren't ya hungry? Better get some Duff before the scallywags eat it all." When Irish didn't say anything, he continued.

"Did you hear we're shovin' off tomorrow?"

"Where are we headed?" Irish anxiously asked.

"Not sure, but I guess we'll find out." Jake casually sat down on the plank floor and stretched out. As he glanced up at the few stars, just starting to appear, he let out a satisfied sigh. Irish had always admired the other man's carefree attitude. However, as he took in the other sailor's sun bleached hair and roughhewn features; he could tell that his life had been anything but carefree. Jake was also shorter than most, but his husky build made up for it.

"So, what do ya think about those young ladies?"

"I'm not sure. Only that they don't deserve to be here against their will. How come the Captain won't let them go?" Irish sat down next to Jake. Although he knew the answer to his question, he wanted to see what Jake Harper thought about the matter.

"It's somethin' to do with the bracelet," he put in, "But I wonder what McNeil wants with it. It doesn't look worth much."

"I hope he doesn't intend to hurt 'em, " Irish sighed. At this, Jake Harper turned to him in surprise.

"Well, you've been on this ship longer than the seventeen

years I have. You know the Captain cares very little of what happens to them. You know how heartless he can be, don't you?" Jake asked and couldn't believe who he was talking to.

You have no idea how well I know, Irish thought to himself. He would have voiced his thoughts if all his horrible memories hadn't begun to haunt him once again. So instead, Irish merely replied, "Aye, I guess I do."

"Well, I'm going to get my duff now." Jake quickly stood then both sailors made their way to the others, who were eating the pudding like treat the cook made once in a great while.

When they finished, some of the men started to mend their clothes, sing, or just relaxed, enjoying the night off from their many duties.

"Well men," Henry spoke up after belching loudly. "Those ladies must be sorta lonely." Irish quickly looked up from his mending and glared at Henry who stood up.

"I think we should give them some company and I'll go first."

"Aw why don't you just sit down and keep quiet," Irish demanded and tried to stay calm for his temper had a way of getting away from him.

"I don't know Henry, I heard those females can sure put up a fight," Jake Harper chuckled and pointed to the deep scratch on Charlie's jaw. "At least you'll have a scar on both sides of your face now," he continued.

"Quiet, Harper!" Charlie shouted in return.

"So who's comin with me?" Henry asked again, but this time several of the other sailors stood up beside him. They all starting walking to the brig when Irish rushed in front of them.

"Stop!"

"You can come with us, but you're not going first!" Henry shoved past him, but Irish grabbed his arm.

"Don't get in my way old man!" Henry growled.

"Yeah!" The other men yelled and pushed Irish out of the way.

"Wait! The Captain didn't say you could...not yet," Irish desperately tried to stop them.

"You never want to have any fun," someone shouted to him. Irish was furious as he watched them climb down into the hold.

I've got to go to the Captain! I can't just stand by and let young innocent girls be mistreated by those scoundrels. Irish hurried to the grand dining room.

He stopped outside the room, located right beside the Captain's cabin, where the officers dined. Before knocking, Irish peered through the small window on the intricately carved door. McNeil, William, and Francis were seated at a large table. When he saw all the wonderful food they were eating, his mouth began to water. All he and the other sailors were fed was dry salt beef and stale ship bread with an occasional plate of duff.

He took a deep breath and pounded on the door. Normally no sailor ever dared to interrupt the Captain's meal, but Irish was determined to give McNeil a piece of his mind or at least learn of his intentions. The very stout second mate opened the door.

"What do you want?" Francis whispered and gave Irish a stern look, warning him to leave.

"I have to talk to the Captain." Francis said nothing. He just stood in the door way and glared at him. Ignoring his signal, Irish shoved past him and quickly walked up to McNeil. William looked up from his plate and nearly choked as he walked by.

"Captain," Irish said quietly, suddenly doubting his boldness. McNeil slowly wiped his mouth and glanced at him irritably.

"And what is so important that you thought it wise to interrupt my dinner?"

"I'm sorry, but it couldn't wait."

"Go on." McNeil slowly leaned back in his chair as Irish gulped.

"Sir, some of the sailors are restless and are on their way to terrorize the young ladies." McNeil started to laugh, "Well, is that all? You're a stupid man Irish. You didn't really think I wasn't aware of it?" He then started to eat again. "Let the men have their fun. Besides, they won't be with us much longer." At this, William, Francis, and the Captain all began to chuckle, but Irish didn't know what was going on. When they noticed Irish's confused expression, they howled even louder.

"What do you mean?" he finally asked.

"It's nothing really. They'll just be getting a little wet in the morning." Francis sniveled.

"Quiet!" McNeil pounded the table so hard that it made Francis' glass of port tip over and spill all over him. He didn't like anyone spoiling his surprises.

"What...you mean to throw them overboard? You can't do that!" Irish shouted angrily.

"Why should you care what happens to them? It's not like you're...." Everyone was silent for a few moments and waited in suspense for the Captain to finish. "Oh that's right...I nearly forgot. In fact, I never really thought about it before now," he sneered.

"What are you talking about?" Irish asked, wishing McNeil would just spit it out.

"Well, you could very well be related to that girl down there. This makes everything so much more interesting!" McNeil smirked. Irish couldn't believe his ears!

Related to me?

"You could almost say the apple doesn't fall far from the tree." McNeil was now laughing so hard, along with the other two men that tears started to fall down his face.

"You can't throw them overboard!" Irish shouted louder than before. Suddenly he had a brilliant idea that would ensure the safety of the young women.

"Oh really, and why can't I?" McNeil's expression immediately became serious as he pierced Irish with the intense anger in his eyes. Nobody said no to Captain McNeil.

"Well," Irish hesitated and wondered if he was stepping over his boundaries. At that moment, he pictured Audrey and Lanna sitting in the musty brig.

They're probably frightened out of their minds. What if she is related to me? Why she could very well be my daughter! Instantly a boldness he'd never known before, rose up in him.

"The lass, whom the shell bracelet belongs to, can't be thrown over."

"Why?" McNeil asked in unbelief.

"Because in order for the shell to work, it must be in the hands of its owner."

"How would you know?" William asked.

"Well, that's the way I was told. Listen or not, I don't think you want to take that risk," Irish sounded much calmer then he felt. He wished he knew what the Captain was thinking, but then again, he hadn't been thrown out yet.

There must be small chance that they believe me.

"I think it's time you leave us to our dinner," Francis spoke up. However, when the second mate realized how boldly he'd been, he quickly glanced over to McNeil. Thankfully, the Captain nodded his agreement. Francis then got to his feet and ushered Irish out of the room without another word.

After the door shut behind him, Irish turned only to hear shouting and laughing coming from the crowded deck.

Oh, no, if those firs know what's best for 'em, they better not bring any harm to those lassies! Irish ran through the mob, but swiftly came to a halt when he saw Jake Harper playing a small accordion and two other men dancing with Audrey and Lanna against their will. Henry had Audrey by the wrists and was twirling her around while the other man was holding the maid, who was nearly sobbing hysterically.

"Leave them alone," Irish marched over to Henry and shoved him to the ground. When Audrey was released, she stood there trembling, but looked grateful none the less. Irish was about to ask if she was alright when Henry quickly got up. He then swung Irish around and angrily punched him in the face.

"You asked for it, mate!" Henry suddenly jumped him and they both went flying to the ground, wrestling.

Audrey didn't know what to do. She quickly scanned the deck for a place to run, but several of the other men who weren't egging Henry and Irish on, were coming towards her.

"Audrey," Lanna cried. Audrey turned to the ladies maid and the large sailor holding her. Although she hadn't the slightest idea what she would do once she got there, Audrey rushed over to her friend anyway.

"Please! Let her go," she pleaded. Without warning, Charlie came up from behind and grabbed her by the waist. He then began to carry her toward the stern of the ship. Audrey was completely helpless. She tried everything to escape, but it was no use. They were almost to the end of this vessel when Joseph stepped directly in front of him.

"Leave 'er alone."

"Get out of my way," Charlie pushed past him, but Joseph rushed in front of him again and hit him in the stomach. Charlie groaned in pain, as the tall young man helped Audrey to her feet.

"Folly me," he shouted and started for the hull. "Hurry!" Joseph admonished and turned to his left. It was only then he noticed no one was behind him that Audrey wasn't behind him.

"Are you alright?" Joseph stopped and walked back to where Audrey stood.

"I can't go without Lanna," She cried and pointed to the frightened redhead.

"Go on, I'll get her," The sailor ordered, but Audrey still hesitated. However, when she glanced back and saw Charlie trying to get up, she made herself run to the dark hull as fast as she could.

Joseph stopped in front of the man who held Lanna. He couldn't remember the last time all the sailors were so riled up! *Why is the Captain allowing this? He's always prided himself on keeping an orderly ship. Maybe he doesn't even know,* he thought as he watched all the commotion. *But I don't see how he wouldn't know with all the racket they're making.*

Unbeknown to the sailor was that McNeil was indeed very aware of what took place, as he peered through the small window of the door. And he had no intention of stopping them. Instead, the Captain was deep in thought over what Irish had said about the precious shell.

"What do you want?" Samuel asked when Joseph approached.

"Aye, let 'er go before this gets any worse." Joseph pointed to what had turned into a huge group of fighting men and shouting bystanders.

"It's my turn, so leave me be," the largest sailor of the St. Carlin crew replied. He then glanced down at Lanna, who trembled on his lap.

"Besides...I can fight any of 'em off."

"Cum on. I'll give yar me duff for a month," Joseph offered. Unfortunately, Samuel shook his head.

"That don't compare to a fair lass," he stroked the side of her tear streaked face. Not knowing what else could be done, Joseph turned toward the large fight.

"'ey! Quit fighten' amongst yarselves. Samuel's been having a bit av craic with the maid," he pointed to Lanna as if she were bait. Several of the crew, who heard Joseph, began to approach.

"No, she's mine," Samuel bellowed as he lifted the ladies maid off his lap and stood between her and the angry sailors.

Joseph's plan had worked! He quickly grabbed Lanna's arm and led her to the hull. Thankfully, no one seemed to notice they were gone. They both quickly entered the hatch that led to the hull and made their way to the brig. Lanna saw Audrey standing safely by the door waiting for them. The redhead nearly choked with tears of relief as she rushed to her side. Both young women then ran inside their strange haven while Joseph lifted the key off of the nail.

"Sorry about all av this, but I think it wud be safer if..," he held up the key to lock the brig.

"Yes...yes, perhaps you're right," Audrey managed to say before she sat down in the hay. She tried to stop the tears that continued to fall for she was still shaken by the horrible events.

Joseph couldn't help but feel more and more sorry for them. *I hope McNeil releases them soon. They don't deserve to be kept here,* he finally made himself turn away and began walking back to the deck. As he did so, Joseph heard something he'd never thought he would hear from two frightened girls being held against their will. Audrey and Lanna started to quietly sing and worship God. Joseph quickly glanced at them to see if what he heard was true. Sure enough, the young women were kneeling, with eyes closed. He watched them for a while in confusion. Then they did something even more shocking than before. They started praying for the Captain and even the men who had captured and mistreated them.

"Starboard watch!" The first mate called from deck. Joseph took one last look at the young ladies then slowly made his way back to the deck. He still didn't know what to think.

CHAPTER EIGHT

*A*s Primrose came into view, Rose sensed that something wasn't right. She glanced at her mother and father, who were sitting across from her.

"What's wrong?" Victoria asked.

"Oh...nothing," Rose stiffly replied and tried to remove the queer notion from her mind.

"You look pale. Is a headache coming on?"

"No mother, I'm quite well."

The carriage reached the front door and came to a halt. Rose slowly climbed out after Victoria.

"What a beautiful day," Harold declared when he took his turn and stepped down, "Perhaps I'll take a walk in the garden before going inside."

"I will join you, but I must first get my parasol."

"That sounds delightful. I'll wait for you." Harold opened the front door for his wife. As she walked in, Victoria was immediately confronted by a very disturbing scene. David sat on a chair in the front hall with Claire stood beside him, holding a blood stained rag to his head.

"Good heavens!" Victoria gasped and Harold moved to her side. "David, are you alright? What's happened?" she asked breathlessly. When Rose heard the strange commotion, she fearfully rushed past her parents. David slowly looked up at her anxiously.

"My lady, its Miss Audrey." It took all of her strength not to collapse.

"No...how?" Rose managed to whisper.

"She's been kidnapped." That was the last thing Rose remembered before she fainted.

"Miss Rose?" She heard someone call. Rose slowly opened her heavy eyelids and saw the housekeeper, standing over her holding a small bottle of smelling salts. Rose eventually recalled all that had happened and quickly sat up.

"No Miss, you must lie down and rest. You took a nasty fall," Claire whispered.

"I can't just lie here when my own flesh and blood has been kidnapped and is out there somewhere." Rose pointed to the window and was surprised to find that the sun had already set. "I must find her," she started to cry.

I've been so horrible to her. All those things I said earlier. For all I know she ran away. Who could blame her? If I were her, I would have, Rose slowly crawled out of bed.

"They've already gathered a search party and are looking for her right now," Claire reassured.

"Where is David?"

"He's looking also."

Rose walked to the window and peered out, although she couldn't make out anything. It was rather cloudy and the moon left an eerie glow.

"What happened to his head?" She asked when she recalled the pained look on David's face.

"One of the men, who took Miss Audrey, hit him over the head with his pistol. Isn't that horrible? What is England coming too? Kidnappers, thieves, and guns," Claire clicked her tongue, but Rose wasn't listening. She was consumed with something else.

They had guns? I hope Audrey's all right. I don't know what I'll do if anything happens to her. Suddenly she realized she hadn't seen her ladies maid yet. Rose turned to Claire.

"Where is Lanna?"

"Oh, she's missing as well. Ever since…she and Miss Audrey decided to have a picnic in the garden this morning."

Audrey was slowly awakened by the distant calls of seagulls. The waves lapped against the great vessel as it rolled steadily over the swells. She stiffly sat up and grasped her aching shoulder.

This floor is so hard. Wait a minute, why am I sleeping on the floor? Where am I? She started to panic.

"Lanna!" the shriek quickly awoke the ladies maid who lay beside her.

"What's wrong?" As their gaze met, Audrey's memory was swiftly restored when she noticed some straw in Lanna's unkept hair.

"Oh, for a moment I forgot where we were," she slowly crawled to the small port hole and gasped for she couldn't see land any longer. The link to the only home she'd ever known was gone.

"We're in the middle of the ocean!" Audrey choked. Lanna quickly put her arms around her and looked out over the large swells.

"We're never going to see Primrose again. What's to become of us Lanna?" Before the ladies maid could answer, they heard someone approach.

"Good mornin'," Irish nervously called. When he saw the grief stricken women, his feigned smile quickly faded. He reached up to the nail that usually held the key, but it wasn't there. "Where did..," Irish began to ask as he glanced around the dim hull. It was then that Joseph appeared.

"Irish," the sailor walked up to him and handed him the key to the brig.

"Where did you find it?"

"I thought it wud be better if no one cud fend it." Joseph moved aside after Irish gave a quick nod and moved to unlock the door.

Lanna slowly got to her feet and approached the door while Audrey wiped her eyes. When she looked up, she found Irish's gaze on her.

Why is he staring at me? Although she felt uncomfortable being glared at, Audrey saw kindness in his dark hazel eyes. With his graying red hair, unshorn face, and brogue; it was obvious how

Irish had obtained his nickname. However, his accent was different than Lanna's soft dialect. It was mild, as if he'd been born in Ireland, but hadn't grown up there for long. But then again, no one's accent was as thick and hard to understand as Joseph's. Audrey had only heard him speak once or twice, but she could immediately tell he had indeed lived on The Emerald Island for many years.

Audrey didn't really know why, but she felt that as long as she and Lanna were on the horrible St. Carlin, Irish wouldn't be a threat. They would be safe around him, along with Joseph. She wasn't the only one who was aware of the sailor's scrutiny. Lanna also noticed. After a while, she cleared her throat.

Irish then realized he'd put the key into the lock, but still hadn't turned to open it. If truth be told, he was too busy trying to figure out if McNeil spoke the truth. Were one of these frightened girls indeed related to him? He quickly finished the job and opened the creaky door and waited for Lanna and Audrey to emerge.

"Where are you taking us?" Audrey looked to Joseph, then to Irish.

"The Captain wants ya, lass," he solemnly replied.

What does that cruel man want with us now? Audrey almost voiced her thoughts, but instead took a deep breath, took Lanna's hand, and slowly followed the men.

They arrived outside of The Officer's dining room a few minutes later. However, Joseph strayed from the group to return to his duties. Before Irish knocked on the door, he turned to the young ladies. They looked so vulnerable as they stood before him, awaiting their fate. He hated the part McNeil was making him play in his cruel plans. Only a few hours ago, when the larboard watch was finished, William pulled Irish aside and told him McNeil wanted him to bring the women to the deck, but then to send Audrey to him alone. Just the thought of leaving Audrey alone with the Captain, gave him a bad feeling. The last thing Irish wanted to do was assist the man in his wrongdoings, but he was at the Captain's mercy.

For all I know, McNeil could make me out to be the villain in all this. I hope I did the right thing by going to him last night.
Then, without warning, William opened the door and grinned.

"My, you two look well rested," he laughed sarcastically when he saw Audrey and Lanna's appearance. Their hair was horribly snarled with straw and their clothes were filthy.

Something inside of Irish told him this wouldn't end well. William grasped Audrey's hand, raised it to his lips, and kissed it.

"My lady, please follow me," he then roughly took her by the arm and began to pull her inside.

"Wait…I'm not going without Lanna!" Audrey cried and reached for Lanna, who was now being held by a hesitant Irish.

"Please stop," Lanna gasped, but it was no use. William easily dragged her inside and shut the door in the maid's face.

He led Audrey to a lavishly set table with delicious food. She had to admit the eggs and sausage smelled wonderful, since the last time she or Lanna had eaten was the previous morning. William pulled one of the chairs out and Audrey sat down. Then, without another word, he left the room and locked the door. Before Audrey could even think of what to do next, the whistling Captain made his appearance from the other door across the room.

"Well, well, don't you look riveting," he sauntered over to the chair opposite Audrey and was also seated. She couldn't stand to even look at him or his condescending smirk.

"You must be hungry. Can't we forget the past and try to have a friendly meal together?" Audrey thought his cheerfulness was revolting as she kept her gaze on the plate in front of her. That is until McNeil pounded the table which made her shriek.

"Stop your pouting! It's very unbecoming," he shouted, but Audrey's downward gaze continued. She couldn't stop the trembling that shook her small frame.

"Fine…you don't have to look at me, but you are going to listen to what I have to say. And you're going to eat everything set in front of you. If you refuse, you will not be given food again for the remaining of the voyage. And believe me… it will be too long to go without, even for your stubbornness," he growled. "Do you hear me?" McNeil pounded his fists again. He loved seeing her flinch, knowing that she was afraid of him.

A few moments of silence had passed, except for the sound of the Captain's chewing. Audrey finally picked up a lovely warm biscuit and took a bite. Trying to keep Lanna from her mind, she finished eating while McNeil began to reveal his plan.

"Good job, Irish," William chuckled when he emerged from the dining room then made his way to the helm. Irish looked down in shame and released Lanna's arm.

"What's happening to Audrey?" Lanna turned and glared at Irish, who still kept his eyes on the freshly swapped deck. "I must be with her!" She started for the door, but Irish rushed in front of her. "Please," Lanna cried and leaned against him. She finally realized her pleading wouldn't do any good. Irish most likely had just as much say in the matter as herself.

"I'm sorry lass, I wish I could," The sailor stated in a whisper, his voice thick with emotion. He couldn't bear the ladies maid's hopeless stare. She then turned from him and slowly sat down on the steps that led to the quarter deck.

"Now that I have your bracelet—"

"What does my bracelet have to do with you?" Audrey cut in between bites, but immediately regretted it when she saw the Captain's angry countenance.

"You will not interrupt me again! It's not only your bracelet I need. It's the shell itself. It was once very large and contains certain powers to protect." Audrey quickly looked up at McNeil to see if he was serious. And indeed he was.

"You've never heard of it?" he finally motioned for her to speak.

"That is preposterous! Surely you jest."

"What makes you think I jest? The radiant shell is a rare

Sunrise Shell. The first person to discover its power was Lord Connor Fintan. He'd won the shell in a tournament during The Dark Ages. Whenever he went into battle, he would never be harmed as long as the shell was with him."

"You believe a mere sea shell can protect? Where did you hear such a silly tale?" she said and almost laughed herself. The Captain quickly stood up, walked to the door, and opened it once it was unlocked.

"Irish!" he called.

After glancing up in surprise, Irish stepped up to McNeil. However, before letting him inside, the Captain moved closer.

"It would be wise to keep your mouth shut...if you know what I mean," he quietly threatened then they walked back into the room.

"There have been stories of the shell's power for many years. But this man was the first to tell me all about it. It's been in his family for years.

"Well, you have it now. Why don't you release us?" Audrey cried and couldn't believe she had been taken from her home for a silly myth.

"Well, I had planned to do just that, until...." McNeil smiled, "Irish informed me the shell has to be in the hands of its owner for it to work. So you can thank him that you'll never see your home again," he now laughed, but seemed to forget to mention Irish had also saved the young ladies from being drowned.

Irish's heart broke when he saw tears come to Audrey's eyes. He felt his face grow warm with anger.

"You can also thank him for all of the ships we're going to ambush with your shell's help," Captain McNeil grinned once again and suddenly walked to the door. He loved breaking people apart, especially when they were probably father and daughter.

I couldn't very well take the chance of them reuniting and Irish helping her escape, now could I? He thought, then silently congratulated himself for his smart planning. How long had he searched for it? McNeil had to admit he'd almost given up ever seeing the shell again. But now here it was, right in his grasp. His thoughts were interrupted by Audrey. She was now quite upset and opened her mouth, trying to tell Irish what a terrible thing he'd done, but instead she only choked on her tears.

"How…could you?" was all Audrey could manage before she started to weep. Irish nearly began to weep himself. Unfortunately all he could do was watch the poor confused girl trying to speak.

Maybe it is all my fault. I should have left well enough alone! Irish scolded himself. But he couldn't let Audrey be thrown overboard. *What else could I have done? I'm such a stupid, stupid man.*

"That's right," McNeil piped up, "What do you think we should do with him, my dear?" Audrey brought her trembling hand to her mouth and tried to calm herself. She didn't really understand why she was so upset.

I'm going to be stuck on this bloody ship forever! I'll never see Primrose again…never read in my garden…never be able to tell my mother how sorry I am, for everything. Her thoughts reeled. Audrey felt light headed and sick to her stomach all at once.

"Please just leave me," she gasped for breath.

"As you wish," McNeil waited until Irish left the room, then followed him out. Lanna was finally allowed to rush to Audrey's side.

CHAPTER NINE

𝒩early three days after Audrey had been kidnapped, the search party had all but given up trying to find her. David, on the other hand, was not planning to give up that easily. He had seen the men who tried to capture Audrey after the carriage accident, and he couldn't stand the thought of her being alone with them again. He was walking in the woods once again, just trying to find one sign of Audrey's capture. One clue. As he made his way through the trees, David came to the small fish market, as he had so many times before.

"David, what brings you here today?" One of the local fishermen called to him. Although, he knew what the answer would be. David had taken it upon himself to meet and question everyone he'd come across at the small harbor to quite an extent. David slowly walked over to Ben Layken.

"I'm just looking for some kind of clue that I may have missed," he sighed.

"Ah, you're never going to give up, are ya? I probably would be looking myself…if someone I cared about disappeared," Ben said, trying to cheer him up.

"I still feel bad that I couldn't help you at all. I don't see how they could have come through here without anyone seeing them."

"I don't either. Someone must have. Perhaps I'm missing someone," David replied.

"Are you sure you asked Frank McGregor and Old Lady Smithson? She prides herself in watching every blessed thing that goes on around here."

"Yes, I've talked with both of them. McGregor was ill, and Smithson was being a midwife at the time," David's shoulders slumped with hopelessness.

"Wait, I don't know why I didn't think of this earlier, but I wonder if Jim Calford saw anything. He's around here a lot," Ben laughed when David quickly stood up from where he was sitting and looked like he'd just been given a gold nugget.

"Where does he live?"

"Just down the road a ways." Without another word, the young man started down the dirt road.

"Sure is strange what women folk can do to a man," Ben mumbled to himself as he went back to mending the net in his hands.

David stopped just outside of the first house he came to. It was pretty run down and it didn't look as if anyone lived there. But he was going to check anyway. He slowly walked up to the entrance, but nearly fell through the stairs on the way. He pounded on the door several times and had almost given up, that is until a stalky man opened the door.

"What do you want?" he asked with a low groggy voice that sounded like he'd just woken up.

"Are you Jim Calford?" The old man slowly nodded.

"I have a few questions."

"What kind of questions?" Jim leaned against the door and yawned. It was then that David smelt ale on his breathe.

"Three days ago, a young lady was kidnapped by two men. They took her into the wood, which only leads to the market up the road. No one seems to have seen them, but I was wondering if you had," David held his breath as he waited for a reply.

"Come on in."

As David followed him inside, he realized this Jim Calford must have been a sailor or a captain for quite a while. There were several ships in bottles and compasses on the mantle over the meager fireplace. He shut the door only to have Jim quickly open it again. He swiftly knew why. It was far too dark with the door shut, for there was only a single window in the one room shanty. After clearing off the maps which were sprawled out on the small table, Jim offered David a seat. Another thing David couldn't miss among the sparse furnishings was the seemingly endless supply of empty jugs and bottles around the room.

What am I doing here? This is a complete waste of time. Oh well, while I'm here I might as well ask this drunk some questions.

Jim sat back in his chair, "So ya say no one else saw her being kidnapped?"

"Everyone I asked said—" David stopped in midsentence when Jim reached for a bottle and took a long drink.

"They're all scared," He put in once he'd finished.

"Scared of what? How would you know? Do you mean to say that you saw who took her?" David quickly asked as he eyed the old man curiously.

"Aye...are ya gonna let me tell you or not?" David made himself stop and let silence fill the room. It was only then that Jim spoke.

"Two days before I saw what happened, I had just gotten to the fish market when I noticed a new ship in the harbor. I recognized it as the St. Carlin and knew I had to find out why they were anchored in our tiny harbor, of all places." Jim caught a glimpse of the young man's confused expression and sighed. "I take it you've never heard of the St. Carlin or its Captain, John McNeil?" David shook his head

"Well, I'll just say Captain McNeil never docks his vessel anywhere unless there's a mighty good reason. What makes me suspicious about seeing the ship is McNeil doesn't usually do business around here."

"He doesn't?"

"No, not when there's a bigger harbor town close by. It was then I knew they must be getting into some kind of trouble." Jim took another swig of his ale when he finished. He noticed that the young man before him appeared to be deep in thought.

"How do you know so much about this Captain?" David finally spoke.

"I used to work on his ship, but that was a long time ago," Jim sighed heavily before continuing, "When the St. Carlin does stop for cargo, they're only anchored overnight. So there's somethin' going on without a doubt, because they don't get their cargo from here, and there's no pub for ten miles," He began to ramble.

"Anyway, I decided I would keep an eye on them for a while."

"So did you see them take the lady?" David once again cut in eagerly.

"Aye, I came a little later that day, so the market was closed. I walked over to the stump hidden behind some trees and sat down for a spell," Jim stopped to take another long drink.

David was getting very weary of this old man's slow tale. He didn't want to lose any more time. Jim must have noticed the lad's anxiety and slowly handed him the bottle. After David took a long sip himself, Jim finally went on.

"Well, I sat there for a few minutes then dozed off."

"What!" David nearly gasped.

"But then I woke up, because I heard a wagon. Two men, on an old wagon, drove in. They sure weren't quiet about it either. When they stopped, they lifted two women with sacks over their heads and set them in a lifeboat. Sure enough, they rowed out to the St. Carlin."

"There were two ladies? Did they appear all right? What happened then?"

"Calm down, son. I couldn't really tell, but they didn't look hurt if that's what ya mean. Well, after that...uh...I didn't watch anymore after that," Jim looked down at the dirty table as David slowly stood up.

"I guess that's all I really need to know," he said, then walked to the open door. "I suppose you don't know where the ship will sail to," he turned to face Jim before leaving.

"Nope, but I do know you'd better be thinkin' twice before getting in the way of Captain McNeil. He and his crew don't have a very good reputation and he doesn't take kindly to people who nose their way into his business."

"Thanks for the warning, but I'll take my chances," David replied and quickly walked out.

"Better steer clear!" Jim called after him.

David carefully made his way down the rickety porch, and suddenly realized that he'd left his horse at the market in his haste. So after he made his way back to the harbor and mounted his steed,

David decided to travel to the next harbor. The one Jim Calford had mentioned. It was about thirty miles north.

Someone there must know more about the St. Carlin and where it usually travels. Perhaps I should first return to Primrose and tell them where I'm headed. Herald might want to accompany me. Audrey's face to mind next, *Or I could rescue her myself…*

He had been sweet on Audrey since she was merely twelve years of age, but she never really returned his feelings.

But there's always hope…especially if I rescue her! He hadn't forgotten how grateful she had been after the carriage incident. His musings were interrupted by a young boy, who was chopping wood in front of a small house.

I'll have the boy deliver a note back to Primrose, so I can get started.

CHAPTER TEN

"**H**oist the mainsail!" Captain McNeil's orders rang out over the crowded deck. "What's our longitude?" he turned to William.

"Ten Degrees west, Captain."

"Good, just keep following them without getting too close."

"Aye, aye."

Early that morning, McNeil spotted another ship while peering through his looking glass. It appeared to be a packet ship. However, it had too many passengers on board to be merely for cargo. But that's what tempted the Captain more than anything.

All those rich people...they won't know what hit them, he smiled to himself. *Since I have the shell, no one will be able to stop me!* Several years earlier, the St. Carlin had ambushed the Florentine; a large merchant vessel. They, in turn, put up quite a fight that McNeil hadn't planned on. Although he was victorious in the end, the St. Carlin came away with more damage than the loot was worth.

It will surely be different this time, the Captain looked through his glass once more.

"When we reach their speed, should we overcome them straight away?" William asked.

"No, I don't want them to know we're following them until tonight," McNeil growled and got an idea.

"Do you think Miss Wesley would like to watch while we conquer them?" he glanced at William, who smiled wickedly. McNeil couldn't remember the last time he'd had such fun on his ship before. As quickly as he'd gotten his idea, Audrey came to mind. Ever since she had breakfast with him, she'd been different. It seemed to have broken her. She was no longer her stubborn feisty self. She never even talked back to McNeil anymore. The

Captain didn't know why he felt disappointed towards her, but he did just the same. He presumed Audrey might break free from her depressed state once he allowed the women to go about the ship as they pleased, but it did nothing to lift her spirits. The only thing she did was either stare out over the swells or read from a small black book in the corner of the bow.

Where did she get that book? She wouldn't dare take one from my quarters. But even if she did, I don't own a book as small as the one she holds.

When he and William went about their business, the Captain continued to think of ways to stir some kind of reaction from the lady. Turning from the rail, he scanned over the deck. Sure enough, McNeil found Audrey reading the mysterious book and Lanna sitting next to her, mending some of the crew's clothing. The Captain figured as long as he had a maid on his ship, he might as well give her some work. He sauntered over to them. When Audrey felt his eyes on her, she tried to keep her gaze on her Bible.

"What are you two ladies doing this fine day?" McNeil clasped his hands behind his back and waited for Audrey to look up. Instead, Lanna slowly glanced up at him, looking irritated.

"Well, since you ask, we're actually wonderin' why your keepin' us on this mingin ship an' when you're plannin' to release us," the ladies maid stated flatly, which made McNeil smile.

Although Audrey no longer put up a fight, Lanna was a whole other matter. He simply ignored her bold question and moved his gaze to Audrey, who still hadn't moved nor said a word. One thing that angered McNeil more than anything else was being ignored. He could feel his temper quickly wearing thin.

"Miss Wesley," his voice lowered. Audrey finally looked up. Her face reminded him of a small frightened child, who'd just woken up from a bad dream. "Why do you look at me so?" the Captain asked, but was only given silence in return. "Say something!" he suddenly yelled, which made several sailors stop their work and curiously glance toward them.

"There is nothing to say," Audrey quietly replied, sounding much calmer than she felt. If truth be told, the very sight of the tall intimidating Captain made her tremble in fear. She didn't know why he scared her so much. The worst thing he could do was throw her overboard, and even that was sounding better every day. She and Lanna had only been on the St. Carlin for four days, but it felt like an eternity.

"Aye, what is it you'd like 'er to say?" Lanna asked as Audrey returned her solemn gaze to her book.

"I think the cook might need some help." McNeil's eyes narrowed, but the maid wouldn't move. "Go, now!" he shouted again. Lanna anxiously glanced at Audrey, then reluctantly made her way to the kitchen.

Audrey didn't know what to do.

If I don't look at the Captain, maybe he'll leave me alone. Without warning, McNeil quickly covered the distance between them. He grabbed a hold of Audrey's waist, and pulled her toward him.

"No one ignores the Captain of this ship, madam," he breathed only inches from her face. Panic began to stir as he moved even closer to her. Before Audrey realized what she was doing, she firmly kicked McNeil's shin. Thankfully, he released her and grasped his leg in pain, all the while cursing under his breath.

When she quickly backed away, Audrey felt shooting pain from the tip of her foot. Clearly, she did not know her own strength. She tried to calm both her violent trembling and pounding heart that beat wildly as she turned to run back to the hull. However, after taking a few steps, the Captain reached for Audrey's Bible, ripped it out of her hand, and threw it over the side of the ship. Audrey spun around only to catch a glimpse of her precious book before it disappeared over the rail.

"How could you do such a thing?" Her cries were completely ignored, for the Captain silently limped toward his cabin. Once he loudly shut the door, she fell to her knees and wept bitterly, not caring that the whole crew watched her from a distance. They all knew better than to come to the poor women's aid with McNeil still close by.

Several minutes passed before Audrey could see through her tears, but once she glanced down, she realized there were several pages that had been torn out of the Bible inside her clenched fist.

Lanna felt her stomach tighten with fear when she saw Audrey rush past the kitchen toward the brig.

I knew I shouldn't have left her alone with the cruel man, she thought and immediately ran after her. She could already hear Audrey's cries as she approached the open brig.

"Oh, you poor wee thing! What did that scrapper do to you?" she asked as she sat down next to her.

"It was horrible," Audrey choked and buried her face in her dirty hands. When she finished telling her what happened, Lanna was completely outraged. But then again, she was completely helpless. She glanced at Audrey's tear streaked face. She looked awful, but Lanna knew she must look the same. They'd been without a hair brush for days, or even a basin of water for that matter. As she looked into Audrey's red eyes, Lanna saw something that made her want to cry as well. They were filled with hopelessness and a fear she'd never seen from the person she admired so much. In all the years Lanna had known Audrey, her faith in God was immovable. No matter what the circumstance, Audrey always knew and professed that God was bigger than anything. But it seemed different this time.

"Audrey—" Lanna placed her hands on Audrey's shoulders, "Somehow…somehow we're goin' to get out of this. God is on our side… everythin' 'ill work out." Audrey only pulled away and walked to the port hole, looking very discouraged. "You do believe that, don't you?" she quietly asked.

"I'm not sure of anything anymore."

"What do you mean?" Lanna could hardly believe what she was hearing.

"Don't you understand? There's no hope of us ever being released. Not as long as Captain McNeil has my shell."

"Aye, that may be, but God is still on our side. He's bigger than the daft Captain!" Lanna now shouted.

"Perhaps mother was right. Maybe God can't help us," Audrey

turned away and muttered under her breath, "Perhaps there isn't a God," she couldn't believe those words had just come from her own mouth. Lanna stood, staring at Audrey. As a tear rolled down her stunned face, the ladies maid slowly walked out of the open cell.

"I never thought I would hear you say such a thing," she said quietly. However, right before she turned to leave, the ladies maid whispered something barely audible, "I looked up to you." Audrey was left with her very guilty conscience. She'd never felt so alone.

CHAPTER ELEVEN

*A*s he made his way to the brig, Joseph began to get nervous. In fact, his heart pounded so loudly, he couldn't believe no one woke up when he'd passed the crew's primitive sleeping quarters.

What is wrong with me? I'm just following orders. I've never felt this way before, he thought as the brig came into view. However, when Joseph gazed down at the sleeping maidens, his pulse quickened. It was then that he realized he didn't even know their names. He'd seen them on deck several times in the last few days but could never make himself approach them, especially where Audrey was concerned. But how could he befriend them? He was after all, part of the crew keeping them from their freedom.

"Miss?" he nervously muttered. Other than the creak of the old ship, his whisper seemed to reverberate much louder than he'd intended. He quickly glanced from Lanna to Audrey, but they didn't stir.

Why does McNeil want me to wake them at this late hour anyway? Why can't it wait until morning? He must be up to something, Joseph asked himself, stifling a yawn. *Why else would I be sent down here?* After he'd fulfilled the starboard watch nearly an hour ago, Joseph was about to go to sleep when McNeil ordered him to bring Audrey and Lanna to him. He stood in indecision for quite a while.

Well, I better carry out my duty. McNeil will be waiting. "Miss, wake up." Audrey slowly turned to her side and finally sat up.

"What's going on?" Lanna yawned.

"It's the middle of the night," Audrey stated sleepily after glancing through the port hole. The sky was pitch black, except for an eerie moon.

"All hands on deck!" the order sounded, along with the bells.

"The Captain wants both av yer on deck also," Joseph stated, but still felt a bit uneasy. Audrey moved her gaze to Lanna, but when she recalled what had happened earlier, she looked down in shame. The ladies maid only sighed in return. After getting to their feet, they followed the sailor through the dark hull.

Audrey knew it was a rather silly time to be thinking it, but she couldn't help notice how handsome the sailor was. Even though his face was unshorn and his white tunic was dirty, she easily overlooked it and only saw his brawny features. Her thoughts were abruptly interrupted as her foot caught the edge of the hatch, causing her to stumble. It was so dark she could barely see one step in front of her!

"Mind yar step," Joseph warned and grasped her arm. For a brief moment the clouds seemed to part and Audrey caught a glimpse of his eyes. She marveled at how blue they were. The moonlight shined over the deck as they emerged from the hatch. Both young women were astonished at how crowded it was. Audrey also thought it strange that not one lamp was lit. Once in a while, Audrey would go for a walk at night when McNeil allowed her and Lanna to do so. Normally, there were a few lanterns lit and only a handful of men on deck.

Everyone is awake and about their duties? Fear slowly washed over her, for she knew something was about to happen, and it would most likely be less than pleasurable.

Why does the dreadful Captain want Lanna and me at this hour? She anxiously thought as they approached the stern and spotted McNeil looking through his glass and William quietly talking beside him.

"Captain," Joseph called once they climbed the stairs onto the quarter deck.

"Ah, I'm glad you're both finally here," McNeil sneered and glared at Joseph. Audrey tried to ignore the condescending, smug tone in his voice. "You won't want to miss what we're about to do."

"What are you talking about?" Lanna boldly inquired.

"Didn't you notice the ship ahead?" William asked, not believing how they could have overlooked the bright vessel only a few yards in front of them. It gave Audrey a cold shiver because the lonely ship looked almost ghostly as it rolled over the swells. Suddenly what the Captain had said four days ago, when they had breakfast together, quickly came to mind.

"You can thank Irish for all the ships we're going to ambush with the shell's help." Audrey was convinced the Captain would be true to his word. Without another thought, she began to march back to the hull. The last thing she wanted to see was a ship taken over. She'd heard about the horrors of what occurred during a siege. Usually, if there were women aboard, they'd be captured and mistreated while the men would be shot and killed if they resisted. And sometimes they were all killed merely for the perverted enjoyment of cruel men.

"Joseph, don't stand there gawking. Go and get her!" McNeil ordered and wondered why the young sailor hesitated. When he finally did go, his steps were slow. Never had McNeil seen Joseph react to his orders this way. He was young, and anybody who'd ever talked to him quickly found out that Joseph's dream was to be a sailor. In fact, ever since McNeil had hired him, he was always eager to perform any kind of duty. Even with Joseph's slow pace, he easily caught up with Audrey. When she realized she was being followed, Audrey didn't run away, but instead, stopped and turned to face him.

"I don't care what Captain McNeil wants, I will not watch what he's about to do," she stated firmly. Joseph couldn't stand seeing Audrey's fearful expression.

"I have to brin' yar back," he quietly spoke so none of the crew or the Captain could hear and moved his gaze to the other ship in indecision. He then grasped her arm, beckoning her to follow him back to the quarter deck.

Once again, Audrey couldn't believe her thoughts. She was again taken back by the sailor's kindness and his gentle touch. He could easily force her to go without hesitation.

"Joseph! We're waiting. What are ya doing?" William called to them while McNeil intently watched from behind and stroked his beard. Lanna also strained to see what Joseph and Audrey were up to.

I wish I could make out what they're saying to each other.

After several minutes, Audrey finally let the sailor lead her back to the small group.

"You can sit here, madam," William smugly pointed to an upholstered chair someone had obviously brought from the Captain's quarters. "But if you refuse, you'll be forced to watch... on his lap," he chuckled. Even though the darkness, Audrey saw Henry step forward and wink at her wickedly. Needless to say, she angrily stomped to the chair. For a minute, she wondered why they hadn't brought another chair for Lanna.

She probably wouldn't want to sit beside me anyway, Audrey thought. Ever since their argument, very few words had been spoken between them.

"All right men!" McNeil's booming voice echoed, "If you haven't figured it out by now, we're going to ambush the vessel before us."

Audrey was surprised when several sailors cheered at his announcement.

Have they done this before? she asked herself.

"Don't light any lamps, for we'll be upon them soon. Larboard, get some muskets. The rest of you, haul out to leeward!" McNeil turned to the lady and grinned.

Audrey had never been afraid of the dark, even as a child. However, the situation at hand was an entirely different matter. She'd never experienced such darkness. The moonlight had made it tolerable at first but soon the sky became cloudy and the rolling waves were black as pitch. Now the only light came from the ship they were about to ambush in a matter of minutes.

The St. Carlin was now at full speed in their pursuit. Audrey marveled at how the crew could keep working in such conditions. Other than the frequent orders from the Captain, the darkness seemed to creep in until it felt isolating, completely smothering her.

Irish, who had been put to work trimming the yards, could hardly believe what they were about to do, nor was there anything he could say or do to stop it. Ever since McNeil made it look as if he was to blame for Audrey's capture, he'd been worked to the bone. But he figured that would be the case, since the last thing the Captain wanted was Irish approaching the young lady and revealing the possible truth.

"Lay, get alongside them," McNeil ordered as quietly as he could. Some of the crew then began to clean their muskets. Audrey wondered if anyone in the ship ahead of them had any idea of what was about to befall them.

"Starboard, collect the grappling hooks," this order came from William, who now lowered his voice as they neared the unsuspecting vessel. As the St. Carlin made its way to the port side of the other ship, everything was quiet. That is, until the lookout, who stood in the crow's nest finally noticed the dark vessel silently stalking them. Everyone aboard the St. Carlin watched, what seemed only seconds, until every sailor on the other ship rushed to the deck, scrambling to pick up their speed, but it was too late. McNeil gave the signal and his men quickly threw their hooks onto the other ship's rail. Then the Larboard sailors, who held the muskets, climbed over and immediately pointed them at the stunned crew. The few men that tried to put up a fight were either knocked unconscious or thrown into the freezing water below.

Several minutes of struggling to gain control went by before a musket was fired. Audrey jumped from the startling sound and quickly leaned forward, trying to see what had taken place. But then again, she wasn't sure she wanted to find out. All was still, until she heard men start to cheer.

Audrey didn't know which crew it was until McNeil shouted, "Well done men!" He happily climbed aboard the conquered vessel. Along with him were a handful of other sailors holding what appeared to be several crates and small trunks. She intently watched Francis run up to McNeil.

"The Captain's been shot, but we have the first mate," he stated proudly. Upon hearing this, Audrey's hands came to her mouth in unbelief at the sudden loss of life.

And for what profit? A little gold? This is preposterous. No one seems the least bit remorseful. Out of curiosity sake, she scanned both decks for Irish. It took a little while, but she finally managed to locate him amongst the crowd. He didn't look very pleased at what they'd achieved. Even from where she sat, she could see Irish, halfheartedly pointing a musket at the defeated men. Audrey then glanced up at Joseph, who stood a few feet behind her because he'd been ordered to make sure she stayed put. His expression was also solemn. Her musings swiftly came to a halt when she noticed the first mate of the other ship being dragged to McNeil.

"Well sailor, what kind of vessel is this?" he inquired.

"Only a merchant ship," the poor man replied. McNeil stepped up to the tall, lanky man and punched him in the stomach.

"That was the wrong answer," the Captain growled through clenched teeth, "I saw how many passengers were on board just this morning, and they appeared to be more than merchants. This is a clipper ship." Audrey quickly covered her eyes when McNeil hit him again.

"Bring me every person on this bloody ship," he ordered, after the first mate fell to the plank floor. She would never forget the shrill screams that came from the women who were dragged from their cabins and brought to the deck in their night clothes.

Nearly two hours later, Audrey was amazed at the large number of men, women, and even some children that were now on deck. When every single one of them and their cabins were thoroughly searched for anything of value, the crew carried the treasure back onto the St. Carlin.

"Well, I hope you all have a safe voyage," Captain McNeil chuckled when he'd returned to the St. Carlin. However, before walking back to the stern, he picked up a nearby lantern and lit it. Turning to the other vessel, he threw it onto the deck. As it burst into flames, Audrey once again heard screams from the women and children. She marveled at the Captain's cruelty.

"All hands ahoy. Sail ho!" McNeil continued to watch the fire growing larger by the minute. The men immediately went about their duties, but Audrey couldn't bear it any longer. She stood up and darted down the quarter deck before anyone could stop her. Francis was just beginning to relight some of the ship's lanterns, so she could see where she was going fairly well.

Audrey marched up to McNeil and realized she had no idea what to do once she faced the broad Captain. She slowed her pace momentarily to come up with an idea.

I know what I'll do. Nearly every day Audrey angrily watched McNeil pull out the shell pieces from inside his jacket pocket, which were now tied onto a small leather cord. She never quite understood what he was doing when he intently stared at it, all the while stroking his beard. Audrey finally started toward McNeil again, but she still wasn't sure how she would retrieve the shell from him. Suddenly, out of the corner of her eye, she thought she saw something glisten. She quickly stopped and tried to locate the shiny object. It was actually her shell, hanging half way out of the pocket of McNeil's jacket! He was so consumed in watching the other crew trying to put out the fire he'd started, that he had no idea what Audrey was about to do. She knew she wouldn't have much time before someone was bound to notice her. Her heart pounded so loudly, Audrey was afraid someone might hear her as she simply reached for the shell then immediately backed away.

As she turned to run, McNeil yelled after her, "Hey!" But his bellowing was no use, Audrey just kept running.

"Where do you think you're runnin' to, lass? There's nowhere to hide," he now laughed as he slowly followed the young lady. However, he felt his temper rising with every step he took.

Audrey knew McNeil's words were painfully true. In fact, his words seemed to ring in her ears. But something inside of her kept her from stopping.

What should I do now? she sighed heavily when she approached the very front of the ship. There was indeed nowhere to go.

What have I done? Oh Lord, please protect me! She finally turned to face the Captain and actually smiled. McNeil was dumbfounded by her expression, but suddenly realized why she was so amused with herself. She lifted the shell with a trembling hand and held it over the rail.

"My dear," McNeil swiftly came to a halt and tried to remain calm. He had no idea how to stop what she was about to do, but he surely didn't want Audrey to know how nervous he was.

She won't hesitate for long. The shell is of no value to her, he anxiously thought.

"You'd better think twice before doing anything hasty." *Worthless crew...why didn't anyone stop her?* McNeil felt completely helpless. A feeling he hated.

With the Captain's serious expression and anxiety in his voice, Audrey knew she was making him uneasy. The consequences of throwing the precious shell overboard hadn't even crossed her mind. She kept telling herself to release the shell, but her hand now felt glued to it.

What's wrong with me? This shell has been nothing but trouble. If it hadn't been for this horrible thing, Lanna and I wouldn't be in this mess. Nevertheless, she couldn't make herself release it. As she hesitated even longer, McNeil remembered Lanna was still being held on the quarter deck.

"Jake, bring the maid to me. Step lightly, man!" he ordered, trying to talk quietly.

Why hasn't she dashed it into the sea yet? Is it possible she's still frightened of me? Audrey was able to loosen her tight grasp a bit, when she caught sight of Jake Harper bringing Lanna toward McNeil.

"Unhand me, scrapper!" the ladies maid shouted.

"Miss Wesley, you give me no choice," McNeil growled and took hold of Lanna's forearm. Audrey seemed to be frozen in place as she stared at her dear friend. She desperately tried to think of a way to escape from the nightmare she found herself in. What she didn't know was, the situation was about to get far worse. The Captain grabbed both of Lanna's arms and swung her over the side of the rail with great ease. The small maid's scream pierced the air and quickly caught the attention of everyone on the ship.

"If you release the shell you'll never see her again...sure as the tide." Now it was McNeil's turn to smile. Tears swiftly came to Audrey's eyes as she realized how foolish it was to think she could outsmart the Captain. He then released one of Lanna's arm which made her swing back and forth. Her cries finally made Audrey rouse from her frozen stupor.

"Wait...don't let her go. Here!" Audrey held the shell out toward McNeil. He gave the word, and William ripped the shell from her hand, then another man grabbed Audrey and brought her to the Captain, who slowly lifted Lanna back to safety.

"My patience for you is gone," McNeil roughly took ahold of her chin to make her look up at him. "You'll regret what you've done this night. Lock her in the brig."

Before being taken back to the hull, Audrey glanced at Lanna, who clutched her arm where McNeil had held it. But she wouldn't look at her in return.

CHAPTER TWELVE

*Q*s David rode over the hill, he saw it. It took a little longer to get there than he'd anticipated, but he arrived none the less. In the back of his mind there was a nagging feeling that he'd traveled all this way in vain. As much as he tried to push it aside, it just kept coming to him.

If I've come all this way and it turns out to be a dead end, there's no telling where Audrey and Lanna could be by now. Trying to dwell on something else, David began to look at the scenery as he got closer to the town.

Scottsford was a very large and beautiful town. Most of the houses were on the hill he'd just ridden over and they all faced the harbor.

Surely someone will know of Captain McNeil and his ship, he hoped. Right at that moment, David recalled Jim Calford's severe warning.

Am I doing the right thing by going after Audrey myself? Should I have gotten someone to accompany me in my pursuit? Oh well, perhaps the drunk old man exaggerated a bit. Why did I tell Lanna to go after her? How did I think she would get past Audrey's captors? By the time David stopped blaming himself for the time being, he was right in the middle of the Scottsford Harbor.

Well, I suppose I should start asking around.

"You there," David called, after dismounting his horse and approached a sailor. However, the busy man, who held a large crate, kept walking as if he hadn't even heard David.

"Excuse me…I was wondering.…" David went after him and tapped his shoulder. It was then the sailor stopped and turned to him, looking annoyed.

"What?"

"Do you know of—" He was quickly cut off by the man.

"Aye, can't ya see I'm busy? Bother someone else with your daft questions." With that, he continued.

How rude, David thought. He was about to ask someone else, but found that everyone appeared to be far too consumed with their business.

Now what should I do? He scanned the harbor until he caught a glimpse of two men entering a pub.

"I've got it!" David suddenly shouted, which caused several heads to turn in his direction, only for a moment. But he didn't mind. He decided a local pub would probably be the best place to ask about the ship he was seeking. It would surely be easier asking a bunch of gossiping fools than try to get another busy sailor to stop his work so David could talk with him.

He weaved through the crowded streets, until he finally arrived at the tavern. He entered the dim smoky room and was warmly welcomed by several hellos.

"What will ya have?" The barkeep asked.

"Nothing. I'm in a hurry, but I need to know if anyone here can tell me anything about Captain McNeil and his ship the St. Carlin?" Several silent minutes past before one man finally spoke up.

"Aye, what would you be needin' to know?"

"Everything," David quickly replied.

Rose abruptly sat up and found herself completely soaked with perspiration. Once she realized she'd had the horrible dream again it still took quite a while to slow her frantic breathing and pounding heart.

I can't believe it happened again, she thought as she wiped her brow. Rose must have had the same dream every night since Audrey's disappearance. Every time it occurred, it seemed so real; she could in fact taste the salty air and feel the mist from the large waves. Her throat ached from her screams as Rose held onto the sides of a lifeboat in the dream.

I wish I knew what it meant. As much as she tried to forget about the nightmare, she couldn't help but ponder over it.

While she held on for dear life, Rose would watch the ship that held her husband captive, drifting farther and farther into the darkness of the raging storm. Then she felt a small icy hand on her shoulder. Turning, her gaze would fall upon a young woman, standing at the stern of the same lifeboat. Her skin was pale almost ghostlike, with her long wavy hair and white silk dress she wore, blowing in the fierce wind. Eventually, Rose would recognize the strange woman as her daughter! What affected her above all else was when Rose looked into Audrey's porcelain face. It was innocent, so peaceful even in the midst of the storm. However, as quickly as she appeared, Audrey would smile, silently step up to the edge, and slip into the raging depths. No matter how many times Rose screamed after her and told her to stop, it was no use. She would then wake up with a start.

It's always exactly the same. What could it mean? Why does it continually affect me so? Rose thought as she realized all the bed sheets were also drenched. She got out of her bed and slowly walked to the window. The sun was already shining through.

Where could she be? Was she indeed kidnapped, or did she merely run away? "Oh, Audrey," Rose fell onto the window seat, and started to weep. "I'm so sorry for what I've done." *Why? Why have I treated her so poorly...when all she wanted was my love.*

As she slowly stood up, Rose caught a glimpse of her father walking to the front door below. *He must have just returned from town.* She went for her robe, then rushed to the door. She had worn her robe a lot lately. Figuring it didn't make much sense to get dressed for the day, when there was no reason to even get out of bed.

When she came to the large staircase, she met Harold entering the front door.

"Is there any word from David?" Rose asked, then held her breath. Harold in return said nothing, but looked down and slowly shook his head. Rose turned to go back to her room after letting out a heavy sigh.

David must not be having any luck in his search for Audrey. Well God, you've let me down once again. It's unquestionably heartless allowing Audrey to be kidnapped, especially when she's been so faithful towards you.

"Here you go, lass." Jake Harper set a plate of food down next to Audrey before stepping out of the brig. Before he could lock it however, he glanced at the poor women. She looked so hopeless as she sat on the plank floor, staring at the small hole where a cannon once sat.

"You brought this upon yourself, you know," he admonished, but Audrey remained silent.

"The Captain's mighty angry," his chuckling made Audrey finally glance up at him. "Aye, I'll never forget the look on his face when you were about to let go of that shell." Upon hearing this, Audrey also recalled the Captain's expression two days earlier, and couldn't help but smile herself.

"Starboard watch!" Someone suddenly called from deck. Jake Harper locked the door and silently made his way back to the deck.

Later that night, Audrey turned over on her side and sighed. She couldn't sleep yet again, for too many thoughts reeled through her mind. Was her family frantically searching for her?

They must all think I'm dead. Or maybe they're not even worried about me. The remembrance of Audrey and her mother's quarrel still made her stomach ache.

Mother probably thinks I ran away. But David was there. He knows what really happened. That is, if he's all right after getting hit. Audrey turned over onto her stomach as if she could turn her back on the troubling thoughts and escape them. However, it wasn't long before Lanna's words came back to haunt her.

I've disappointed her. We were closer than sisters and she admired me, but I let her down. Tears came then, but she didn't bother to dry them. "I'm sorry Lanna," she cried aloud. *I didn't mean to.*

Strangely enough, after the sailors were ordered to lock Audrey into the brig, she had no idea where Lanna had gone.

I hope she's alright. For all I know, she could have asked not to stay with me, she mused.

After a while, Audrey fell into a fitful sleep that only lasted an hour or so, for she was awakened by her anxiety.

Why didn't God protect me from getting captured in the first place? Or at least warn me. She'd gone over the events many times since then, but it wasn't until that moment Audrey finally saw the truth. Minutes before Henry had grabbed her that day, she sensed it might not be safe for her to be in the garden.

"But I didn't listen!" Audrey quickly sat up, and glanced through the small window. "It was all my fault," she sobbed as she scrambled to the corner of the small cell and began sifting through the straw. She could see fairly well because there were no clouds and the moon was full as it shone through the port hole.

After recovering the few pages that had been ripped out of her Bible, Audrey breathed a sigh of relief that she hadn't thrown them away. She hadn't looked at them since McNeil threw her precious book overboard, though she needed some answers and something inside her told her she would find them in the pages her dirty hands now held. However, before looking through them, Audrey gazed up at the ceiling.

"Lord," she whispered, her tears starting anew. "I've come to my wit's end…I don't know what to do, but I can't do it alone. I'm sorry I've turned my back on you. Help me, Lord!" Through blurred vision, she glanced down at the pages. Most of the pages were torn, but thankfully a few remained undamaged. There were about fifteen in total, but amazingly enough, the very first page was the ninety first chapter of Psalms.

"He that dwelleth in the secret place of the most High shall abide under the shadow of the Almighty. I will say of the Lord, He is my refuge and my fortress: my God; in him will I trust. Surely he shall deliver thee from the snare of the fowler, and from the noisome pestilence. He shall cover thee with his feathers, and under his wings shalt thou trust: his truth shall be thy shield and buckler. Thou shalt not be afraid for the terror by night; nor for the arrow that flieth by day; Nor for the pestilence that walketh in darkness; nor for the destruction that waistth at noonday. A thousand shall fall at thy side, and ten thousand at thy right hand; but it shall not come nigh thee. Only with thine eyes shalt thou behold and see the reward of the wicked. Because thou hast made the Lord, which is my refuge, even the most High, thy habitation; There shall no evil befall thee, neither shall any plague come nigh thy dwelling. For he shall give his angels charge over thee, to keep thee in all thy ways. They shall bear thee up in their hands, lest thou dash thy foot against a stone. Thou shalt tread upon the lion and adder: the young lion and the dragon shalt thou trample under feet. Because he hath set his love upon me, therefore will I deliver him: I will set him on high, because he hath known my name. He shall call upon me, and I will answer him: I will be with him in trouble; I will deliver him, and honour him. With long life will I satisfy him, and shew him my salvation."

Upon reading this, an overwhelming peace swept through Audrey. It was as if God had written it just for her, and in a way He had. God had never left her, *He* was with her in trouble. And *He* had given his angels to watch out for her.

I can't believe how blinded I've become these past few days. She glanced at the ceiling again. *God I'm so sorry. I was the one who didn't heed your warnings...I wasn't dwelling in your secret place, away from harm. I see now that Your warning was Your protection. I could have prevented this whole thing!* Well, *no more! From this day forward, Lord, I'm going to listen to You.*

After reading the Psalm once more, Audrey began to worship and praise God. It made her feel so good to be right with her heavenly Father. It felt as if a large weight was lifted from her.

By the time the sun's first rays shined on the horizon, Audrey felt like a new person. If Captain McNeil hadn't ripped her Bible from her hands, she would've never found and read the Psalm. She was no longer afraid of anything because she knew God was always with her.

I just wish I could talk to Lanna and tell her how sorry I am.

CHAPTER THIRTEEN

"**I**fn you're in a hurry, there won't be enough time for me to tell you what you want to know about John McNeil," the gruff looking man, who was probably in his early sixties, informed the young man. David then slowly walked over to the small table in the corner.

"By all means, please tell me everything you can," he sighed and figured it might be important to find out all he could about the Captain. Furthermore, it wouldn't do him any good to be in a hurry if he hadn't the slightest idea where Audrey and Lanna were in the first place.

"I'm David Lawrence," he extended his hand and the man took it.

"Peter Sterling, but everyone just calls me Pete," As he leaned forward into the light, David immediately noticed a horrifying scar where Pete's left eye should have been. It began at his cheek bone and nearly went up to his gray hairline. He couldn't believe he hadn't seen it right away, but the light in the pub was poor.

"Might I be askin' why you want to know about this McNeil?" Pete asked.

"Uh…well, some of his crew kidnapped a young woman and her maid. I'm trying to find them," David replied and tried not to stare at his partially mauled face. "I want to know of the man who would kidnap two innocent women and take them away from their home," he finally sat down across from Pete.

"I'll tell ya, everything I know. John McNeil grew up in Bonnie Point , a small town right on the coast of Ireland. He worked as a blacksmith with his father. There he married an English woman...Lenora. And they had a son," Pete momentarily stopped and sighed heavily as if it were painful for him to speak of it.

"One night, he came home drunk and beat Lenora like he'd done before. But this time she'd had enough. As soon as he passed out, she took their son and fled. They secretly boarded a ship bound to America. Needless to say, John was none too happy when he'd found out where they'd gone. He then boarded a ship also. That is, when he managed to save up enough money. When he arrived in Boston, it had been more than a year since they'd left. It took quite a few months for him to find his family but when he did, John wished he'd never come to America......"

McNeil set out once again to the busy market in Boston to search for them. He didn't really know why he stayed in the town so long, but something told him Lenora was close by.

She always said Boston was a wonderful place and we had to visit or move there one day. I just know she's here, he kept telling himself as he walked through the market.

Nearly an hour later, his suspicions were confirmed! There, at the very edge of the market, McNeil was shocked to see Lenora with child, and holding the arm of a well-dressed man. She was dressed in an elegant gown as well. They were just getting into a grand carriage. It was only then that he saw the person he'd truly been searching for. McNeil's small son climbed into the carriage with the help of the strange man.

Get your hands off my son! he clenched his teeth, his hands now curled into tight fists. It took everything in him not to run up to the man and kill him right then and there.

Lenora, how could you do such a thing? McNeil carefully followed the carriage all the way through town where he was once again taken back when they stopped in front of a magnificent mansion.

"Welcome home Mr. and Mrs. Baits," the butler opened the door and greeted when the three approached the entrance.

My wife married another man? Now McNeil had really lost his temper......

"At that moment, John swore to himself that he would go back to the mansion that night and indeed kill the wealthy man who'd stolen his wife and son." Pete took a quick sip of his drink then continued. "Needless to say, John was full up with ale when he returned after dark......."

McNeil stumbled up to the front door and knocked as if they would simply hand over his son.

"Yes?"

"I've come for my son. He's mine and I want him back," McNeil's statement was slurred.

"Go away, fool. Sleep it off somewhere else," the old butler snapped when he realized the stranger was intoxicated. He then shut the door in his face.

McNeil wasn't about to give up that easily. He crept to the side of the house. He tore the sleeve from his tunic, wrapped it around a large rock he'd found, and poured some ale on it. As soon as he located the room where Lenora and her new husband sat in front of the fireplace, McNeil lit the cloth on fire and threw it into the large window. When he heard Lenora's scream, he chuckled and quickly climbed through the shattered window. He quickly found himself face to face with Mr. Baits.

"John, what are you doing here?" Lenora gasped.

"Don't talk to me you...you—" Suddenly Mr. Baits attacked him and they fell to the floor.

The last thing McNeil remembered before being knocked unconscious was a loud explosion and Lenora's shrieking. He finally awoke to see the room, engulfed in flames. McNeil coughed and wheezed as he slowly got to his feet, but couldn't see anything through the smoke! His first plan was to rush up the stairs to find where his son, Dennon most likely slept. But now he realized it to be impossible. Instead, McNeil ran outside to catch his breath. To his horror, he found Lenora holding a lifeless young boy. Fear rose up in him at his wife's hysterical cries.

"Leave us alone," Mr. Baits marched up to him, but McNeil quickly pushed him to the ground and rushed to Dennon.

"Look what you've done!" Lenora cried hoarsely, "You've killed him...you've killed him!" she said over and over. But McNeil hardly noticed as he pulled Dennon's small body out of her arms and into his own.

"My son, what have I done?" He fell to his knees and tightly held Dennon against him as he wept bitter tears, groans came from deep within him.

Never had Lenora seen McNeil cry.

"John...he's gone," she slowly approached, then ever so gently took Dennon from his father.

"Now leave." Mr. Baits got to his feet.

"I'll leave when I want to," McNeil was finally able to speak, "I came here to kill you and take my son. Now get out of my way before I finish the job." Mr. Baits slowly backed away as McNeil grabbed Dennon and walked back into the darkness. His cries could be heard for quite some time......

After that, McNeil was in and out of jail for causing other trouble in the town for about four years. Eventually he got a job with the Princeton Shipping Company. Been working for them ever since. In fact, now that I think of it, he's even a minor partner now." Pete moved his gaze to the mug in his hands.

"May I ask how you know so much about him and his past?" David asked.

"Lenora is my sister. She came to me that night after being brutally beaten and I helped her escape. It was about ten years before John and I bumped into each other again. He forced me to listen to everything I just told you. Then he gave me this," Pete pointed to the left side of his face. It was then a wry smile suddenly shone on his face. "Right after John did this, I managed to shoot him," Pete proudly stated. "I didn't kill him of course...only got his leg. I used to be a pretty good shot...until I lost my eye."

"Do you have any idea where I could find him?" David asked.

"Not sure. John is unpredictable...always has been. Although, I think he goes back to his hometown, Bonnie Point every few months." Upon hearing this, David stood.

"Thank you for the information. You've been a great help." he walked to the door.

"Keep your wits about you, son. John doesn't show mercy in his dealings," Pete warned and David nodded in return, then made his way back to the still busy harbor.

Now all I need to do is find a ship that's going to Ireland.

CHAPTER FOURTEEN

May 1839

"**L**and Ho!" The sailor in the crow's nest called.
Audrey quickly sat up and rushed to the window.
Land! I wonder where we are. Unfortunately, all she could see was fog. *How can they be certain we won't crash into anything?* She thought as she began to pace back and forth in her cell.

As far as she could tell, it was the seventh of May, a Wednesday. This meant that Audrey had been kidnapped for nearly two weeks, and locked in the brig for five horrible days.

I don't know if I can bear being cooped up here any longer. "I pray they'll let me go to shore." Then, as if on cue, Audrey heard someone approach. When she turned toward the noise, she spotted Charlie digging in a barrel close by.

"Are we going to shore?" she anxiously asked.

"Not we, lass. You're not going anywhere," he smiled and must have found what he'd been searching for, because he simply walked back down the narrow hallway.

"Wait!" Desperation was clearly evident in her voice, "Please come back," Audrey breathlessly called after the retreating sailor and grasped the bars on the door, but it was no use. Charlie was gone. She let out a long sigh and wandered over to one of the crates. She once again strained to see any sign of land through the heavy fog. It seemed ever since Audrey's small talk with Jake Harper days ago, no one ever spoke to her anymore when they brought her three meager meals a day.

The Captain probably forbids anyone to talk to me. I just wish I knew where Lanna was. Who knows what's become of her in these past few days, she thought, trying to push her worries out of her mind.

Audrey had never felt so restless as she tearfully watched McNeil and most of his crew row to shore, leaving her behind. Hopeless thoughts swiftly began to creep in and tried to claim her newly found joy.

Will I ever set foot on land again? She tried to make her sadness leave by turning away from the port hole, but they remained. Finally she wiped her moist face.

"No, stop this," Audrey reprimanded herself, "I refuse to worry. Lord, I put my trust in You and I cast my cares on You in Jesus' Name, amen." She lay down upon what had become her very uncomfortable bed, made by gathering all the straw from the brig floor into a pile. It did little to soften the hard planks. She then retrieved the few pages from her Bible and began to read. Eventually, sleep claimed her.

Nearly two hours later, Audrey was awakened by someone whispering her name. She had no idea who it could be, but the voice was familiar just the same. When she opened her eyes, she quickly had to shield them from a bright light. For a moment, she thought she must be dreaming.

Am I dead? Audrey thought, slowly sitting up, only to find that she was still indeed locked up in the hull. She felt a shiver run through her after rubbing her eyes in disbelief, straining to see where or what the light was coming from. It definitely felt like a presence, as if someone was in the brig with her. Then, as quickly at the light entered the room, it disappeared, leaving the dark, dingy place exactly the same. She sat there in stunned silence for quite a while.

What was that? Was I only dreaming of the bright light? she asked herself many times. *I've been in here so long I'm starting to see things.* However, what she saw next confirmed the mysterious thing that had just happened was not a dream. The brig door was now wide open! Audrey could scarcely believe her eyes. In fact, she blinked several times to be sure.

"Thank you Father," she cried and put the precious pages back in her pocket. As she slowly got to her feet, her knees were wobbly at first. Without another thought, Audrey walked through the open door.

When the realization of being freed from her cage hit her, she didn't know what to do next.

All right, first I must find Lanna. Then we'll have to find a boat and row to shore without being seen.

Almost every day she thought of ways to escape, but having to row all the way to shore had failed to cross her mind before. It all seemed so much more difficult now that she was actually free. She also had no idea where to start looking for her ladies maid. She crept through the hull and slowly took a breath of the fresh salty air once she reached the stairs. After going up a few steps, she carefully peeked out of the hatch.

Lanna, where are you? She scanned the deck. There was no sign of her dear friend. Suddenly, to Audrey's horror, she caught a glimpse of her. She was tied to the large mast right in the middle of the deck.

Oh, what have I done? How am I to get to her without being seen? She couldn't take her eyes from the ladies maid. There was a gag over her mouth and she sat on the plank floor with her back against the mast. She appeared to be sleeping.

Poor thing. She looks awful.

Audrey had to quickly duck back down under the hatch when she heard a noise.

"Hey, as long as the Captain's gone to shore, we can have us a little fun," Henry sneered just as she slowly glanced out. A handful of sailors were standing outside of the officer's dining quarters. Audrey cringed and wondered what kind of *fun* they had in mind this time. Thankfully, they all seemed so preoccupied that she knew this might be her only chance to make a run for it. After taking one last look at the men, Audrey dashed toward Lanna. Just as soon as she reached the mast, she quickly hid behind it and tried to slow her wild breathing. Her heart felt like it was going to beat out of her chest. She glanced at the sailors and found they'd all entered the room and shut the door behind them. Since the coast was clear, Audrey quickly knelt beside the sleeping young woman. The sight was almost too much to bear.

How long has she been tied up like this? her anger rose up in her, but at the same time she felt sick. *It looks as if she's been here ever since I was locked up five days ago!* The poor ladies maid was horribly sun burnt. As Audrey untied her, the skin where the ropes had been was all red with several blisters. And the gag was tied so tightly Lanna's face was bruised.

"Lanna, wake up," Audrey's voice broke with emotion.

"What...what's happenin'?" Lanna asked after she awoke. Her voice was hoarse from lack of water. She began to rub her sore wrists until Audrey spoke.

"We're getting out of here," she helped the weak maid to her feet.

"How did you get out av the brig?" Lanna whispered as they made their way to the lifeboat as fast as they could.

"There's no time to explain. We must get this boat into the water. Do you think you're strong enough to help me?" Lanna nodded eagerly, although she felt far from it.

Before they knew it, Audrey and Lanna had gotten the boat onto the side of the ship and were now lowering it.

"I'll get inside and get the ores ready and you finish lowering it..," Audrey glanced at the ladies maid. She was completely out of breath from what they'd already done, and her hands were shaking.

"Perhaps you should get in. I'm stronger than you are right now," Audrey admonished. Her arms burned as she slowly lowered the heavy lifeboat using pulleys. All of a sudden the rope became tangled which jammed the pulley.

"What happened?" Lanna called.

"The rope is stuck!" Audrey cried, "I can't get it loose." *It's almost in the water…just a little further!* She began to pull the rope back and forth in desperation.

"Audrey," Lanna gasped loudly when she saw someone standing behind her. Audrey froze as if she wouldn't be seen if she kept still. She finally gulped and slowly turned around to find Joseph standing only a few feet from her. He appeared to be watching the whole ordeal, but strangely enough, he didn't appear to be angry. Audrey didn't know what to do as he moved closer. Instead of grabbing her, Joseph took the rope from her hands. He easily untangled the pulley, then retrieved a ship's ladder and let it down over the rail. With kindness in his eyes, he turned to Audrey when he'd finished and gently helped her climb over. She was seated across from Lanna while Joseph finished lowering them the rest of the way. Both young ladies were completely speechless as Joseph nodded to them and simply walked away.

Surely a miracle had occurred for no one seemed to notice the two women who'd rowed from the St. Carlin all the way to shore. Since dusk, the fog was nearly gone so they were in perfect view from the small town.

After Audrey and Lanna hid the lifeboat, they slowly climbed up the rocky bank. Thankfully they were able to stay out of sight behind some cargo piled up by the edge of the small harbor.

"What should we do?" Audrey whispered as both women searched for a place to better hide.

"Aye, look," Lanna pointed to what appeared to be an old storage shed about forty feet from where they stood.

"We'll have to make a run for it," Audrey was saying, but suddenly they both ducked behind the crates as two men walked by. They silently watched them saunter toward a rundown pub just up the road. Right when the men approached the pub's entrance, they nearly ran into another man who emerged. Audrey immediately recognized him as Jake Harper.

"Aye, what's the craic?" One of the men asked Jake.

"Well, the bar maids are ugly and the drinks are lousy, but it's worth gettin' off the ship for a while," Jake Harper replied.

"We're in Ireland."

"How can you tell?" Audrey asked, turning to Lanna.

"Well, the way those men talked. And I believe the church over there is Catholic."

"Are you certain?"

"Aye," After taking one last look to make sure it was safe, they both ran as fast as they could to the shed.

I hope no one is inside, Lanna anxiously thought as she slowly opened the heavy door and crept inside.

"I can't see anything," Audrey gasped after shutting the door.

"I know, but there's nathin' we can do." Once they're eyes adjusted a little, Lanna found a lantern, but it didn't have any kerosene.

"How did ye manage to get out av the brig?" Lanna inquired some time later, once they'd gotten somewhat comfortable. Fortunately, they were able to find some sort of tarp to sit on.

"Oh Lanna! I've so much to tell you. But first, I want you to know how sorry I am. I was entirely wrong about everything. God wasn't at fault… it was me," Audrey found it very hard to talk to her friend when she could hardly see her face in the dim light. But she continued anyway. "I've asked God to forgive me, but I've yet to ask you. I'm so sorry. Please forgive me for my doubts." All was silent until Audrey thought she heard Lanna try to stifle a sob. Suddenly out of the darkness, she was embraced by the ladies maid.

"Of course I forgive you. You're me dearest friend. I'm the one who should be apologizin'. I was too hard on you." When Lanna finally released her hold, Audrey began to tell her about the glorious, but at the same time mysterious light that had entered the brig.

"Why were you tied against the mast?" She quickly asked, once she remembered the horrible state she had found her friend in.

"Well," she sighed, "After you'd been locked up, I slept in the kitchen. But two days later, I was put to work cleanin' McNeil's cabin. One day I was tidin' up a bit when I heard someone enter. I turned an' saw the Captain come in an' close the door behind 'imself. I knew it wouldn't be good. Just when he reached for me, I bit the daft buggar before he could even touch me!" Lanna smiled proudly.

"You bit Captain McNeil?" Audrey gasped, hardly believing what she'd just heard.

"Aye, right on the arm, as hard as I could."

"Lanna Ryan, you are a corker!" Audrey stated, then they both burst out laughing. However, when they recalled where they were, they immediately covered their mouths to keep quiet.

"It's queer hearin' that from you, especially with your English accent," Lanna grinned, but kept her voice at a whisper.

"What shall we do now?" Audrey asked.

"I was just thinkin' the same."

"I suppose we'll have to stay hidden until the St. Carlin sails away, but I don't know what we'll do for food until then."

"Well, if God has gotten us this far, He's well able to take care av the rest," Lanna admonished. Audrey silently thanked God for such her dear friend.

"What do you mean they're gone?" McNeil's booming voice sounded. Just before dark, McNeil and his men made their way back to the ship. To say the least, the Captain was not pleased when Francis informed him that the women had escaped.

"How could two incompetent females get away without being seen, much less make it to shore?" he yelled even louder.

"I'm sorry Sir, I just don't know." What Francis failed to mention was the reason why no one had seen them.

"None of the men saw them." All was revealed as McNeil instantly smelled port on his breath.

While the first mate braced himself for what he knew was coming, the Captain did indeed strike the stout man.

"Men, take this dog to the brig, but first flog him. See this as a warning for the rest of you. My patience is wearing thin, so keep in line. Tomorrow we're going to find the damsels," McNeil sneered then made his way to his cabin.

CHAPTER FIFTEEN

" *A*lright, we both need a little rest. You from carrying me, and I need to walk a bit," David jumped down from his horse and stretched. It had always been a habit for David to talk with his steed. Since he was around horses most of the time, they were his only company. In fact, he had been taking care of them since he could remember. One of his dreams was to one day own a livery in a large town somewhere.

With Audrey at my side. David let out a sigh and began to walk down the road. The young man had never been much for traveling. The past week had been the first time he'd been on a ship, much less away from Augustine. It took nearly six days from England, but once he arrived in Port Shire, he soon found out his search was far from over. That did nothing to lift his spirits. He was already feeling a sense of hopelessness from the long voyage to Ireland for he'd asked everyone on the ship if they'd heard of Captain McNeil, but it was no use. The only thing that beckoned him to continue was Audrey and Peter Sterling's story that David hoped was true.

"Come on, old boy. We should reach Bonnie Point anytime now," David turned to his steed. Sure enough, the small town slowly came into view.

Thank goodness I'm finally here! I just hope I haven't wasted too much time already, his pace quickened at the thought.

Once he came to the center of town, he easily located the pub. His plan was to visit the local place to ask about Captain McNeil because of the luck he'd found in Scottsford.

David tied his horse on the post just outside of the pub then glanced out at the misty water. There weren't any ships docked in the shoddy harbor, but one was anchored out much further.

That's odd, why wouldn't they dock in the harbor? David asked himself. But since he hadn't the slightest idea about the workings of ships and such, he quickly forgot about it. He was about to go inside when three men cut in front of him and quickly entered the pub.

Why are they in such a hurry? He asked himself then followed them. The men approached the bar and leaned against it. The tallest of the three wore a very serious expression and was dressed much better than the other two.

A few minutes had passed when David was going to ask everyone about Captain McNeil, but the strange men beat him once again.

"Excuse me," the well-dressed man turned around. "Have any of you seen two young ladies in town today?" Several drunk men began to chuckle.

"Not many young ones round here, unless you mean Christy over there," the barkeep pointed to a toothless bar maid across the room and laughed. At that another round of laughter broke out, with the exception of the three angry men and David.

"Well, if you do see them, they belong to me. I'll be willing to pay if they're returned to me as soon as possible."

Audrey's here and she's managed to get away? David glanced at the man whom he'd been pursuing. *So this must be Captain John McNeil. He does look quite intimidating.* His gaze was intense, almost penetrating. David's thoughts were then confirmed to be true.

"What's the matter, McNeil, lost another one of your females? How'd you lose this one?" Someone continued to joke and once again they all started hollering.

When David was sure no one was watching him, he slipped out of the pub unnoticed.

I've got to find where Audrey and Lanna are hiding. They must be terrified. He swiftly mounted his horse and rode back to the harbor. It was then he realized he hadn't the slightest idea where to start looking for them.

Audrey, where could you be? He scanned the shore as if he could ascertain where the young ladies were, although he obviously didn't see any sign of them. David pulled the reigns to go further up the shore. He continued until some children, playing near an old shed, gained his attention. They appeared to be playing some sort of hide and seek.

"Hey, we could 'ide in there," a young boy pointed to the shed, but the girl standing beside him slowly shook her head.

"I'm not goin' in there!" she replied.

"Why not?"

"Because thar's ghosts!" The boy then started to laugh.

"You doss, thar's naw such things as ghosts, especially in Callaghan's storage shed."

"But I heard them," the girl stared at the old building with wide eyes.

"What?"

"Aye, I heard a lady ghost laugh jist last night when I wus walkin' home." she claimed and finally ran back into town.

That was all David needed to hear. He quickly jumped off his geld, tied it to the nearest tree, and marched to the shed.

Audrey slowly awoke and put her hand on her stomach. It had been growling all night it seemed. She knew she wouldn't be able to bear it much longer.

I should have eaten the food Jake Harper brought me before I left the cell yesterday morning. "Lanna," she whispered and meekly touched the small maid's shoulder.

"What is it?" Lanna roused.

"I'm so hungry. We have to find something to eat, or at least some water."

"Aye, but how?" she yawned.

Lord, please help us. Audrey silently prayed. All of a sudden they heard a noise. It sounded as if someone was approaching the entrance. Audrey gasped, which made Lanna immediately sit up. A shudder ran through her as she glanced around the dark room for a place to hide, but dreaded that it was too late. When they heard the door about to open, both women clung to each other in sheer panic. Audrey shut her eyes as if she could make Lanna and herself disappear.

"Whatever happens, Audrey, I'm certain we'll be alright," Lanna reassured in a hushed tone. Suddenly Audrey felt the warmth from the sun hit her face.

"Jaykers! David, it that really you?" Upon hearing Lanna's gasp, Audrey's eyes shot open in disbelief. Sure enough, David Lawrence slowly walked into the shed, but his expression was that of complete bewilderment. If truth be told, he wasn't entirely certain if the two young women who sat before him were truly the ones he'd been searching for. They were unrecognizable! However, once the ladies maid said his name, he broke the stunned silence.

"Audrey, Lanna, I've found you at last!" Audrey's hair, once smooth and silky, was now tangled and ratty. And Lanna's hair was uncontrollably frizzy. Nevertheless, David overlooked their tattered clothes and dirty faces and only saw Audrey's charming features and the way she smiled at him. He now felt certain he'd done the right thing in pursuing them so diligently.

"Forgive me for being so informal. I meant to say Miss Wesley. Are you both all right?" David covered the distance between Audrey and himself.

"You followed us all this way?" Audrey asked, still completely astonished. David grasped her hand to help her stand up.

"I couldn't rest until I found you," his voice lowered, her hand still in his own.

At first Audrey thought he was only being considerate, but as time went on, his actions began to make her more uncomfortable. While her and Lanna told him about everything that had happened, she tried to figure out what was different about him, but to no avail.

Oh well, it doesn't really matter if he's acting strangely. We'll be going home soon! She thought.

"Miss Audrey?" David interrupted her thoughts.

"Oh, I'm sorry." Audrey blushed when she realized she'd been ignoring their conversation.

"Your stomach was growlin'," Lanna quietly chuckled.

"Yes, and you looked as if you were miles away. May I ask what you were thinking?" David smiled warmly and intently gazed at her, which made her discomfort worsen. Lanna must have sensed it for she swiftly cut in.

"Is there any way we could get some food?" We haven't eaten since yesterday morn."

"Why yes! I'll go and fetch some straight away." David stood up.

"Wait, first tell me. How is my family? Are they terribly worried?" Audrey asked, tears welling in her eyes. She wasn't entirely certain if she wanted to know or not, since her and her mother hadn't been on good terms.

"Of course, they're worried. They probably would have accompanied me, but I left in quite a hurry."

"My mother is worried?" she persisted.

Why is she asking such strange questions? It's obvious that her family should be worried, isn't it? David thought. He was fully aware that Rose Wesley could be a bit high strung, but he'd never seen her treat Audrey badly.

"Yes, she's very worried. In fact, I recall your mother fainted when she first found out about your disappearance." After saying this, David turned to leave.

She fainted? I wish there was some way to assure them I'm safe and finally on my way home. Perhaps I could have David send a letter to them. She thought, and then once again realized Lanna still sat before her.

"Oh Lanna, I'm sorry." Audrey chuckled, "I don't know what's wrong with me today."

"Quite alright. Did you notice how strangely David is actin'?" Lanna asked.

"Yes, he is different, isn't he?"

David snuck back to the shed and couldn't help but feel proud of himself. After buying some food, he managed to find Audrey, Lanna and himself passage back to England. The only problem was that it wasn't going to be leaving until the tenth of May. Still a full two days away.

Surely we can stay hidden until then. David approached the shed. At that moment, he caught a glimpse of his horse still tied to a tree.

Well, I can't very well have him standing outside of the shed. And I can't bring him to the livery, for someone might start asking questions. "All right old boy. It's time we parted ways," he walked up to his steed and removed the reigns from the tree.

"Someone will be happy to have found you." With that, David struck the back of the horse and watched it wander into town.

He began to move back to the door and was about to reach for the latch, but suddenly hesitated. He could hear Audrey and Lanna talking about him inside. He then leaned in a little closer.

"Why do you suppose he's actin' so differently?"

"I'm not sure," Audrey replied.

"Aye, would you like to know what I think?" Lanna asked. "I dare say he fancies you quite a bit."

"What? It can't be." Audrey gasped, but she was starting to think the ladies maid spoke the truth.

"Why not? Yer man couldn't take his eyes off you from the minute he foun' us. Hadn't you noticed?" Lanna chuckled. "Well, do you feel the same?" she finally asked.

David held his breath when all he heard was silence in return.

"I've known him forever, but I can't say that I've ever been inclined toward him…I consider him to be a good friend." Upon hearing Audrey say this, David sighed heavily. All of his plans were instantly crushed.

Everything I've done…coming all this way…for what? I pictured this entirely different. His thoughts reeled as he slowly backed away from the shed. *I couldn't possibly barge in now.* David glanced down at the food he held. As he moved to at least leave the packages at the door, he heard the end of their conversation.

"I still can't believe we were able to escape without bein' seen."

"Except for Joseph that is," Audrey reminded her.

"Why did he let us go?" Lanna asked.

"I hardly know. There's a kindness in his eyes unlike any other." At that moment, they heard a noise just outside of the door. They both froze with fear! When nothing else was heard, Audrey and Lanna glanced at each other.

"What was that?" Audrey stood up and slowly reached for the latch. She then held her breath as she opened the door just a crack. Fortunately, the only thing she found was a loaf of bread and some cheese laying on the ground, in front of the door.

How strange. If David left this for us, where did he go? Audrey asked herself before shutting the door. But she didn't ponder it for long because her hunger was calling.

CHAPTER SIXTEEN

*L*anna slept soundly considering their meager surroundings. That is until she was awakened by someone singing nearby.

What is that noise? she thought she must be hearing things, but slowly sat up and strained to see if Audrey was awake or not. Even through the darkness, the ladies maid could tell by her even breathing that she didn't hear the strange howling. Lanna started to lay back down, when she heard it again, this time much louder.

That's quite enough. She got up and carefully opened the door.

It took a little while, but she finally recognized the strange singing man as David, who was stumbling toward them.

Is he full of spirits? He is! I've got to stop him before he wakes everyone. Lanna forgot to shut the door behind her as she boldly approached him.

"Are you daft? Do you want the whole mingin town to hear your screechin'? Why are you singing?" The ladies maid tried to keep her voice down although she'd clearly lost her temper.

"What do you mean? I ain't singin'. I have to see Audrey," David replied innocently. Upon hearing his slurred statement, her anger worsened.

"You're drunk! Have ya completely lost your senses? Someone could find us," she spewed.

"I want to see Audrey." he demanded.

"Well, she doesn't want to see you, especially like this, so ya might as well leave!" Lanna stood her ground between the shed and the tipsy man before her.

"Get out of my way," David shouted then angrily shoved Lanna.

Audrey slowly awoke. However, as soon as she noticed that Lanna was missing and the door was wide open, she rushed over and peered out.

Oh no, what's happened?

"Get out of my way." In the dim light, Audrey gasped as she witnessed David push Lanna to the ground. When he heard her, David turned and their gaze met. Something in his eyes frightened her. A sort of longing mixed with anger.

"Audrey…I," he began.

After witnessing his treatment with Lanna, Audrey backed away in fear when he began to stumble towards her. Thankfully, he was nearly upon her when he suddenly passed out. She breathed a sigh of relief as she stepped into the doorway to see if Lanna was all right. She found the ladies maid already on her feet and coming towards her. She was about to speak when Audrey spotted a large figure standing right behind her! What she saw next nearly caused her to faint. Henry, quickly covered Lanna's mouth before she even knew what was happening.

"Got ya!" he triumphantly shouted as Audrey ran back inside before being seen.

What should I do? Audrey began to cry as a sense of helplessness swept over her.

"You better hope we find your little friend, lass. The Captain has no use for you, other than bait," the sailor sneered and carried Lanna into the darkness.

"David, wake up this instant!" Audrey shook his limp arm. It took everything in her not to go after Lanna right away, but Audrey knew it would be impossible to do anything, except get captured herself.

Oh Lanna, I'm so sorry, Audrey wiped away yet another tear.

It seemed like an eternity until David finally stirred.

"Where am I?" he groaned.

"You have quite a bit of explaining to do," Audrey stated

angrily.

"What do you mean?" he rubbed his eyes.

"Lanna's been captured! I must go after her, but you have to help me," she simply explained which made David sober a bit.

"What? How are we—you, going to get Lanna back? It's impossible."

"We can't return home without her." she cried, "Lanna's like a sister to me and I'd do anything for her." David scrambled to his feet and stepped in front of the door.

"I can't let you. You're clearly not thinking straight."

"What?" Audrey shouted and also stood. "Of course I am. Now let me pass." But he wouldn't budge.

"Wait…we must consider this more."

"What is there to consider?"

"Perhaps we should at least wait until daybreak, then go after her," David continued.

"So you will help me?"

"Yes, I'm not sure how, but I'll try to do everything in my power to rescue Lanna."

"Oh thank you, David. And thank you for coming after us." David felt himself blush as Audrey placed her hand on his arm in gratitude. "Now then…we just need to come up with some sort of plan..," she walked back to her makeshift bed of old tarps, but David wasn't listening to her. His thoughts were consumed on something entirely different.

Everything is going splendidly. Surely Audrey returns my feelings. She just doesn't know it yet. Although, if we get killed trying to save Lanna, all will be ruined. We can't possibly rescue her from a whole crew of sailors…impossible. With that, David made his way to the other side of the room. He covered the dirt floor with another old cloth then laid down on it.

By morning Audrey should realize that as well. Perhaps the ship will have already left.

Early the next morning, David was still sleeping soundly until he felt someone nudging him.

"David, it's morning."

"Very well," he sat up and yawned.

"Come on, there's no time to waist. I hope they haven't mistreated Lanna, but the longer we wait...." Audrey couldn't finish. All night her thoughts had haunted her. Thoughts of what might be happening to the poor ladies maid.

"First we must retrieve the lifeboat Lanna and I hid, then row to the horrible ship once again."

"Audrey...Miss Audrey," David tried to cut in, but she continued.

"Then we'll have to—" He suddenly stood up and walked to the door. When Audrey noticed his nervous expression, she finally stopped. "What's wrong?"

"Well...that is to say...I'd hoped you would've come to you senses last night. I tried all night to think of a way, truly I did, but I just don't think we can help Lanna any longer," David lied, for in truth, he'd slept wonderfully.

"You mean we aren't going after her?" Audrey glanced up at David, tears brimming in her eyes.

"It would be completely impossible. What if they've already sailed away?"

"But you said—"

"I know, but there is no way. And I won't stand by and allow you to be killed, saving a common maid." David covered the latch with a calloused hand. Audrey couldn't believe it. He was completely unfeeling.

"Why would you say those things last night? You lied to me!" she stood up angrily. "You come along after two weeks and want to take control of everything? I'll have you know, Lanna and I escaped perfectly fine without your help," Audrey regretted the statement as soon as it came out of her mouth, for it wasn't entirely true.

"You might have escaped, but I found you both nearly starved." Audrey moved her gaze to the floor until David moved closer to her and put his hand on her shoulder.

"Audrey," he began, forgetting formalities. "I care about you and I don't want to see anything happen to you. That's why I can't let you go. Can't you see?" For a moment, he thought he'd gotten through to her, but he was sadly mistaken. They broke eye contact and Audrey quickly slipped out of the shed. David wasn't about to give up that easily.

He had better not follow me, Audrey hoped, but when she heard David behind her, she quickened her pace.

"Wait!" he called, running up to her and took ahold of her hand. "Why can't you understand what I'm trying to tell you?"

"Let me go! I'll save her myself." she knew she sounded ridiculous.

"Please," David pleaded.

"Leave me alone and go back home," Audrey shouted for she no longer cared who might hear them. She then pulled away from his hold, but David persisted. When she finally realized there would be only way to get rid of him, Audrey stopped and held up her hand, signaling David to a stop.

"If you don't let me go, you're acting the same as the men who captured me."

"Audrey…I love you," David suddenly blurted in desperation.

"Well, I don't feel the same. I'm truly sorry."

He was cut to the heart, especially when Audrey compared him to her horrible captors. David now knew there would be no hope. The beautiful woman he adored would never love him as he did her. Suddenly he felt very foolish in his pursuit. He glanced up at Audrey, but her pleading look was too much for him. The last thing he'd wanted to do was cause this poor girl more pain and that's exactly what he had done. David finally turned and slowly walked into town, his shoulders slumped in defeat.

CHAPTER SEVENTEEN

"Captain! The lass... she's on her way out here," a sailor shouted from the crow's nest. McNeil quickly turned and glanced to the shore. Sure enough, he saw Audrey slowly rowing toward them.

Well, that was easy enough, he smiled. "When she gets here, make sure we give her a warm welcome," the Captain sneered sarcastically. However when Irish, who was swabbing down the decks heard the news, his reaction was entirely different.

"Why would she come back here after escaping?" he whispered.

"Mighty strange indeed," Jake Harper leaned back on his heels and wiped his brow with his sleeve. Both sailors gazed at the young lady until the first mate walked by.

"Forward there!" William ordered before leaving.

She should just turn around, Irish sighed as he returned to his duty. After witnessing what the cruel Captain had done to Lanna, Irish didn't know if he could bear watching what might happen to Audrey once she boarded the ship.

Audrey couldn't believe she was actually rowing toward the St. Carlin in the same lifeboat her and Lanna escaped in.

Lord, please let her know I love her and I'm on my way, Audrey's thoughts reeled. She'd only seen a glimpse of McNeil's temper, so she could hardly imagine how he felt when he'd found out they'd managed to escape.

I can't believe how controlling David is…impudent man, Audrey felt her anger momentarily return as she clumsily rowed toward the vessel. *Lord, I'm not sure if I did the right thing in telling David to leave, but I couldn't abandon Lanna. Help me to do Your will, but in the meantime, please help me just make it to the ship,* she silently prayed. Her arms were aching so badly they began to shake.

After what had seemed like hours, Audrey arrived on the port side of the St. Carlin.

"Well, well, well, I'm glad to see you've finally decided to grace us with your presence." McNeil stepped up to Audrey after the crew helped her out of the lifeboat and led her to the forecastle.

"I've come for one reason and one reason alone," she stubbornly stuck out her chin. "To retrieve Lanna." After her statement, Audrey cringed when she heard the Captain's all too familiar debased laugh.

"I don't recall ever taking orders from you," he calmly replied and kept his gaze fixed on the young lady. There was something different in her eyes. And the way she spoke held some sort of authority he'd not seen before.

She's trying to be bold, but inside she's scared to death of me. McNeil told himself. The Captain didn't say anything for a time which caused Audrey to wish she knew what he was thinking. She hadn't noticed until actually facing the frightening man, but Audrey felt like a new person! Ever since she'd gotten right with God from reading the torn pages of her Bible, she finally realized she didn't have to be afraid of what man could do. She was no longer afraid.

"Men, we'll have to make room in the brig for our returning guest. Bring Francis to me," McNeil ordered to the gawking sailors. When the Captain spotted Irish among the small crowd, he smiled and got an idea. "And Irish, bring the maid out here. I'm sure Miss Wesley would like to be reunited with her wee friend..."

Audrey intently watched Irish make his way to the Captain's quarters. However, when he entered the cabin, she felt sick to her stomach.

McNeil once again prided himself for his quick thinking as he watched Audrey shriek and fall to her knees when Irish led Lanna to them. Audrey's newly found boldness swiftly left as she gazed at the bruised and beaten figure hunched over in front of her. Lanna looked completely terrified! She was trembling and flinched at any small movement.

Lord, what have I done? I should have run out to Lanna right when she was captured...instead of hiding like a coward! Audrey began to sob when Lanna came closer. Her left shoulder was bear where her dress had been ripped. There was also a deep yellowish purple bruise that nearly covered half of her dirty face.

When Lanna spotted the cruel Captain, she seemed to finally come to life and tried to hide behind Irish.

What have they done to her? Audrey asked herself. Once Irish managed to place Lanna beside Audrey, she tried to get Lanna's attention, but the ladies maid kept her gaze on the plank floor for she was too frightened to look up.

"Lanna, look at me," Audrey whispered when McNeil's attention turned to Francis, who was dragged from the hull, but she wouldn't respond.

"Francis, you're a disappointment and I'm releasing you from your duties. Get off my ship," the Captain sneered, a smile slowly crept onto his bearded face. As Francis turned to get his things from the hull, McNeil quickly pulled his musket from his belt and shot the sailor in the back! Audrey and Lanna screamed, then a deadly silence fell over everyone. That is, until the Captain spoke.

"See this as an example to anyone who thinks he can cross me," McNeil moved to Francis's lifeless body, but found that he was still alive. Audrey covered her eyes when McNeil kicked Francis in the stomach. And since he was close to the edge of the forecastle, the Captain's act sent the first mate flying down the steps. Even though she didn't see it, Audrey would never forget the groans that came from Francis.

"Get this worthless dog off my ship," McNeil growled. With that, two men lifted him up to the rail. Francis's cries did indeed confirm he was still alive when they threw him over the side. Once she opened her eyes, Audrey couldn't take her eyes from the dark red stain that covered the wooden steps. The Captain turned to the young women.

"Bring them to the brig." It was then Audrey felt her boldness now mixed with anger, return.

"Captain McNeil!" She shouted and pulled away from the sailor who was trying to bring her and Lanna to the hull. "I am no longer afraid of you or anything you do to me, for I am fully convinced that He who lives in me is far greater than you!" McNeil slowly held up his hand, signaling the sailor to a halt. He then sauntered closer to her and feigned a smile.

"And who do you have?" he asked.

"My Lord Jesus. He promised to protect me from the likes of you. How do you think we possibly escaped earlier? The only reason I returned was for Lanna, and I'm certain we'll be rescued again." Audrey began to tremble, not with fear but with authority.

"Get them out of my sight!" McNeil shouted angrily. "Faith is for women and children...superstitious nonsense. You should have thought twice before leaving my ship. Mark my words; you haven't seen me lose my temper yet...just ask your maid. Oh wait, she's lost her mind." He patronizingly spewed then stomped to his cabin as both women were taken to the brig.

The Captain slammed the door and plopped down on the nearest chair. He couldn't believe how one woman could make him so frustrated.

Well, there was Lenora. She could get me riled up in minutes. As much as he tried not to think about it, McNeil's past came back to him like a reoccurring nightmare. Usually quite a bit of port followed those times. The Captain got up and pulled a bottle of the very drink out of the cabinet and took a long swig.

Alright, back to the situation at hand. Good thing I killed Francis...what a fool. Surely that will keep everyone in line. I still have their respect. Keeping fear in the crew was every Captain's main goal. McNeil had heard of far too many mutinies around the area. Whenever he heard about another one, it made him more and more concerned to keep order.

I will not let Miss Wesley ruin everything I've worked so hard for. If McNeil let a petite woman get to him, how could he expect to keep the men's respect? Suddenly a smile broke across McNeil's face as he got another brilliant idea. It had actually been on his mind for quite a while, but now it would be perfect!

She'll finally see why no one crosses Captain John McNeil and gets away with it.

After the barred door was locked and the sailors had gone back to the deck, Audrey rushed to Lanna's side and put both of her hands on the shorter maid's shoulders.

"Lanna, speak to me! Say something," Audrey pleaded, but she just stood there, gazing straight ahead. When all her attempts had failed, Audrey finally sat the ladies maid down and began to tend to her many wounds as best she could.

"Don't worry, dearest. I'm here now and I'll never leave you again." *Lord, I pray she'll come back to me and be made completely whole.*

Later that night, Lanna finally fell into a fitful sleep. Audrey sat against the side of the ship, peering out of the small port hole. The full moon shined on the still black water. She had been praying all night, but was now silent. Suddenly she heard someone approaching.

"Miss?"

"Yes, who's there?" Audrey squinted at the bright light coming from the lantern he held.

"It's Joseph. Joseph Brioney, ma'am… thought yar might be hungry," he set down several pieces of ship bread. It wasn't long before Audrey took one and started to eat. Since being locked up that morning, no one had come with any food.

After what seemed like only seconds, she'd finished the last stale morsel and looked up at Joseph. She was surprised to see that the sailor had pulled up a crate just outside of the brig and sat down.

"Oh, I nearly forgot. Thank you for helping Lanna and I lower the boat earlier. It was very kind of you," she waited for a reply, but Joseph only nodded in return. She thought he was about to leave when he suddenly spoke.

"Yer shouldn't 'av cum back." Although Audrey thought him rather nice in worrying about her, she also wondered why he was so concerned.

I know he's helped Lanna and I, but I can't make myself trust him entirely.

"Why did ye return?" Joseph asked.

"I came for Lanna," Audrey's voice broke as she glanced over at her dear friend. "I was afraid of what Captain McNeil would do to her if I didn't return, but I...was too late," she couldn't continue.

"You couldn't 'av stopped him. It jist would've been yer instead," Joseph tried to comfort her, but it wasn't working.

"It should have been me," Audrey tried to dry her tears, but it was no use. *How humiliating.* She thought, for they were now coming in torrents.

Joseph felt horrible.

Why did I come? I've only made the lass feel worse, he scolded himself and quickly tried to come up with something to change the subject.

"What did ye mean earlier...about someone livin' inside av yer?"

Audrey forgot that nearly every sailor on deck had witnessed her and the Captain's heated exchange.

"Christ resides in me. I live to serve Him." Joseph nearly smiled. His plan had worked and Audrey was beginning to calm down.

"Do you know of Him?"

"Aye, the sovern judge," Joseph sighed heavily as if he was referring to a heartless dictator.

"But He's a loving Father." When she noticed his confused expression, Audrey continued, "His love is fathomless. In fact, we could never fully comprehend just how much He truly loves us. Is something the matter?"

"No, I guess I've never 'eard anyone spake of God that way before," Joseph hardly knew what to think. He'd never met anyone like the young lady who sat before him. The only problem was, he couldn't figure out what his feelings were towards her. At that moment, the solemn reminder came to mind yet again.

She doesn't trust me and never will. You're just a poor sailor. Not to mention, you're of the same crew who took her from her home, Joseph tried to push the thought aside, but it lingered just the same. The only thing that seemed to free him from it was trying to come up with some way to help Audrey escape.

"Sum av the men say the Captain's gonna make me the second mate," he changed the subject so quickly that Audrey could barely keep up. "An' if he does, me chance wud be greater…." The sailor tried to come up with the right words. He'd always been sort of a shy man, but never tongue tied. This was a newly found attribute whenever the young lady was around. Unbeknown to Audrey was how hard it was for Joseph to come down to the brig and actually speak with her.

"There cud be a chance ter 'elp ye escape once an' for al'," he finally managed to say, although by now, Joseph was sweating a little.

Once again Audrey was taken aback by how kind the mysterious sailor was.

"You would risk your life to help Lanna and me when you don't even know us?"

"Why not? Ye risked yar life for yar friend. I don't want ter see ye go through what she did." Joseph suddenly blushed when he realized how forward he'd sounded. "Besides, once I steal the shell from McNeil, we'll be able ter git away safely."

What? She couldn't believe what she'd just heard. *Does everyone on this bloody ship think the same?* "The shell is like any other. It can do nothing." The sailor's eyes widened at Audrey's statement.

"But the Captain said—"

"The shell is a myth…nothing more. God is the only one who can protect," Audrey tried to get through to him.

"Then how do yer explain how we seized that ship so easily? I nu the Captain, he doesn't believe in myths or superstitions. Surely the shell 'as power."

"Well, I had the shell when I was kidnapped. Why wasn't I saved then?" she countered, her frustration quickly rising.

"Aye, I 'adn't thought av that." The conversation came to an abrupt stop, for the sailor was deep in thought. Now it was Audrey's turn to change the topic. For some reason she wanted to learn more about Joseph Brioney. She just couldn't understand how someone so kind could work for such a cruel Captain.

"How long have you worked on this ship?" *There must be some logical reason. Perhaps he was captured like me and has been forced to work on the St. Carlin ever since.* Her thoughts quickly came to a halt when the bells rang, signaling the shift change.

"I must go," Joseph breathed as he quickly kicked the crate to the side. However, when he started to rush down the hall, he nearly ran right into Henry!

"What are you doing down here?" he stared at him suspiciously. "Oh I see."

"See what?" Joseph slowly took a few steps away from the other sailor.

"You came down here to see if the brig was unlocked, didn't you?" Henry smiled.

"Surely not...I wud never—" Henry suddenly put his hand up,

"No need to deny it. You can't fool me. I just wish I would have beat you to it," he laughed.

Joseph was completely speechless, although he knew it would be wise to play along.

"The brig is locked, right?" Henry's seriousness momentarily returned.

"Aye,"

"Well then I have no reason to be down here I guess. I'll just follow you back to the deck." With that, Joseph and Henry walked down the hall, leaving Audrey thanking God that she was indeed locked inside. As the sailors were leaving, Joseph glanced back one last time.

Don't worry, lass. I won't let anyone hurt you.

CHAPTER EIGHTEEN

" $\mathcal{N}$o please! I don't know where Audrey is. Please stop!"
Lanna cried helplessly.
"You'll be sorry for lying to me," McNeil's voice
lowered before he struck the small maid again, sending her to the
floor.

Audrey sat up and realized she'd just had a horrible dream.
She could still hear Lanna's whimpering. She then looked around
the brig and found her ladies maid cowering in the corner.
"Lanna, don't worry. You're safe with me now," Audrey
comforted and crawled over to her, but she trembled at her touch.
Audrey felt sick as guilt washed over her.
"It's me…Why can't you remember?" she embraced Lanna
even though she tried to pull away.
"What did the Captain do to you?" She held her and caressed
her hair until Lanna finally began to relax a bit. Audrey then wiped
the angry tears from her own face.

As the sun dropped under the green swells, Audrey began to
grow weary in trying to get some kind of reaction from Lanna.
She'd been trying all day, but to no avail.
I wonder if Joseph will come to make plans to escape. Then,
as if on cue, Audrey heard someone coming down the hall. She
rushed over to the door to see if it was the sailor. As much as she
wanted to make plans to get off the St. Carlin, Audrey found
herself eager just to speak with Joseph again. Much to her dismay,
the person who approached the brig was Henry instead.
"'Ello deary," he sneered and pulled the key from his pocket.
Audrey began to feel panicked when he dangled it in front of her

and chuckled.

"What do you want?" she gulped and asked breathlessly.

"Well, I want a great deal of things."

"I hope you're not planning something that would anger the Captain, for you saw what happened to the second mate."

"Aren't you a feisty one." She tried to remain calm and hide her fear as the pompous sailor unlocked the door, all the while staring at her intently. "Especially when you're all alone," he swung open the door.

"I'm not alone."

"Sure looks that way to me, except for that other little lady." Audrey silently prayed for protection as Henry started to move closer. Suddenly he stopped as if frozen. She didn't know what to do, other than hold her breath and watch his every move.

"Uh, you have to come with me...the Captain wants you."

"Alright," she agreed and let him lead her to the deck, but she continued to wonder what had stopped him from his intentions.

When they walked out of the hatch and went to the stern of the ship, Audrey was surprised to find that none of the crew was about their duties, but instead whistled and called to her. The merriment seized however, when Captain McNeil sauntered from his cabin. All eyes were on him as he silently stepped up to Audrey and grabbed her arm. As McNeil began to lead her to the officers' quarters, Audrey tried to pull away, but his grip was too tight. She actually winced in pain from the strong hold.

"Let me go! Please, you're hurting me. Where are you taking me?" she cried, but knew it wouldn't do any good.
When they approached the door, Audrey caught a glimpse of a wicked smile on his face. He was about to push her inside when William ran up to them.

"Captain," he said, but immediately regretted calling him when he realized what was going on.

"Do you think it wise to be interrupting me right now?" There was obvious frustration in his voice.

"But, Sir, there's a ship up ahead that's close enough to overrun," William nervously explained. While they talked, Audrey quickly glanced around for somewhere to hide if the Captain decided not to take William up in his offer.

Lord, what should I do? She frantically prayed as she looked around the dark cabin. All of a sudden, she saw it! A penknife on the edge of the desk was within reach. She tried to nonchalantly grab it. However, she must have pulled too much, because McNeil quickly yanked her to him.

"Not so fast, girly," McNeil's tight hold squeezed Audrey's wrist so hard that she couldn't hold the penknife and it fell to the floor.

"You're a tricky one," he looked down at the young lady and chuckled. "Well, there's no time for that now... perhaps later." the Captain brought her up the stairs to the quarter deck then finally released her.

Audrey slowly walked to the rail and realized what was happening. McNeil planned to take over another ship.

Oh no, not again, she thought and sighed. She then glanced down at her sore wrist and hoped it wasn't broken.

"Men, we're going to take over that ship up ahead. Get the muskets ready, hoist the mainstay!" the Captain gave his all too familiar orders. Because Audrey didn't want to witness the same thing as last time, she quietly snuck to the corner of the deck, overlooking the main deck. As she watched the men performing their duties, Audrey suddenly caught a glimpse of Lanna, aimlessly roaming around the deck and trying to dodge the sailors who were accomplishing their tasks as quickly as possible, but she wasn't fast enough, and was shoved to the ground.

Henry must have left the brig open. She must be scared to death! Audrey was about to run towards the ladies maid, when William quickly caught her.

"Hey now, the Captain wants ya up here."

"I have to go to Lanna," Audrey cried, but finally gave up when William wouldn't budge.

When all the sails had been loosed, the St. Carlin finally caught up with the other ship and was now broadside. The men used their grappling hooks to get onto it. They must have been on the other ship for nearly thirty minutes when all of a sudden, a blast was fired! It made the St. Carlin jolt, sending everyone aboard to the floor.

What was that? Surely it wasn't the sound of a musket being fired. It was much too loud! She fearfully thought as her ears rang horribly. But Audrey soon found out. Through all the commotion she overheard that a cannon ball had ripped through the hull. Fear tried to wash over her at the thought of sinking, but she pushed it aside.

The other ship fought back but Captain McNeil won in the end with only three deaths. One of the casualties was a St. Carlin sailor, but no one seemed to mind.

"Is the ship still seaworthy?" McNeil asked William.

"Yes Sir, just some damage to the hull. The carpenter is repairing it now."

Audrey scanned the deck for Lanna, but there was no sign of her.

Did she rush back to the hull? she thought, but continued to look for the ladies maid. Her gaze suddenly fell upon Joseph standing against the port side rail, looking out over the water. A feeling of dread came over her when she realized what Joseph was holding. It appeared to be a torn piece of Lanna's tattered apron.

"Lanna's fallen overboard!" her scream echoed. Before anyone could stop her, Audrey ran as fast as her feet would carry her to where Joseph was. However, when she got to the sailor, she didn't stop. Instead she rushed past him toward the rail and peered over it. All she could see was pitch black water. Audrey could barely breathe with panic.

"She wus standin' right beside me...when the cannon fired...I tried to grab 'er, but she wus gone before I knew it," Joseph managed a whisper. Audrey began to try and climb over the rail to jump in after her dear friend.

"What are ye doin'?" Joseph reached for her waist and easily pulled her from her death even though she continued to fight him.

"It's too late." Audrey was nearly hysterical, but eventually she stopped resisting him. It was then Joseph realized he still held her. As soon as he released her, Audrey rushed away; leaving Joseph with a feeling that someone was watching. Sure enough, when he looked over his shoulder, he found McNeil intently watching him from the quarter deck. He wasn't sure what the Captain was thinking, but Joseph knew he must be more careful around the young woman.

Otherwise, I might end up like Francis, he anxiously thought, quickly getting back to work.

Once inside the hull, Audrey almost tumbled over a barrel. She caught her footing then glanced up and gasped. It was amazing at how much damage a single cannon ball had made. There were several inches of water on the floor and jagged pieces of wood everywhere. Audrey slowly weaved through the sailors and debris, then ran into the brig and slammed the barred door although it just swung back open behind her.

"What am I to do without her?" she fell to her knees and wept harder than she'd ever done before.

Nearly an hour had gone by and Audrey thought she would rather die than ever return home without Lanna.

If I ever do see Primrose again. She was now lying on the damp straw for she didn't have any strength left. A scripture came to her memory and seemed to speak to her.

"I would not have you to be ignorant, concerning them which are asleep, that ye sorrow not, even as others which have no hope. For if we believe that Jesus died and rose again, even so them also which sleep in Jesus will God bring with him."

"But Lord, what hope do I have left?" Audrey asked aloud.

"How could you have forgotten?" something spoke to her heart, *"You have the promise that you'll see Lanna again.* But Audrey wasn't comforted by this.

"It's going to be so hard without my dearest friend. I'm all alone now."

"I will be with you always."

"Oh Lanna!" Ignoring the voice inside of her, Audrey's cries grew louder. Her throat burned and her head began to ache. Then, without warning, she felt someone gently grasp her hand. Audrey looked up to see who it was and thought she must be dreaming. Joseph sat just outside of the brig and had reached through the bars to take her hand in his own. She met his gaze, but he said nothing. For a moment she thought she saw tears in the sailor's eyes as well.

Joseph didn't know what had gotten into him. It was about midnight by the time he'd finished the starboard watch and made his way to the sailor's sleeping quarters. He was exhausted, but sleep wouldn't come. Every time he closed his eyes, he saw Audrey's grief stricken face. So he finally got up, carefully crept back to the brig, and found Audrey still sobbing.

What if someone sees me here? Joseph asked himself, but amazingly enough found that he didn't care any longer. Because Audrey's hoarse cries were too much for him, Joseph looked away to keep his own tears from falling. Unbeknown to the sailor was how much Audrey had needed his kindness. Even though he didn't say a word, his presence seemed to comfort her. An unknown amount of time had passed when she slowly fell asleep.

CHAPTER NINETEEN

*A*udrey slowly stirred as the sun hit her face. She sat up, but immediately winced, for her head pounded in pain. When she remembered that Lanna was gone, tears tempted to fall once again. But for the time being, her grief was pushed aside as she recalled what else had happened the night before.

Was it all a dream? Was Joseph truly here with me? As hard as she tried, Audrey wasn't sure of anything. She glanced over to where she thought Joseph sat, and there, laying on the plank floor was the cloth that had been torn from Lanna's dress.

Since the brig was still unlocked, Audrey rushed over to the pastel material, picked it up and held it to her face. Although it was clear that Joseph had been there, it all was a bit hazy to her.

For the remainder of the day, Audrey neither left the hull nor ate one bite of the food brought to her. Something inside her told her that she was being foolish, but it didn't matter. She'd never been so depressed in all her life even though God was trying to comfort her. She not only was responsible for Lanna being mistreated so badly that her mind had left, but above all else, she was accountable for the ladies maid's death. Because of that, Audrey could never forgive herself and she was certain God wouldn't either. In her mind, she didn't deserve God's forgiveness or comfort.

Before she knew it, the sun set under the never ending sea and the darkness eventually took over the brig. How she hated the view of it. Never did Audrey think she would tire of the ocean, but that was before. She was about to fall asleep when a large barrel tipped over by the brig door and made her nearly jump out of her skin. Audrey quickly sat up and turned to see who had knocked it over and found a man hiding in the shadows. At first, she feared it might be Henry that is, until he spoke.

"Sorry if I scared ya. It sure gets dark down here," Irish shyly stepped a little closer. "Joseph told me to meet him here…says we're going to figure out a way to help you escape."
Audrey sighed with relief. When the dim moon light fell upon the sailor's face, she thought he looked rather nervous about something.

"I'm sorry about your friend," he finally said.
McNeil says she's my daughter, but how can I know for sure? That one question had burned inside him ever since he'd first laid eyes on the beautiful young lady who strangely resembled his wife. He'd wanted to ask her so many questions, but didn't know how to go about it without scaring Audrey away.

Besides, what had she been told about her father? Probably wouldn't believe me if I told her the truth. But something inside Irish told him that she was indeed his daughter and this might be the only chance he'd get to speak to her. As the silence began to feel more and more awkward, Irish began to sweat.

Maybe I should be sure we're related before I make a fool of myself. The older sailor wiped his brow and hoped Audrey didn't notice his anxiety. He then finally took a deep breath and broke the silence.

"I heard the Captain say your last name was Wesley. Any relation to Harold Wesley?" Irish inquired. Audrey's head abruptly jerked up at the mention of the name.

"Why yes, he's my Grandfather."

It's true then! A joy washed over him as tears swiftly came to his eyes. *Rose did live…and my daughter is sitting before me.* One of the main reasons why Irish had never left the St. Carlin after so many years was out of fear of what he might find if he would have searched for his family. He didn't want to get his hopes up, just to find that his wife never made it. When he finally pushed aside his musings, he found Audrey staring at him.

What should I do now? Irish asked himself. *She's truly my daughter, but what has she been told of me?*

"Aye, what a small world we live in. I know your parents," Irish tried to remain as nonchalant as he could.

"You must be mistaken. My Father passed away many years ago...but...how could you possibly know them?" Audrey quickly stood up and gazed at Irish indignantly.

So that's what she thinks? That I'm dead? Irish now knew he could never tell his daughter the truth for she would never believe him. He wanted nothing more than to leave before he broke down right in front of the young lady, but he firmly made himself continue.

I can't leave now that I've found her. I'll just play along.

"How did he die?" he asked and tried to hide the emotion in his voice.

"I hardly know. I presume he died before I was born," Audrey couldn't believe the conversation she was having with a perfect stranger. "You must be thinking of someone else."

"Are you sure about that now?" Strangely enough, the sailor's persistence caused Audrey to doubt herself.

"What do you mean?"

"I know him...he's alive and well."

"Where are you goin' in such a hurry?" William asked Joseph, who was on his way to the hull.

"I wus jist...jist on me way ter the steerage since me watch is over," Joseph nervously turned to the first mate.

"Your watch isn't over yet, get back to your station."

"Aye, Sir," as he heeded the officer on watch, Joseph found Henry leering at him. He tried to ignore the gaze and returned to his duty, but it obviously didn't work. It wasn't long before Henry sauntered over to him.

"I bet I know where you were off too," he winked at Joseph, who didn't know what to say, so he remained silent.

"Sorta wished it was me the lass was takin' a liking too. She's a pretty little thing, ain't she?"

"Uh, yes...that she is," Joseph blushed and tried to appear uninterested. He was relieved when Henry left, saying no more.

I've got to be more careful, Joseph scolded himself.

William then called for the Larboard watch. Joseph couldn't be sure, but he thought he caught a glimpse of William smiling at him smugly, for he ordered the sailor to walk back across the deck, only to discharge him a moment later.

This time he waited until the coast the clear before sneaking off to the brig, but knew he wouldn't be able to stay long.

"I don't believe you...I can't." Audrey countered after hearing Irish's outrageous statement. *It can't be true. That would mean my mother has lied to me all these years,* she thought.

"Irish!" Joseph rushed up to the brig and quickly glanced from Audrey to the sailor. "Ye'd better go. William's callin' for yer watch. He might nu we're up ter somethin', but I'm not certain."

"Wait, he can't leave. I have more questions," Audrey interrupted, but tried to keep her voice down. Her request was ignored as Irish quickly left without another word.

"If Captain McNeil finds out about Irish an' I tryin' ter help ya, thar's no tellin' what he might do," Joseph said, "I 'av ter go, but I'll cum back as soon as I can."

Early the next morning, the Captain slowly made his way to the quarter deck from his cabin.

"What's our heading?" McNeil asked William the same question he asked every morning. However, the first mate didn't give his normal reply. Instead, he turned from the large wheel to face the tall Captain.

"I have a suspicion." he said quietly, looking around to see if anyone was nearby. There were several sailors going about their duties. One of which was Joseph Brioney, who was eyeing them suspiciously.

"But not here," he finished.

"Jake Harper! Take the helm," McNeil called then led the way to his quarters.

Once inside, the Captain took a seat at his large desk. William got right to the point.

"You're right. Joseph and Irish are up to something."

"What did you find out?" McNeil asked hastily.

"Last night I found Joseph quickly walking to the hull, right before his watch was over. I told him to get back to work. However, when the starboard watch was over, I followed him. I only watched from the hatch, but I noticed that he didn't go to the sleeping quarters, but to the brig."

"What does Irish have to do with this?" McNeil asked again.

"Well, a few minutes after Joseph left, Irish suddenly appeared."

"And?"

"He also came from the brig. He must have been talking to the lass." William quickly finished then watched McNeil stand to his feet and began to angrily pace the room.

"I told Irish not to go near her, and what's the first thing he does? Goes behind my back!" the Captain came to a halt and glared at William with fire in his eyes. The first mate didn't know what to think. He'd seen the Captain get angry, but never like this.

"I will not lose the control of my ship!" McNeil spewed, although William wasn't sure if he was talking to him or not.

"He'll be sorry. Bring him to me straight away."

Irish dressed quickly, for he had a plan. Before anyone noticed his absence, he was going to go to the brig and reveal the truth to his daughter. However, right when he finished and looked up, he saw William, Henry, and Charlie marching toward him.

"The Captain wants you," William coldly stated.

"Oh, a....alright," the older sailor took a step, but Henry and Charlie suddenly took ahold of his arms.

"Aye, take it easy on these old bones," Irish tried to stay calm, but dread began to wash over him as the sailors dragged him away.

Joseph was working on some rigging when he saw Irish being taken across the deck and into the Captain's quarters.

Oh, no. What's happening? As they entered the cabin and slammed the door behind them, Joseph absently returned to his work, all the while wondering what was befalling the other sailor.

Henry and Charlie shoved Irish to McNeil's feet. The Captain was so angry, he could barely speak. When everyone remained silent, Irish slowly glanced up.

I'm such a coward, why didn't I tell my daughter the truth when I had the chance? Now it's too late. The Captain will kill me just like he's done to many others. And if I'm gone, who'll see to Audrey's safety? Without warning, McNeil drove his fist into the side of Irish's face.

"Do you know why you were brought here?" he growled while Irish groaned in pain. The sailor was then hit again.

"I say, do you know why you were brought here?"

"No," Irish finally replied and wiped the blood from his lip.

"Yes, you do!" the Captain shouted, kicking Irish in the stomach. He thought he was about to black out when McNeil motioned to Henry and Charlie to pick him up from where he lied on the floor, holding his stomach.

"You didn't think I would find out about your little chat with Miss Wesley? I know of everything that goes on aboard my ship!" As much as Irish regretted his actions, he found that he was beginning to care less and less of what McNeil did to him now; as long as it was done quickly. Unbeknown to him was that McNeil also realized this and was swiftly making plans to make the sailor truly sorry for disobeying him.

"Flog him," he ordered.

He's not going to kill me? Irish slowly raised his head, although he wasn't certain if that was a good thing of not. After being pulled to his feet, McNeil clenched him by the neck.

"If you ever so much as look at the lass again, I'll kill her, right in front of you." With that, McNeil released his tight grip and walked out of the room.

CHAPTER TWENTY

early three days after finding out that her father was actually alive, Audrey couldn't help but think about him and where he could possibly be. She needed to know more, much more. She tried to find Irish countless times, but he seemed to have disappeared.

He must be somewhere on this horrible ship, Audrey told herself after she woke up and was about to make her way to the deck to search for the sailor again.

Perhaps Joseph might know of his whereabouts.

After being beaten by McNeil, Irish had been flogged. Then he'd been tied up and thrown into the corner of the officer's dining quarters, unconscious and bleeding. He was kept there until the next day, without food nor water. When he was finally released late that night, McNeil made the weak sailor take both the starboard and the larboard watch, which meant that Irish had been put to work for nearly twelve hours without given any provisions whatsoever.

When he was about to pass out from exhaustion the next morning, he was then forced to repeatedly swab down the decks. Irish's back ached from swabbing the large area and from his many lashes that hadn't even begun to heal yet.

"Hey Irish," William shouted from the quarter deck. "Get back to work!" he ordered then turned back to the helm. Irish wasn't even aware that he'd stopped.

Some minutes had passed when someone called his name once again, but this time it was Joseph, holding a small bucket.

"I thought you might nade sum water," he whispered and held

the ladle out to him. Irish slowly stood up, but immediately felt his knees give out from under him. Joseph quickly set down what he was holding and caught the tired sailor to steady him. He knew he was risking a lot by even approaching Irish, but he couldn't stand watching the poor man suffer any longer.

"Hurry an' take a draink before someone sees," After Joseph made sure Irish had regained his balance, he picked up the ladle, dipped it into the cool water, and once again handed it to him. When he finished drinking, Joseph caught a glimpse of William watching them, so he quickly took the water and started walking back to the bow of the ship, all the while, wondering if he'd done the right thing or not.

Audrey still sat on the crate inside the brig, staring at the darkening sky through the port hole as she'd done time and time again. She then sighed in frustration. She wanted to know more about her father so badly, and Irish was the only person who held the information. That morning, Audrey had finally found Irish, swabbing the deck, but she couldn't get a chance to speak to him because it was so crowded. William seemed to hover closely to the sailor, so she finally gave up and decided to wait until later before she tried to approach him again.

Once she heard several men making their way to their meager sleeping quarters, Audrey gathered her tattered skirts and made her way to the deck. Amazingly enough, she found Irish still washing the plank floor with a lantern sitting beside him. He was in the exact same spot as that morning.

Has he been out here all day? I've never seen anyone washing the floor this late, Audrey anxiously thought and glanced around to see if it would be safe to approach the sailor. Thankfully, the only person nearby was Joseph.

When Joseph turned and saw her, he suddenly stopped what he was doing and felt the color drain from his face. The night Irish had been taken to McNeil's cabin, Joseph had crept up the door very carefully and strained to hear. There, he'd overheard the Captain say he would kill Audrey if Irish ever spoke to her again. Because of that cruel threat, Joseph knew he couldn't let her go anywhere near the sailor.

"Miss," Joseph called as he quickly stepped right in front of her.

"Yes?" Audrey momentarily came to a halt and looked up at him in question. He tried to think of something to say, but to no avail.

"Could you excuse me please? I must speak to Irish as long as he's alone," she started to walk around the sailor to continue toward Irish, but without thinking, Joseph grasped her hand in a desperate act to stop her. She quickly glanced at Joseph's large calloused hand that nearly covered hers then met his gaze.

"Maybe ye cud spake ter him later. Right nigh is not a good craic," Joseph blushed slightly when he noticed the way Audrey was looking at him, although he had no idea what her expression meant. He released her hand.

"I have to speak to him." Audrey insisted and turned away from him, but she could still feel the warmth of his hand holding hers.

"Irish, may I talk to you?" she abruptly stopped when Irish didn't look up but kept working.

Perhaps he didn't hear me, Audrey thought, so she tried again.

"I'm sorry to bother you, but I just have so many questions." There was still no response.

"Irish, why won't you look at me?" she cried and reached out to touch his arm. Angry tears stung her eyes in confusion mixed with frustration, for it was now apparent the sailor was purposely ignoring her.

"I don't understand. Why are you doing this?"

When Joseph realized that he was standing in the middle of the deck, staring at Audrey, he quickly returned to his duties before someone saw them.

"Don't cry, lass. I love you and I couldn't bear it if anything happened to you, Irish had never felt so horrible in all his life. All

he wanted to do was tell Audrey he was her father and that he loved her. But instead he was causing her more pain.

I should have kept my distance, he scolded himself, but knew it would have been impossible to keep from finding out more about his daughter. Ignoring her was undoubtedly the hardest thing he'd ever done.

Audrey couldn't keep her temper any longer.

"How could you tell me you know my father and then turn around and ignore me? I thought I could trust you," With that, Audrey turned and rushed to the hull. However, as she was leaving, she glanced back at Irish, who continued scrubbing. In doing so, she ran right into Joseph's broad chest.

"Pardon me," Audrey began to walk away before the sailor could see her blush.

"I must tell ye somethin'." She heard him whisper. She turned to look at him, although she was in no mood to talk. "Its aboyt Irish—" he began, but Audrey quickly interrupted.

"Well, I refuse to talk about him," she started to leave once again.

"Well, jist listen then…before me watch is called." Because he was so persistent, Audrey reluctantly agreed to listen to what he had to say. They both moved closer to the rail.

"Irish is ignorin' ye for a reason."

"Well, that's apparent."

"Naw, what I mean ter say is, he's merely tryin' ter protect ye."

"Why would that protect me?" Audrey touched her forehead. She was getting very weary of being confused. The sailor wanted to avoid going into too much detail to keep from frightening her, but now knew he would have to reveal the whole story.

"The mornin' after Irish spoke ter ye, he wus taken ter McNeil's quarters an' beaten."

"What?" She gasped.

"I don't nu for certain, but I overheard the Captain threaten him that if he ever approached ye again, yar wud be….killed." Audrey stared at the sailor.

Why doesn't McNeil want Irish talking to me? she asked herself. However, her questions were temporarily forgotten when she recalled how angry she had been at Irish when in fact, he was only trying to keep her from harm.

"Starboard watch!" William called. Hearing this, Audrey and Joseph parted ways. What they failed to notice, was McNeil standing against the rail of the quarter deck, pretending to look through his glass, but in truth, he'd been intently watching them the entire time.

"Lord, I'm sorry for being so horrible to Irish and I ask you to forgive me. And Father, I pray that I'll be able to find out about my earthly father. But until then, help me to put my trust in you for your timing. In Jesus' name, amen," Audrey quietly prayed while she sauntered down the hall back to the brig.

When Joseph's watch was finished, Irish was ordered to complete his four hour watch. Only after that was he allowed to return to the hull to sleep. Which meant he still wouldn't be able to eat anything until the next morning.

"Evan," a female voice softly called. "Evan." Irish slowly turned on his side and glanced around to see who could possibly be calling him by his given name. To his amazement, a woman stood before him. Irish blinked several times only to realize who she was. His wife looked exactly the same as he remembered her. It had been etched in his memory.

"Rose, is it really you?" the sailor rubbed his face in disbelief. "How—what are ye doing here?" he wanted to run up to the woman to see if it was truly her, but something wouldn't let him.

"I came to tell you that you're running out of time," Rose stepped closer.

"Running out of time?"

"You need to tell our daughter the truth before it's too late."

"What do you mean?" he slowly sat up in his small hammock.

When he saw a single tear fall down Rose's cheek, Irish wasn't sure he wanted to hear her answer.

"You will never set foot on land again. Soon this ship will be going down…with you on it." Irish sat in stunned silence for a while, trying to take in what she had just said. As much as he hated to think about never seeing land again, somehow he had always known he would perish on the St. Carlin sooner or later.

Pushing his fears aside, Irish sighed.

"How long?"

"Tonight," Rose breathed. He knew it was foolish, but ever since he was certain that Audrey was truly his own, he'd pictured himself reuniting with his daughter, catching up, then bringing her home and seeing his wife again.

That will never happen now. Suddenly an urgency swept over him. He had to tell Audrey the truth. But then another thought came to mind.

What about Audrey? I can't go near her without harm coming to her.

"Wait!" Irish spoke up, "If this ship is going to go down, then will she…will she…." he abruptly stopped when Rose put her hand on his lips ever so gently. How he longed for her touch.

"Don't worry, Audrey will be saved." With that, Rose leaned in closer. When her lips almost touched his, Irish's eyes quickly opened.

"Hey Irish, didn't you hear the bells? Breakfast!" Jake Harper called before climbing the stairs to the deck.

"Uh, I'm comin'," Irish sat up and glanced around the dim room. He couldn't help but sit there, contemplating what Rose had said. He kept telling himself it was only been a dream, but something told him otherwise. Irish got to his feet, then quickly knelt beside his meager belongings that sat on the floor, in a small wooden trunk. Everything he owned in the world was inside. After opening it, Irish pushed aside everything until he found it. He grasped the scarlet cloth and slowly pulled it out of the trunk. Irish held the scarf up to his face to see if it still smelled of his beloved wife, but it was gone. It had been much too long.

When he recalled Rose's words about never setting foot on land again, the same urgency he'd felt earlier immediately came over him again.

I have to tell Audrey the truth before it's too late! Irish quickly stood up. *Wait, I can't risk my daughter being killed.* Rose's last words suddenly struck him.

"Audrey will be saved." Irish stuffed the scarf into the pocket of his trousers and took off running to the brig, not caring who saw him.

I'll just have to say it. That is, if she'll speak to me after I completely ignored her. Irish sighed anxiously. *Oh, well, she'll listen after I reveal the truth like I should have long ago.* When the brig came into view, he found Audrey still fast asleep.

"Miss Wesley?" he called in desperation because he knew that it wouldn't be long before McNeil or William would be making their appearance.

"Miss, wake up," Irish did all he could not to rush inside the brig, take hold his daughter, and tell her everything would be alright. But instead, he only grasped the barred door. After what seemed like an eternity, Audrey finally stirred. When she turned and saw Irish, she quickly sat up. He was the last person she thought would be calling her.

Oh no, what's wrong? Dread tried to grip her when she noticed how anxious the sailor appeared. *He wouldn't be here if it wasn't important.*

"What's the matter?" she asked. Irish glanced down the hall. *Empty.* "There's not much time to explain...." Suddenly he stopped. He opened his mouth to speak, but nothing came out.

I have to say it! He told himself.

"What's going on?" Audrey got to her feet. It was then she saw that Irish was covered in sweat.

"It's about your father. I don't have much time, but I'll tell you everything I know of him," Irish was about to begin when Audrey suddenly spoke.

"I must know one thing. What is his name?" she whispered as if it was the most important question she's ever asked.

"Evan Fintan."

"Evan," Audrey repeated wistfully.

"He was born in Ireland. While playing on shore, he fell into a deep ravine and was knocked unconscious from hitting his head. It wasn't until much later that he was found. It was a miracle he was still alive. The man who'd found him couldn't find his parents, so he brought Evan to a nearby orphanage. The last thing he remembered his parents tell him was they would soon be going to England. He wanted to go there to look for them, but no one believed the boy. He lived at the orphanage until he turned eighteen. When he was finally released, he immediately traveled to England, but there was no way to know where to even start his search. He probably wouldn't have even recognized his parents if they did meet again." Irish and Audrey heard voices down the hall growing louder by the minute.

It will only be a matter of seconds now. Irish thought and swiftly continued.

"Evan finally gave up his search and got a job as a gardener on a large—" Irish was abruptly cut off by William, who marched up to him with three other men behind him.

"What do you think you're doing?" He shouted and was about to grab Irish when Joseph came running into the room as well, holding a musket.

"Leave Irish alone," he ordered and pointed the gun directly at William.

"Joseph, no," Irish admonished. Joseph, who couldn't believe what he'd just heard, stared at Irish blankly.

"'Don't be overcome by evil. Overcome evil with good.'" Unfortunately, while his eyes were on Irish, William quickly stepped up and took ahold of the tip of the gun. However, the sailor wasn't prepared to give up that easily. Both men struggled to gain control of the musket, until suddenly, it went off.

For several seconds Audrey thought the blast had missed everyone. That is, until she saw Joseph grasp his bleeding arm in pain. He quickly glanced up at William, who now held the gun. His rage was evident just by the look in the young man's eye. Forgetting his pain, he attacked the first mate, but before they both fell to the ground, William managed to hit the side of Joseph's face with the back of the heavy musket. One hit was all it took.

"You'll be sorry for that," William growled as he pushed the lifeless man off of him and swiftly got to his feet. He and the other men then silently dragged Irish down the hall.

As soon as they were out of sight, Audrey finally came to life and fell to Joseph's side.

"Oh, why did you do such a thing?" she asked and quickly searched for the wound. It wasn't hard to find where the blood was oozing from. Audrey ripped back the sleeve of his left cuff and carefully rolled it up. When she found that it was only a deep cut, surrounded by a few minor burns to the upper part of his arm, she breathed a sigh of relief.

Thank goodness…it only grazed his arm, she moved her gaze to the sailor's face when it hit her. Irish's last words before they'd been interrupted, struck her the moment they left his lips.

Was I merely hearing things or did he quote the very same verse as…as my…it can't be. It just can't! Audrey asked herself for what seemed like the hundredth time. Tears came to her eyes as she recalled the heated words her mother had said to her during their argument.

"Your father made me sick! Always quoting the Bible to me like I was a child. 'Don't be overcome be evil, but overcome evil with good.'" Audrey's musings were swiftly interrupted by Henry, who had come to fetch her.

"The Captain will see you, lass."

CHAPTER TWENTY-ONE

lthough it was morning, the grey clouds and fog darkened the sky. It also made what little light there was eerie and depressing.

Once on deck, Audrey saw Irish being held near McNeil's cabin through the light rain that began to fall. Henry continued to pull her toward them, but Audrey hardly noticed. She felt as if she was in some sort of daze. All she could think about was what Irish had said before being taken away.

After William pounded on the door, McNeil emerged.

"Well, well, well. What do we have here?" he asked. His voice was still a bit groggy, but it held the same degrading manner.

"Irish was talking to the lass," William replied. McNeil pierced the sailor with his eyes, but instead of looking down in fear, Irish met his glare with a boldness no one had ever witnessed before. It was then two men roughly set Joseph down between Irish and McNeil. Audrey gazed down at the poor sailor and she felt a pang of guilt, as if it was her fault he was unconsciously lying a few feet from her. However, she seemed to have forgotten that her life was the one now in jeopardy.

"Irish, I warned you, but you didn't listen," A sly grin slowly formed on McNeil's face.

"Don't worry, she will be saved...Audrey will be saved." Rose's words played over and over in Irish's mind as McNeil sauntered over to Audrey, who was now being tightly held by Henry. When he reached out to touch the young ladies cheek, Irish violently tried to free himself from the two men holding him. Even though he was confident his daughter would be all right in the end, he never took into consideration that she might be taken advantage of before it was over.

"Take your hand off her!" Irish growled. Audrey shut her eyes for she too couldn't bear the Captain's touch. Thankfully, McNeil turned from her and started to stroke his beard. The rain began to fall harder.

As he contemplated his next move, the Captain once again congratulated himself for his quick thinking. Before Audrey realized what was happening, Joseph was dragged to the port side of the ship.

"Wait…what are you doing?" Audrey started to panic, but the sailors listened only to the orders of their Captain.

"You can't do this! He's not conscious." McNeil then turned to her.

"Well, that won't really matter now, will it?" he chuckled and nodded to his men.

"No, please!" she cried. Amazingly enough, the sailors who held Joseph's lifeless body, hesitated.

McNeil wanted to watch the young woman's grief stricken expression when the sailor was thrown over, but when Audrey sighed with relief instead, the Captain's gaze shot in their direction. The two men were actually arguing.

"What are you waiting for?" Charlie shouted to Jake Harper who held Joseph's legs.

"I said throw him over!" McNeil intervened, but Jake wouldn't move. McNeil's face grew red as he marched over to him and grabbed the sailor by the collar.

"Do you want to join Joseph as well? Heed my orders!"

"But what did he do? Joseph has always followed orders."

"Unlike you," The Captain growled and pushed the incompetent man out of his way. He then picked up Joseph's legs himself, and helped Charlie swiftly throw him over the side of the ship.

"Why do you look so solemn?" McNeil sauntered up to Irish; Audrey's cries could still be heard.

"How could you do that?" the sailor asked through clenched teeth. He could scarcely believe the young sailor was gone.

"That? That was nothing!" he leaned in and was now only inches away from his face. "It is now Miss Wesley's turn." Irish managed to free his right arm and grabbed hold of the Captain.

"What about the shell? It won't work without her." he desperately pleaded as McNeil turned and hastily pulled away.

"You've been lying to me for a while now, how do I know you aren't lying about that as well? Besides, I haven't forgotten that you once owned the shell. Surely it will work with you on board. Although, you won't be as easy to look at, as your daughter," McNeil grinned as his voice lowered. He then finally walked away from Irish, who felt as if he'd been punched in the stomach.

I was certain she'd be saved. He could hardly breathe as he watched Henry pull Audrey toward the rail.

"Make sure he watches this!" the Captain ordered.

I never thought I would see the day that Jake Harper would question my orders. I will not lose control of my men! But if Jake won't heed me any longer, who'll be next? Well just let them try to take this ship from me. I won't let it happen...I won't!

All was quiet, until a shrill cry pierced the silence and caught the attention of everyone on board. Irish's head jerked up and he gazed at his daughter, through blurred vision. Audrey had managed to pull away from Henry's hold and now ran toward him.

"Father," she threw herself into his outstretched arms, after he too miraculously freed himself. Time seemed to stand still as Irish spoke, his voice hoarse with emotion.

"How did you know?" It felt so good to finally hold his daughter in his arms.

"I hoped it would be you. Somehow...somehow I always knew it might be," Audrey choked for she was nearly sobbing uncontrollably.

"I'm so sorry that I didn't tell you the truth. I was afraid you wouldn't believe me," Irish replied, letting his own tears flow freely. The young lady swiftly pulled away from his embrace and put both of her hands on the sides of his face.

His eyes are so similar to mine, she thought. "I have so many unanswered questions."

"I do as well. I can't explain everything, but know this; I love you so much. I've never stopped loving your mother. Tell her that I love her and always will," Irish slowly caressed Audrey's hair before they embraced one last time. Then the sailor remembered something. He quickly dug his hand unto his pocket and pulled out a beautiful sheer scarf.

"This was hers. Will you give it to her?" Audrey carefully grasped it with trembling hands.

"Yes, but couldn't you give it to her yourself? I know we'll get out of this...somehow," she cried.

"Just promise me you'll give this to her." Before Audrey could say anymore, the spell was broken. Henry grabbed her and two other sailors tried to pull Irish back.

"Everything will be all right, I love you," he shouted as they were abruptly ripped apart.

"I love you!" Audrey cried in return. The sailor dragged her back to the rail and very slowly lifted her up, for she continued to struggle in her final attempt to free herself.

Irish would never forget the expression on his daughter's face, seconds before she was dashed into the sea. It was completely peaceful. There wasn't a hint of fear etched on her face. Their gaze met at the very last, and then she was gone. He was silently taken to the brig after that and locked up along with Jake Harper, who was unconscious from being roughly thrown into the cell, hitting his head.

As Audrey hit the icy water, her breath instantly left her. She fought as hard as she could to reach the surface, but only seemed to sink further. She was about to die, but surprisingly felt at peace. Audrey would be going home soon, her true home. The darkness began to consume her, but the strangest thing happened. One of her favorite verses came to mind.

'Whither shall I go from thy spirit? or whither shall I flee from

thy presence? If I ascend up into heaven, thou art there. If I take the wings of the morning, and dwell in the uttermost parts of the sea, even there shall thy hand lead me, and thy right hand shall hold me.' If I dwell in the uttermost parts of the sea, God will hold me...'

No matter what she did or where she found herself, God was there. He'd always been with her. Audrey knew that now.

Lord, I'll see you soon...face to face. And Lanna as well. That was the last thing she recalled before giving up what little breath she had left. Suddenly someone took hold of her wrist and pulled her upward. As soon as the salty air hit her face, Audrey immediately started to violently cough and flail about. She glanced up to see Joseph trying to draw her to him.

"Joseph!" she managed to choke, for her lungs burned from swallowing the cold, salty water.

He's alive! Audrey tried to clasp her hands behind his neck as Joseph held her against his chest but she could hardly hang on because her hands were so cold. It wasn't very comfortable, but the sailor's broad shoulders helped to shield the fierce wind that seemed to come up from nowhere. The sky began to darken with black storm clouds and it began to pour. The swells swiftly became higher as every horrible minute passed.

"It's...so cold," Audrey gasped. She still couldn't seem to catch her breath. Joseph tried his best to keep as much of the young lady out of the water as possible, but it proved to be an impossible task. It was hard enough keeping his head above the growing waves.

The storm worsened as time slowly wore on. The wind was ripping the St. Carlin's sails apart, and the raging waves were now washing into the deck.

"All hands!" William rushed to the edge of the quarter deck and shouted the order with all his might, although he knew it wouldn't be loud enough for everyone to hear through the roaring winds.

"All hands ahoy!" the first mate hadn't seen a storm like this in a long time.

McNeil couldn't believe this was happening with the shell still in his possession.

Perhaps throwing Miss Wesley overboard was a mistake. Though, it was almost worth it to see the look on Irish's face, he grinned and held onto the wheel with all the strength he could muster.

I thought she would be saved. I thought she would be alright. I've failed her and it's all my fault. Irish gazed out of the port hole for any sign of his daughter, although it was getting difficult with the water washing in more and more. After making sure Jake was propped out of the water, Irish sat down on one of the crates, but it wasn't long before he fell from the steep angle the ship now took on as it rolled heavily over the waves. Irish had to kneel on the wet floor instead. He buried his face in his hands.

"It's all my fault. Will this nightmare ever end?" his voice broke. Irish suddenly realized he was in the very same place when he helplessly wept over losing his wife nearly twenty years ago.

Why is this happening to me? How much sorrow must I endure before it's enough? It would have been better if I had just died that night. At that moment, he caught a glimpse of something. It was a piece of tattered paper underneath the deluged straw. He carefully picked it up and realized it was a page from a Bible.

"Where did this come from?" the sailor asked himself, but then remembered seeing Audrey reading from a small black book once.

So that's what she was reading. That's my girl. Even though the pages were quite soggy, he held them up to his face and cried.

Once all of his strength had been spent, something inside him beckoned him to read the worn paper. Irish was in no mood for reading but he figured it might comfort him. The page was torn nearly in half, but what he could make out was the tenth chapter of Romans.

"If thou shalt confess with thy mouth the Lord Jesus, and shalt believe in thine heart that God hath raised him from the dead, thou shalt be saved. For with the heart man believeth unto righteousness; and with the mouth confession is made unto salvation. For the scripture saith, Whosoever believeth on him shall not be ashamed. For there is no difference between the Jew and the Greek: for the same Lord over all is rich unto all that call upon him."

When he finished reading it a second time, he marveled that he'd never heard of this before. Irish always thought of himself as a God fearing man by going to church, at least when he was on land, which was hardly ever, and keeping the Ten Commandments. He also thought he was what people would call holy because he found pleasure in reading the Bible. But according to what he'd just read, the only way to be saved was to confess the Lord Jesus and believe God had raised Him from the dead.

The sailor resolved that if he was about to die, he'd make sure he would at least be saved on judgment day.

"God, I haven't prayed to you for quite some time…I can't even remember the last time, but God, I need You. I should've gotten off this ship a long time ago and returned to my family, but I was afraid. I've made so many mistakes that I'm not sure if You can forgive me, but I…I believe you raised Jesus, Your son, from the dead. I'm sorry for all of my sins. Please forgive me and save me." Irish was still kneeling on the plank floor, looking up at the ceiling when Jake Harper began to stir. The minute he heard the how loud the vessel was creaking and the cargo moving about the steerage, Jake tried to stand, but quickly fell. Irish had barely been able to stay on his knees long enough to pray.

"How long have I—" Jake started to ask.

"Not very long."

"Did the Captain still?"

"Aye, they're both gone…Joseph and Audrey, my…." Irish

couldn't finish. Without warning, a large wave suddenly hit the side of the ship causing both sailors to painfully fall against the wall.

"This storm is pretty bad. We're going to die down here, aren't we?" Jake Harper sighed. "I'm not ready to die," he whispered, mostly to himself.

"Neither am I, but you can be," Irish now spoke.

"How is that?"

Jake could scarcely believe the peace that came over him the minute he finished praying. In fact, it was the best he'd felt since he could remember. He looked up at Irish, who gazed at the port hole.

"What is it?" Jake Harper asked.

"Nothing, but I must keep looking…to see if they're alright," Irish replied.

What? They couldn't still be alive. It's impossible, Jake thought, but remained silent.

Nearly an hour later, the water was up to both sailors' waists and almost covered the port hole. But Irish continued to watch. Jake Harper was about to tell him to give up when the ship struck something just outside of the brig wall. The crash was deafening as the water washed in so fiercely, both men were nearly crushed. Amazingly enough, it didn't completely fill the cell.

Jake Harper managed to get to his feet, only to feel a searing pain in his left leg, so painful he cried out.

Must be broken. "Irish?" He quickly glanced around for the other sailor. To his horror, he found him pinned against the bars of the brig by a large wooden beam. The water was now up to his shoulders.

"I'm here," Irish was conscious, but his face was gravely pale and blood trickled out of the side of his mouth.

"Don't fret, I'll get you out of there," Jake Harper carefully limped to his friend.

"This should be easy to move with all the water in here." He tried to keep the tone of his voice light. However, when he wrapped his arms around the beam and pulled a bit, Irish let out a low groan.

"No please...leave it," Irish begged breathlessly. It was then Jake Harper saw it through the red tinted seawater. A jagged piece of wood was pierced through Irish's mid-section. Jake tried to withhold any expression from his face, but knew he wasn't doing a very good job of it.

"Don't worry about me. I'm not afraid anymore. Just do one thing for me."

"Anything," Jake Harper replied. It was now harder to hear the other sailor, for his voice was swiftly becoming faint and his breathing was irregular, as if it was forced.

"Can you see them? Can you see Joseph and Audrey?" Jake turned to look even though he knew he wouldn't find anything.

Even if they were out there, there's no way I could see them through the pouring rain. Sure enough, there was nothing. He was about to break it to Irish, but swiftly came to a decision.

"Yes, I see them," he lied.

"Do they look alright?" Irish strained to see, but his vision was going dark.

"Yes, they're above water," Jake Harper turned back to Irish when he heard him cough. It was then confirmed that he'd done the right thing. Peace watched over the dying man's face.

"I knew she would be saved...thank You Lord," he used all of his strength to reach out and touch Jake Harper's arm. "You must tell her...tell my girl, that I love her and I'll see her again...soon."

Joseph strained to hear for he couldn't tell if the agonizing cries came from Audrey or the howling winds as they watched the St. Carlin slowly sink into the deep. He was completely confused, since he hadn't witnessed the brief reunion between the father and daughter.

Why is she so upset to finally be rid of the ship and crew that has caused her so much pain? Strangely enough, Audrey found she wasn't only mourning for her father, but she was also thinking about all the men who would most likely die without making peace with God.

I could have told them about you, Lord. But instead I only thought about myself and what I was going through. Please forgive me.

"They must 'av struk a reef."

"What will happen to us?" Audrey asked, but wasn't sure she wanted to find out.

"Don't worry, jist 'ang onto me," he replied, but she could hardly make out what he had said because he was shivering so badly. He tried to sound reassuring, but he knew the chances of them living through the night, or even more than an hour, were next to impossible.

As much as Audrey tried to keep her eyes open, she was so cold. Sleep was beckoning her to give in to it. Although the impression of needles piercing her body had seized, her numbing limbs frightened her even more. The last thing she remembered before drifting off to sleep was thanking God for the kind sailor, and praying they would somehow be saved. Audrey then let go of Joseph and was nearly swallowed by the sea. Joseph quickly grabbed her and pulled her up.

"Lass!" he gently touched her face, but she didn't move. A fleeting thought came to him.

You might have a chance to survive if you release her. She'll never wake up again. She's as good as dead, but you could live.

CHAPTER TWENTY~TWO

*T*he crashing waves sounded so close. Joseph tried to open his eyes, but they were so heavy. He thought he was still on the St. Carlin. That is, until a large wave washed up onto the shore and nearly overtook him. The sailor's eyes then shot open and he quickly sat up.

Where am I? Joseph glanced around the rocky shore, but the sky was such a dark hazy blue, he couldn't see very far. The sailor couldn't tell if it was dusk or dawn. Once he looked down and saw the wound on his arm, it suddenly all came back to him.

How could I have fallen asleep...or even survive the freezing water for that matter? I thought we would only live about an hour or so. Perhaps Audrey's God had something to do with it. It was then Joseph's gaze fell on Audrey's still figure. She lied only a few feet from him. He scrambled over to her. However, once there, he wasn't sure what to do.

Is she alive? The sailor feared the worst as he moved a bit closer to see if she was breathing. She was!

"Miss," he touched her shoulder. "Audrey!" She quickly sat up and started to cough up water, gasping for air. Joseph pushed her onto her side and her choking seized.

"Are ye alright?"

"I...I believe so," she couldn't believe how sore and hoarse her voice was. If it didn't hurt to speak, she would have asked one of the many questions reeling through her mind.

Joseph apparently wasn't convinced for he continued to stare at her in concern.

The bright morning sun slowly rose up in the eastern sky.

Sunrise. We outlasted the sea for a day and a night. How can it be? Joseph marveled as he scanned the horizon.

"Where do you think we are?" Audrey tried to clear her throat and slowly asked.

"I don't nu for sure."

"What are we going to do?" When the sailor didn't answer, the same awful dread came over her along with a new sense of loss over all the things that had taken place.

I found my father, only to lose him. Lord, why wasn't he saved? Did he act as I did, in not heeding Your warnings? The one thing that upset her above all else was the possibility that Irish had died without turning to God.

I wish there was some way to know.

Joseph could tell Audrey needed a moment to come to grips with everything. But yet, he still didn't understand why she was so shaken, even sorrowful over the death of her captors.

"I'm gonna luk raun a bit." Joseph carefully interrupted her deep thoughts.

"Oh, alright." With that, the sailor started to slowly make his way down the shore.

"Wait," she suddenly called after him.

"Aye?" Joseph rushed back to her and even crouched down beside her.

"Your arm...is it alright?" she asked.

"Oh, 'tis gran'. Don't worry aboyt me," he glanced down at his arm again and was about to stand when she spoke.

"May I see it?"

After he apprehensively let her examine the wound, Audrey was able to make a bandage with a piece of cloth from the hem of her dress.

"Thank you," was all the shy sailor said before going on his way. Because he didn't want Audrey to know what he was doing, Joseph was relieved that she hadn't questioned him. He carefully scanned the shoreline, looking for any signs of what might be left of the St. Carlin. But in truth, that wasn't what bothered him. It was *who* might have survived.

If Audrey and I made it, there could be a good chance some of the crew did as well. And if there are, I have to be sure they're not a threat to us. Joseph picked up a jagged rock then went on with his search.

When Joseph was gone, Audrey touched her forehead and found salt crusted on her skin. It was horribly worse in her hair. She cringed and tried to arrange the tangled mass into a braid.

Oh bother, she finally gave up with that and slowly got to her feet. Her legs were quite weak. She stepped toward a large boulder and sat down on it. When she moved her gaze out over the water, Audrey sighed heavily. Part of her actually wished she could have stayed on the St. Carlin longer.

So much time wasted. I could have talked with my father all that time. I could have asked him so many questions. Audrey pulled her knees up against her and rested her chin on them. Another question she desperately wanted answered began to nag her once again.

Did mother know he was alive? Has she been lying to me all these years? But then again, why hadn't her father come searching for his family if he said he still loved them?

"I just wish I could know for sure." Audrey whispered to herself. Suddenly, she noticed angry tears streaming down her face.

"Miss...Miss Wesley!" Joseph came running up the shore.

"It's actually Fintan now," Audrey didn't know why she'd said it. Somehow it felt good to hear herself say it. She glanced up at the breathless sailor and found that he was completely frantic.

"What is it?"

"You'll never guess...who I've foun'!"

"Who?" The young lady quickly got to her feet and felt light headed all of a sudden. Without answering, Joseph grasped Audrey's hand and pulled her in the direction he'd just come from.

She desperately tried to make out the lifeless figure lying in the dirt and sand as they approached. However, once they finally arrived, she couldn't believe her eyes. She gasped and felt her legs give out from under her, but Joseph was right at her side for support. Audrey burst into tears as she quickly knelt down next to the ladies maid.

"Lord, please let her be alive…let her be alive!" Audrey desperately pleaded and listened for Lanna's heartbeat.

"She is alive, but jist barely," Joseph finally spoke.

"What can we do?" she glanced up at him in earnest.

"Try to warm 'er. I'm gonna fend a spring, for she needs water."

As soon as the sailor left, Audrey wasn't sure how she could possibly warm her dear friend without anything.

"Lord, what should I do?" she quietly prayed and began to rub Lanna's bear arms. "Dear heavenly Father, I pray that she will be all right," Audrey finally moved to Lanna's lower legs and started to fiercely rub them as well.

Ten minutes had passed before Joseph finally found a small brook farther inland. It trickled through one of the countless ravines that were carved into the sea cliffs. In fact, almost the entire island was mountainous except for a few small areas where the shoreline was only a gradual incline. It was there the sailor also found a cave like ravine that would shelter them from the brisk wind and rain.

Joseph ran back to shore, all the while hoping Lanna would be all right.

For Audrey's sake.

When the young ladies came into view, Joseph saw Audrey holding Lanna close to her, trying to get her warm.

"I foun' water to draink an' sum shelter not far from 'ere," he gently picked up Lanna.

If we survived along with Lanna, who else lived through the storm? The same suspicions from before slowly came back to him.

I'll have to come back later…just to make sure. Joseph lay the ladies maid down, quickly took off his jacket, which was just about dry, and covered her. While he went to get some water, Audrey knelt down next to her and fervently prayed again. And she continued to do so late into the night before sleep finally claimed her.

Two days later, the fog slowly lifted as the sun rose. Audrey turned over onto her side and realized she was shivering.

How am I to keep Lanna warm, when it's so cold? she quickly moved closer to the ladies maid, laid up against her, and put her arm over Lanna's waist. She was about to fall asleep again when she thought she heard a quiet moan. She didn't really think anything of it at first. That is, until she heard it again a few minutes later. Audrey's eyes suddenly shot open when it finally dawned on her that the noise might be coming from Lanna! Sure enough, she quietly moaned yet again.

"Joseph," Audrey gasped as she sat up and stared down at the Lanna's still form. "Joseph?" she turned to see why the sailor wouldn't come, or at least answer her, but he wasn't there. She let her tears flow freely as she intently watched Lanna slowly open her eyes. When she looked up at Audrey, she seemed to smile faintly. However, recognition was clearly evident on her face.

"Do you know me?" Audrey choked. It was then Lanna stirred, as if she was straining to say something.

"Don't speak, dearest. It's alright," she admonished, but immediately stopped when something barely audible came from Lanna's salt crusted lips.

"A...Audrey...."

"You do know me! Thank the Lord," Audrey cried all the more. It wasn't long before the maid shut her eyes and fell back into unconsciousness.

Finally! Joseph sighed as his gaze fell on a small bush. The sailor could hardly keep from running up to it. He was so hungry. When he finally came upon it, Joseph began picking the small berries and stuffing them into his mouth at a fierce pace. However, Audrey swiftly came to mind.

I've got to bring these back to her. And the maid will need some as well...when she comes to that is. Joseph continued to pick and reached further into the bush when one of the branches hit his bandaged arm. It shouldn't have hurt him, but strangely enough, he winced and pulled away as a searing pain shot through him.

I thought it was merely a scratch, Joseph slowly pulled back the cloth to see if any damage had been done. What he found made him cringe. The swelling around the cut hadn't gone down, but had grown worse.

Oh well. It's just sore because I hit it. Joseph simply presumed and went back to picking berries. *We won't be able to live for long on a handful of berries. Then what will we do?* He continued to ponder, *Well, I'm not going to worry about that now, especially not in front of Audrey. The only thing to do is to keep watch until a ship comes along...if one comes along soon enough.* Somewhere in the distance, he heard a splash, a big splash.

That was definitely someone. He got to his feet and intently scanned the shore. He feared this might happen. Another alarming noise sounded next. It was Audrey and she was calling his name.

She sounds upset, Joseph immediately forgot about the task at hand and rushed back to their ravine as fast as his feet would allow.

"What is it? What 'appened?" the sailor bounded into their dwelling and found Audrey sitting next to the ladies maid, wiping her eyes.

Oh no, she's gone. We were too late.

"Lanna awoke. She knew me...she said my name!" Audrey informed. Joseph felt a bit foolish in worrying so.

"Where did you go?" she glanced up at him in question.

"Well, I foun' sum berries," He blushed when he reached into his pocket and found only a handful of them. He'd dropped most of them in his alarm.

"I'll get more, but hopefully she'll be able to ayte sum for 'er strength to return." Joseph glanced down at Lanna.

Audrey scooped up some cold water from the brook and held it in her hand as best she could. While she made her way back to Lanna, she once again thanked God that her dear friend was alive and slowly regaining her strength. In the past few days, the ladies maid was only able to stay awake long enough to drink some water and eat some berries.

But her mind has returned, Thank you Lord...I thought I'd lost her. How Audrey longed to talk with Lanna and to tell her all that had happened.

She had just approached the shelter, when she came upon a most frightening scene. Lanna was awake and actually trying to stand.

"Lanna!" Her loud gasp startled the ladies maid. Audrey rushed up to her and tried not to spill the water in her cupped hands.

"Don't try to get up just yet. You need your rest. Here, drink some water." After Lanna sat down, she let Audrey help her take a drink.

"Where are we?" Lanna weakly asked as she laid back and looked out of their sheltered ravine.

"We're on some sort of island. Joseph thinks we're near Ireland though," Audrey replied.

"How...how did ya get off av the St. Carlin. Wait, how did I get off the mingin ship?" Lanna gasped as if she'd just realized where she was.

"I can't remember anythin'," she then whispered, turning her gaze to Audrey. "What happened to me?" Her worried expression was almost too much for Audrey. Although, she was relieved the ladies maid couldn't recall the abuse she had endured.

"Well, what's the last thing you remember?"

"I can remember getting angry at David, who pushed me to the groun'. Then I was taken back to the ship, but that is it. Audrey, what's the matter? What's happened?" Lanna asked when she noticed the tears that welled in Audrey's eyes.

"Well," she began, "After you were captured and taken back to the St. Carlin, I went after you."

"What about David?"

"He refused to go with me. In fact, he barely let me go. When I boarded the St. Carlin, I found that you had been...treated badly," Audrey's voice suddenly broke with emotion, so Lanna decided not to question her further.

"Then the Captain tried to take over another ship a couple of days later, and we were hit by a cannon ball. That's when you fell overboard. It was horrible! I thought I would never see you again," she began to cry so Lanna grasped her hand.

"Joseph tried to grab you, but he was too late...I felt so alone."

"You poor, wee thing. Don't cry now, I'm here," Lanna's soft familiar accent comforted her. She had missed her friend so much.

"What is that?" Lanna suddenly asked and pointed at Audrey.

"Oh this—" Audrey glanced down at the sheer scarlet scarf that was tied around her slender waist.

"I have something else to tell you. I found someone," she smiled, but it was a strange smile. Along with the joyous expression on her face, there was sadness also.

CHAPTER TWENTY~THREE

" $\mathcal{I}$ t was a pretty bad storm a few days back. How did your ship fair?"

"We barely came out of it, but there was another ship close by us that wasn't so lucky."

David had just walked into the small pub at Bonnie Point and sauntered over to his usual seat in the corner, after getting himself a drink. Ever since Audrey went after Lanna, confirming that she didn't care for him, David had remained in Bonnie Point. He didn't really know why he hadn't left, but he didn't know where else to go. And he decided he couldn't go back to Primrose without Audrey. Because he felt like such a failure, he figured it would be easier for everyone if he just disappeared and was never heard from again.

As he sipped his drink, he began listening to the conversation, the barkeep and a sailor were having.

"Do you know what ship it was that went down?" he asked.

"The vessel must have hit a reef. It was the St. Carlin," the sailor replied.

"What? Are you certain? You can't mean McNeil's ship."

"Aye."

"Do you think anyone survived?" the barkeep asked again.

"Not in that storm. Pretty near impossible I'd say... Nobody will miss him though."

David couldn't believe what he'd just heard.

Audrey, dead? I told her not to go after Lanna. He was about to take a sip when another thought crossed his mind. *Her poor family. They'll never find out that she's gone. I suppose it's only right to inform them.* David slowly stood and started for the door, but then stopped.

But I can't go to Audrey's family. I can't face them. Perhaps I'll send them a letter.

Three days in a row? How long is this rail going to last? I can't bear it much longer. Audrey glanced over at Lanna then Joseph and was swiftly convinced they felt the same. They'd made conversation for as long as they could, but there wasn't anything left to say.

When Audrey sighed with boredom, Lanna finally came to the rescue.

"Joseph, now that I come to think if it, we know nothing about you and your past." Joseph's head jerked up at the ladies maid's statement in horror. Who would care to listen to anything he had to say? His poor speech and shyness had always kept him from speaking his mind.

Surely they know I'm a man of few words by now, Joseph thought and tried to calm himself, hoping the subject would just pass.

"Well…a," he stuttered.

"How did you come to work as a sailor? And how long had you worked on the St. Carlin?" Lanna didn't relent, for she was oblivious to Joseph's anxiety. She had no idea how intently Audrey was awaiting his answer as well. She had longed to find out why such a kindhearted man could work for the late Captain John McNeil, for quite some time now.

Had he been forced? Did his family need money? Does he even have family? Audrey's thoughts reeled with questions while she gazed at Joseph.

"If I remember right, about five years nigh."

"Oh," Audrey tried to hide her surprise and continued. "Do you have family?"

"Naw, they were al' killed." Joseph quietly answered.

Perhaps McNeil had something to do with that, Audrey thought again.

"May I ask how?" Lanna then asked.

"It's quite a long scayle," Joseph sighed but in truth, he was beginning to warm up to the idea.

"Well, seein' that there's nothing else to be done, we have all the time in the world. But you don't have to tell us," Lanna suddenly realized the sailor's apprehension. "Just trying to get my mind off this endless rain."

"Aye, you are right. Me parents, two sisters, an' I lived in a wee town in the norn part of Ireland. The mingin house we lived in 'ad been in me family for nearly four generations. It wus right on the coast an' the land surroundin' it wus fruitful. When I wus almost ten an' three years av age, a man came an' wanted ter buy the land, but we didn't want ter sell. Well, the man wus none too 'appy when we turned down 'is generous offer, but finally left when me da threatened 'im with a gun."

Lanna momentarily glanced at Audrey. They were both slightly taken back for they'd never heard Joseph speak more than a few words at a time.

"Shortly after that, me da died av pneumonia an' a famine ruined our crops. I 'ad ter find a way ter support me family so I searched an' searched for a job an' finally got one on a ship. I worked for two an' a 'alf years before I went home. But when I got there, al' I foun' were the remains av me home which 'ad been burned ter the ground," Joseph rubbed his face, but Audrey knew he was trying to hide tears.

"And your family?" she slowly asked.

"I foun' out later that the man who'd wanted ter buy the land that day 'ad gotten drunk an' started the house on fire in 'is rage...he said me mum and sisters were inside," his voice broke so he quickly stopped. Several silent moments passed before Lanna quietly spoke up.

"But how could the man know for sure? They could have escaped." Joseph only shook his head in return.

"How do you know for certain?" Audrey asked.

"Cos he swore they were inside," his voice grew louder.

"But if the man was drunk—" she persisted without thinking.

"You don't understan'! I 'ad a musket pointed at 'is head when he swore. He wouldn't 'av lied to me." Joseph covered his face with his large, calloused hands.

"Did you kill him?" the ladies maid finally asked in a whisper.

"Naw...I left, but I didn't nu where ter go. The ship I 'ad worked for had already set sail. A few weeks after that, Captain McNeil foun' me. He fed me an' gave me a job aboard 'is ship," he slowly replied.

"And you've been working for McNeil ever since," Audrey finished.

"Aye...I wus indebted to him. Don't nu where I wud be if he 'adn't cum along when he did."

"I'm sorry," Audrey looked away to blink back tears.

"And I'm sorry I forced you to bring up such painful memories," Lanna was ashamed of herself.

Another one of my horrible ideas. She knew fully well how a sorrowful past could haunt someone. She never spoke of her own. Audrey had questioned her about it several years earlier, but it only ended in tears. One of the most wonderful times in her life was when Lanna was able to give her past to her Heavenly Father. It was only then that she truly felt free.

Joseph was especially quiet for the rest of the long rainy night.

Ten days after Audrey and Joseph arrived on the mysterious island, there was still no sign of a passing ship. As much as they tried to keep their hopes up, they grew more discouraged as every hour dragged by. They were also having a hard time finding food and keeping warm. Without any fire, the nights were very cold. Audrey and Lanna would lie close to each other to stay warm, but Audrey was beginning to worry about Joseph. He seemed to have made it his duty to take care of them. In doing so, the sailor was getting weaker every day. Every bit of food he found, he gave to them.

"Lord, I'm trying to trust you. I truly am, but I don't know how much longer we can survive here." Audrey quietly prayed as she rubbed her hands together for warmth as she scanned the cloudy horizon like she had so many times before. Time seemed to have stopped ever since they'd arrived on the island. In fact, Audrey was starting to have trouble keeping track of how long they had actually been there. As she watched Joseph slowly walk along the shore, she silently thanked God for him. She was so grateful for him.

If not for him, Lanna might not be alive. I wouldn't have even found her, she thought.

Lanna was now back on her feet, although still a bit frail. But knowing her dear friend was alive and well was probably the one thing that kept Audrey going, besides her Heavenly Father of course.

"Do you see anything?" Lanna asked as she stepped up to Audrey.

"No, nothing yet. Someone is bound to come along soon," Audrey replied, trying to sound reassuring.

"It looks like it's going to rain." Lanna stated and linked her arm with Audrey's. Sure enough, several minutes later, large rain drops began to fall and a cold wind suddenly came up.

"Joseph, are you going to come back to the ravine with us?" Audrey shouted, but the sailor's gaze was fixed over the water.

"Joseph," she called again. It was then that he raised his hand, but still didn't turn to look at her.

"There's a ship!" Upon hearing this, Audrey and Lanna both gasped.

"How are we to gain their attention?" Without answering Audrey, Joseph took off his dark jacket, revealing his white shirt.

"Get out av this rain an' go back to the ravine!" he admonished and began to wave his arms about. He never did turn back.

"This may be our only chance."

Joseph continued to wave and even began to shout; hoping against hope the ship would see him. After a few minutes, he quickly ran to find a higher ledge to stand on for a better chance of being seen. Unfortunately, it was now pouring. But there he stayed, until the ship was nearly out of sight. Joseph tried not to let hopelessness overcome him, but he couldn't help thinking the vessel might have been their very last chance of being rescued. In desperation, the sailor decided to try his very last idea. He jumped down from the boulder and looked around for a long branch, which was no easy task on the bear rocky shore. Joseph quickly removed his shirt, tied it onto the end of the branch, and began waving it back and forth. By now the ship was gone. He dropped his make shift signal in defeat when he suddenly noticed something. Even though it was soaking wet, the bandage on his arm seemed much tighter than before.

How did that happen? Joseph thought as he inspected the skintight cloth. Once he loosened it, he swiftly found the problem. The swelling was much, much worse. And now some sort of thick discharge was coming from the wound and all the burns around it.

Oh no. What should I do? Maybe the wet cloth will help it somehow. With that, Joseph recovered his arm and dolefully made his way back to the ravine.

"Where is he?" Audrey asked for the third time.

"Don't worry, maybe he's watchin' the ship come in to take us home," Lanna comforted. Then, as if on cue, Joseph walked in and sat down across from Audrey. He leaned back against the wall to catch his breath. He was completely drenched.

"What happened? Is the ship coming?" They hastily asked in unison. However, the sailor remained silent. Audrey was about to speak, but Joseph beat her to it.

"They're not comin'. Withoyt any fire, it's impossible to signal them," When his gaze met Audrey's, she only saw hopelessness. He'd given up. She then felt dread wash over her.

Audrey quickly ran into their cave like shelter when she heard her name being called.

"What's happened?" she gasped when she found Lanna trying to hold up Joseph, and rushed over to help her set the large sailor down on the ground.

"He was about to say something when he collapsed!" Lanna stated.

"Why, he's burning up. I told him to take care of himself, but he didn't listen!" Audrey said after feeling Joseph's perspiring forehead.

It had been three more long days since the mysterious ship had sailed by the island. Ever since then, Joseph sat on the shore day and night, hoping and waiting for another ship to come along. That is, when the sailor wasn't searching for food. And when they tried to get him to take some of the food for himself or at least get a little sleep, he was completely immovable.

And now look where your stubbornness has gotten you? A single tear ran down Audrey's cheek as she gazed down at Joseph's pale face.

"What should we do?" she turned to Lanna, all the while panic rising up in her. What would they do without him? They surely wouldn't survive more than a few days.

No...I will not be afraid! Audrey sternly told herself and made herself start thinking of all the times God had protected her in the past several weeks. One of Audrey's favorite scriptures came to mind. *'I will never leave thee nor forsake thee.'* However, her attention swiftly turned to the sailor again, when he began to shiver horribly.

"Poor lad...wish we had some heavy quilts to lay on him," Lanna finally breathed. "Wait, what is that red stain?" she pointed to Joseph's left arm where the old blood stain had remained

"When he tried to protect Irish and I, a musket was fired close to him and grazed his arm. It wasn't very severe." Audrey replied.

"Well, it looks quite swollen now." Hearing the ladies maid's observation, Audrey knelt down beside the sailor and slipped his arm out of his tunic. When they removed the bandage, Audrey quickly covered her mouth. It was a horrible seeping mess and the stench was worse, like rotting flesh.

"Ah! Well, now we know why yer man has such a fever. What should we do?" Lanna spoke, but kept her mouth and nose covered as well.

"I suppose the only thing we can do is clean the wound."

"And we can pray," Lanna put in.

Late that night, Lanna was taking her turn sitting beside Joseph while Audrey tried to get some sleep. However, when the sound of waves crashing against the large rocks along the shore began to lull her to sleep, the ladies maid was reminded that she must get some more water for Joseph before sleep claimed her.

She made her way to the small brook just outside of the ravine, carefully cupped the icy water in her hands, then walked back to Joseph. When he wouldn't drink anymore, Lanna sat down beside him again and started to hum very quietly. She tried not to dwell on the seriousness of Joseph's condition, but the fever was swiftly getting worse, and he was now beginning to thrash about. She couldn't help but be concerned.

Several hours later, she was just about to fall asleep again when the sailor suddenly awoke and grabbed Lanna's arm. She gasped so loudly that she marveled at how Audrey had slept through it.

"Help me," Joseph breathed heavily. A shiver ran through Lanna at the desperate tone in his voice. It was hoarse and unnatural.

"Please," he cried out.

"Aye, what is it?" She moved closer so she could hear him better.

"Please, please—" Joseph used every ounce of strength to speak, but had to stop to catch his breath.

Although Lanna hoped these weren't the poor sailor's last words, waking up Audrey hadn't even crossed her mind.

"Pray...." Joseph's grip tightened around her arm and nearly made her wince. "Pray for me." Lanna could hardly see through her tears as she watched Joseph staring at her with pleading eyes, glazed over with fever.

"All right," she replied, only to relax him, for she didn't know if he was delirious or not.

"I don't…I don't want to die."

"Joseph, don't talk like that." He managed to lift up his head.

"I'm afraid," he then fell back against the hard ground and had to gasp for breath. "Ask yer God to save me!" It was as if he was just trying to hold on long enough.

Because Lanna was convinced the sailor was going to die and he knew it, she knew she must hurry. She didn't even have to think of what to say. It just flowed from her heart.

"Just ask Him. Ask Him to forgive you of your sins an' to save you," she grasped both of Joseph's hands. They were ice cold even though he was burning up and nearly soaked with perspiration.

"God, please save me. I'm sorry…for me sins. I'll serve ye wi' all that I am." With that, Joseph fell back into his delirious state just as fast as he'd come out of it.

Lanna continued to stare at the sailor for quite some time, wondering if what she'd just witnessed had indeed happened. When she finally realized it was unmistakably true, she scrambled over to Audrey, woke her up, and told her what had happened.

CHAPTER TWENTY~FOUR

"**A**udrey, come back here. Where are ya goin'?" Lanna called after her through yet another heavy rainfall, but Audrey only quickened her pace. She ran as far as she could until she came to the edge of the misty shore, where she fell to her knees and wept. She couldn't bear to watch Joseph waist away in front of her eyes any longer.

Audrey glanced up at the large waves that rolled heavily as the storm steadily continued. She was tired of being stuck on the island, wondering if she would ever live to see her home again. She was tired of the constant gnawing hunger in her stomach. She was tired of feeling dirty. But most of all, Audrey was tired of wondering if the man she was beginning to love would live or die. Although she was overjoyed that Joseph had given his life to God, his fever and delirium was getting considerably worse as every hour passed. He now flailed about so horribly that her and Lanna couldn't hold him down. It was painful just looking at the poor man.

"Lord, I can't take it any longer. We have to get out of this miserable place. Joseph needs help," Audrey cried out in desperation.

"Audrey…what are you doin'?" Lanna came running up to where Audrey still knelt. As she approached, the ladies maid heard her friend's cries.

"Don't lose 'eart. Come out av the rain. What am I to do if you become ill as well?" she grasped Audrey's arm in an attempt to pull her to her feet, but she wouldn't budge. She only began to cry harder. Lanna then fell to the ground beside her and put her arm around her trembling shoulders.

"I know what you're goin' through, but feelin' sorry for

yourself is not gonna help anythin'. It's only going to make matters worse. God has helped us before…He will again," Lanna comforted. She was about to get back up when Audrey finally spoke.

"But I just feel so helpless." When she began to sob again, that was it! Lanna couldn't take it anymore. She quickly stood to her feet.

"You know, you're not the only wan who's cold an' hungry! You nade to stop feeling sorry for yerself because this isn't only 'appening to you." Lanna's accent thickened as her anger rose. "Joseph is not gonna die. We are goin' to git off this islan' an' we will see Primrose again. Do you hear me? Now get up an' come out av the rain this instant!" With that, Lanna marched back to their shelter without another word.

Audrey only stared at the shorter woman and marveled at her faith. Even though Lanna was a few years younger than herself, she admired her feisty ladies maid quite a bit. She also felt ashamed of herself.

God, please forgive me once again for my unbelief. I'm so sorry for forgetting all that You've done for me, Audrey silently prayed. She now knew what she must do.

"Lanna, wait," she quickly got up and called after her. "You're right."

Because they couldn't do anything else, Audrey and Lanna passed the day sitting in cave, staring at the rain. It seemed like the storm would never end. Along with the thrashing and tossing, the women had gotten used to the sailor's delirious gibberish. It never made any sense. However, Joseph swiftly gained Audrey and Lanna's attention when his nonsense turned into something much different. He started talking.

"God…." he jerked his head to one side and fitfully licked his dry, chapped lips. "God, I don't want to die."

Audrey hated seeing Joseph like this. He was always so strong and she felt safe with him. It was so strange seeing someone so tall and broad, laying on the ground, weak and pale. He was wasting away right before their eyes. As hard as it was to watch the poor man, she couldn't seem to look away as he desperately pleaded with his maker.

"I can't die…for Audrey." Hearing this, Lanna quickly looked at Audrey, but her gaze was fixed on the sailor.

"God, I…I love 'er. I can't die…now that I've foun' 'er. Please…." When they couldn't make out Joseph's words any longer, Audrey and Lanna both sat in stunned silence for some time. However, Audrey's mind was anything but silent.

He loves me? We hardly know each other. She sighed and glanced up at Lanna, only to find her smiling. *But I guess I've loved Joseph for a while. Yes, ever since he allowed Lanna and me to escape. And when he held my hand to comfort me, without a word. At least, I think he did that. It all seems like a dream.*

Joseph's fever grew even worse, only now he was too weak to writhe. He lay on the ground now, gravely still. When the rain finally seized, Lanna went in search for something to eat, leaving Audrey alone to watch the sailor's labored breathing. She couldn't take her eyes off him, fearing that she would miss something. When she'd sat beside him for several minutes, Audrey slowly grasped his cold hand and just held it.

You were there for me when I needed you most. And now I'll stay by your side until you get through this…until you get through this.

An hour went by, but Audrey was true to her word. She prayed until her eyelids began to get heavy and she slowly drifted off to sleep.

Somewhere in his incoherent state of delirium, Joseph found the strength to pull himself out of the haze and slowly open his eyes. He glanced down at his hand, then moved his gaze up to

Audrey's peaceful face. He didn't know where he was, nor what was wrong with him. All he knew was that Audrey was there. Suddenly, the sailor fell back into the reverie. It was only then that the uncontrollable convulsions began to rack his body.

"Lanna, Lanna, come quick!" Audrey cried as she desperately tried to hold the sailor down so he wouldn't hurt himself.
Joseph stop. You can't die... you can't! Stay with us.

When Lanna finally came running, Audrey was in hysterics because it was now impossible to hold him down. The ladies maid quickly dropped the few berries in her hands, rushed over, and knelt down beside Joseph.

"I don't know what to do," Audrey choked. After a few moments, Lanna glanced up at her.

"I know of nothin' when it comes to fever and sickness!" she cried. Time and everything around them seemed to slip away. All that mattered was Joseph. Even though neither would admit it, both Audrey and Lanna knew too well only one thing followed convulsions.

Audrey backed away from Joseph's side and turned her face upward.

"God, please help us!" she pleaded aloud. Lanna bowed her head and began to pray as well. Suddenly, they heard a twig snap just outside the ravine. Audrey glanced up to see what it was, but couldn't believe her eyes at what she found. A man of medium build, slowly limped toward them. When he came closer, his weary gaze quickly moved from Audrey to Joseph. He must have immediately noticed the horrible wound, for he rushed over to inspect it closer. Only seconds had passed when he turned and began building, what appeared to be a small fire with the few pieces of brush and twigs on the ground.

Are my eyes playing tricks on me? Audrey asked herself once again, but then something inside of her spoke up.

"No, this is an answer to prayer."

As soon as the fire was burning, Jake Harper turned to the still silent young ladies.

"One of you hold this in the flame," he ordered as he pulled a knife from his pocket. Lanna quickly heeded the sailor, but Audrey continued to gaze at Joseph. Then, right at that moment, the convulsions seized and Joseph was still breathing, just barely.

"Thank God," Audrey sighed.

"You'll need to hold him down." Strangely enough, Jake Harper took this opportunity to place a small stick between Joseph's teeth. After he took the searing hot dagger from the ladies maid, Jake knelt down next to Joseph.

"What are you going to do?" Audrey came out of her stupor and quickly asked.

"I have to cut the infection out," he simply replied and didn't notice their worried expressions swiftly change to horror.

"Now hold him down."

"But you can't do this!" Audrey reached out and took a hold of Jake Harper's hand that held the blade. "He must be coming out if it."

"No," Jake interrupted, "This is his only chance. Now you must hold him down!" he shouted much louder than he meant to. But that was all it took for Audrey and Lanna to finally heed him.

It was a horrible ordeal when the cut was made. Even in his weakened state, Joseph put up quite a fight, bruising Audrey in the process. Hours later, it was all over. He was now sleeping with his arm wrapped tightly.

"Thank God you came along when you did. I don't know what we would have done without you," Audrey finally broke the silence as she wiped Joseph's forehead. However, when she didn't hear a reply, she looked up but Jake Harper was gone.

"He left just a moment ago," Lanna stated when Audrey glanced over at her in question.

"But I have so many things I need to ask him."

"Well, yer man probably has a few of his own."

"What do you mean?"

"I would think that he was just as surprised to see us alive as we are av him. The last time he saw you was when you were bein' thrown overboard. Am I right?"

"Yes, I guess you have a point," Audrey replied.

"I'm jist glad he was able to make this wonderful fire. We won't be so cold tonight," Lanna said, but could tell Audrey was deep in thought.

"Why don't you go an' see where he went. Maybe he doesn't think he can stay."

"Alright. Surely he must know that he's welcome. He saved Joseph's life!" Audrey stood up and left the ravine.

Jake knew he wasn't wanted so he left as soon as Joseph was taken care of. The longer he stayed the worse he felt. The guilt was almost more than he could bear. Even though he'd tried to stop McNeil from throwing Audrey and Joseph overboard, Jake Harper was still part of the crew that mistreated them.

Besides...I didn't try and stop the sailors from using the fair young ladies for entertainment. I was right along with them and found pleasure in it as well. I didn't even try to stop anyone when McNeil ordered his men to beat the poor maid until she was scared to death. Jake looked up at the full moon. He was a changed man, but still ashamed of his past. Every time he closed his eyes, he would see everything he'd done.

God, I've asked you to forgive my sins. But can you really forgive me for everything? Just like that? It all seems too simple...too good to be true. Right then, he stopped and grabbed a hold of his leg. It was burning again. He had to stand still for a few moments until the pain seized. Jake made himself a crutch, but the pain was still constant. He knew he probably shouldn't even be walking on it, but there was far too much to do.

Well, they might not trust me, but I'll try to help them get home anyway I can. Maybe then they'll see that I've changed and that I'm sorry. To his amazement, Audrey slowly made her way toward him and quickly glanced down at his leg. He had constructed a splint out of a few sticks and pieces of cloth tied around it.

"Thank you."

"For what?" Jake Harper shyly asked.

"For helping Joseph. We...Lanna and I, hadn't the slightest idea of what to do." After a few moments of awkward silence, Audrey couldn't help but ask one of the questions that continually burned inside of her.

"Are there any others who survived?" Unfortunately, she swiftly knew what the answer would be when the sailor's expression darkened.

"No, I'm the only one." *Tell her what she wants to hear! Tell her about her father!* Something inside of him spoke.

Why should I tell her anything? She wouldn't believe me, Jake doubted himself.

"I'm going to get some more wood for the fire," he lamely changed the subject and started to leave, but Audrey spoke.

"Please stay. There's enough wood for tonight. You've done so much already. And you should rest your leg."

"How can you act as if I've done nothing wrong? Have you forgotten I was among the men who mistreated you? I was a part of the men McNeil ordered to torment the young lass," Jake Harper's shyness momentarily left as he finally voiced his thoughts.

Audrey was taken aback by the sailor's boldness, but she quickly pushed it aside.

"You were only following orders. You tried to stop the Captain from throwing Joseph overboard," she then fell silent. When she caught a glimpse of his solemn expression, Audrey meekly stepped forward and touched the top his hand. The simple act made the sailor's head jerk up in surprise.

"I forgive you Jake Harper," she sincerely stated.

The gruff sailor didn't know how to respond. He just stood there and stared at the remarkable woman before him. When he finally realized she truly meant what she said, he sighed. It was as if he'd been holding his breath under water and finally came up for a breath of fresh air. He was forgiven! Then another thought crossed his mind.

Audrey might have forgiven me, but the maid is a whole other matter. What I took part in towards her is unspeakable. But instead of keeping his doubts to himself this time, Jake Harper glanced up at Audrey once again. He felt like he could trust her.

"And what of the lass? Would she forgive me…for what I did to her?" he bowed his head in shame. As a compassion for the guilt stricken man rose up in her, Audrey began to smile.

"I've spoken to Lanna. She doesn't even remember any of that. The last thing she can recall is being taken back to the ship." Jake Harper had never felt so relieved. There were still some lingering doubts left in his mind, but they were forgotten for the time being as Audrey led him back into the warm cave.

Audrey decided not to press him for answers until he brought it up. She knew it would be difficult, but she had witnessed how hard it was for the sailor to talk about the ship wreck. Besides, the St. Carlin had been his home and the men, his family. He had lost them all in one horrible night. Audrey figured he might need a little time.

And all we have is time, she thought. She turned over onto her side and felt pain in her shoulder when she set it against the hard rocky ground. She then glanced outside of their shelter, but all she found was the same fog that slowly lifted from the island every morning.

I don't know how much longer I can bear sleeping on the ground. At least it's warmer now, since Jake Harper has come and brought the wonderful matches with him. When she realized the sailor wasn't sleeping in the opposite corner of the ravine, Audrey slowly sat up and yawned. It began to rain, yet another thing Audrey was getting weary of. It seemed to rain every day, for hours on end. Being stranded was bad enough, but being stuck in their small musty shelter made it seem far worse.

Jake Harper came running in from the rain. He grinned at Audrey and held up two large fish.

"How?" was all Audrey could say.

"I was able to take quite a few things from the ship before I left, one of which was a net," he proudly replied. Audrey's stomach growled loudly at the sight of the lovely fish. But then she glanced over at Joseph, who was sleeping soundly.

"We'll have to give Joseph as much of it as he'll take."

"Yes," Jake Harper agreed while he prepared to gut the fish to fry it.

"Jaykers, what is that wonderful smell?" Lanna asked when she awoke from the aroma that now filled the inside of their ravine. There was still plenty of fish to go around once they were able to get Joseph to eat some.

When they finished, it was still raining so all they could do was to keep dry and make conversation.

"Did ya see the ship that passed by several days ago?" Lanna asked.

"No, Joseph tried to signal it, but he said it was impossible to get their attention without any fire," Audrey put in.

"Aye, I've been thinking about what to do once we finally see someone come by, so I've started to collect some wood to make a big pile to set on fire."

"Oh good!" Audrey and Lanna both sighed.

After several minutes of silence had passed, Jake finally spoke, but very quietly.

"I, well...I know about Irish...bein' your father and all." Audrey didn't quite know how to respond, because she wasn't sure if she'd heard him right.

"What?" she quickly asked.

"I know that Irish was your father." Tears immediately stung Audrey's eyes.

"But how? You were hit by the Captain before...."

"I was locked in the brig with him before the ship went down," he replied solemnly. All of a sudden she wasn't sure if she wanted to know about her father's last few moments. Then again, she was a bit curious and hopeful that he had made peace with God. When Lanna moved closer to her and grasped her hand,

Audrey finally made herself ask.

"What happened?"

"When Irish and I were locked in the brig, I was still passed out. But when I finally came to, the ship was rolling pretty badly. That's when I knew…it wouldn't end well for us. Irish told me about a piece of paper he'd found. Since, I'm not much of a reading man, he read it to me."

"What was on the paper?" Lanna asked, but was almost certain it was a page from Audrey's Bible. Sure enough, Jake Harper confirmed her notion.

"If I remember right, it was something from Rom…romans. Anyway, it said if you confess the Lord, and believe that He raised His Son from the dead, you would be saved," the sailor went on. Audrey could scarcely believe it. It was too good to be true!

"Irish had done it before I came to, then I did the same. I can't really explain it, but some sort of peace came over us. It no longer really mattered if we lived or died because we weren't afraid anymore," his voice began to sound husky with emotion. It was then Audrey realized that she and Lanna were crying openly.

"After we hit the reef, he told me to tell ya that he loved you and would see you again soon. Then…he was gone. I'd never seen him so calm and peaceful."

"Thank you for telling me," Audrey finally spoke. However, what Jake Harper failed to mention was some of the more gruesome details. He told of Irish's last moments, but Jake purposely left out the part when the water rose above his head, finally claiming his life. The cries of the panicked sailors so loud, Jake could hear it in the brig. And worst of all, the deathly scene he'd come upon when he swam out to the horrible wreck several days later to see if there were any supplies he could use. Even after overlooking the details, his heart broke when he saw how upset Audrey was. Though she wept with grief, she was also overjoyed that she would indeed see her father again.

Thank you so much, Lord. Thank you for saving him, she silently rejoiced and wiped her tears.

CHAPTER TWENTY~FIVE

"**M**a'am!" Claire pounded on the Rose's bedroom door. She kept knocking until the door finally opened.

"Why are you waking me at this hour? It better be important." Rose yawned and shielded her eyes from the sun that shined through the window in the hall. It was already eleven in the morning, but all Rose did anymore was sleep and mope around in her room. Ever since Audrey had been taken, Rose had completely given up and no one was able to get through to her.

"Claire, speak up. I don't have all day," she snapped.

"A letter came for you."

"Is that all?" Rose snatched the letter out of her hand and was about to shut the door when the maid spoke again.

"It's from David, ma'am." Rose immediately stopped and slowly looked down at the now very precious letter. The last anyone had heard from the stable hand was that he was off to go searching for Audrey. Day after day everyone at Primrose waited for some kind of word from him and now it was finally here.

She carelessly slammed the door in the maid's face and ripped open the envelope.

Dear Miss Wesley,

Rose momentarily stopped to retrieve her handkerchief and to wipe a tear from her cheek.

Dear Miss Wesley,

I'm sorry I haven't written earlier. The search for your daughter proved to be more difficult than I had hoped. While I have learned of her whereabouts, I'm afraid I don't have good news. Miss Audrianna was captured and taken aboard a ship. Just today, I found out that the very same vessel hit a reef just off the coast of Ireland. It was a terrible storm and everyone has said no one could have survived. I'm sorry I've failed you and I wish to offer my condolences. I will not be returning to Primrose, but I thank you for all the kindness you've shone me,

 sincerely,

  David.

After reading it once more, Rose dropped the letter to the floor. Her whole body trembled. She now knew what had to be done. She slowly stumbled to her bed stand and pulled the top drawer open so quickly that it crashed to the floor and everything in it fell out. There it was. When the light hit it, it glistened, as if calling to her. Rose knelt down and grasped the knife in her shaking hand, staring at it intently. She'd had it sitting in the drawer for weeks now, just waiting for the right time. The only thing that kept her from using it was her daughter.

And now she's gone! I have nothing left. Rose raised the knife to her chest and was about to finish it when suddenly, a blinding light filled the room. She was so frightened that she quickly dropped the knife and leaned against the wall. She shook uncontrollably.

"Don't be afraid," a low, comforting voice called to her. It almost sounded like several voices were speaking at once, in a low whispering tone. Rose tried to see who was talking, but the light was too bright. She blinked several time to see if she was dreaming, but the warm light remained.

"Who—" she tried to ask.

"'Come unto Me if you are heavy laden and I will give you rest. Take My yoke upon you and learn of Me. Learn of Me and you shall find rest unto your soul. For My yoke is easy and My burden is light.'" With that, the warm light disappeared, leaving Rose feeling numb.

When Claire, who stood near the outside of the door, heard the crash inside the room, she feared the worst!

"Miss Rose, are you alright?" There was no answer. Under normal circumstances, Claire would have never entered the bedroom of the quick tempered mistress, especially when the door had been slammed in her face. But panic beckoned her to enter.

"Ma'am?" she meekly opened the door only to confirm her anxiety. Rose was sitting on the floor, next to a dagger. That was all it took to make Claire run downstairs to fetch Harold and Victoria.

"What's happened?" Victoria couldn't believe her eyes as she rushed over to her daughter.

"Did you hear that?" Rose was finally able to speak, but only in a whisper.

"Harold, send for a Doctor," Victoria cried and turned to her husband, who still stood in the doorway.

"No. I don't need a doctor. I need a Bible."

"What? That's preposterous. You need a doc—"

"Bring me a Bible, right away!" Rose shouted desperately.

"We need to do as she says," Harold spoke up when Victoria glanced up at him again.

"This is utter nonsense," she got to her feet and stomped out of the room. Harold, on the other hand, marveled at how his wife could have missed the glow that radiated on Rose's face. It seemed to fill the whole room as well. Along with that, Harold noticed the letter lying on the floor along with the knife. While everything in the room told him otherwise, somehow he knew his daughter would be alright.

Victoria reentered, holding their family Bible that sat on display in the parlor and quickly handed it to Rose.

"Now, what are you going to do, read? You need to see a doctor!" Victoria insisted again.

"Help me to the bed," Rose pleaded, completely ignoring her mother, "Then leave me be!"

"What? We're not going anywhere. You've obviously had some sort of spell that requires attention."

"Leave me!" Rose shouted again.

After helping her to the bed, everyone finally left. All Rose could think about was what the divine voice had said. It played over and over in her mind.

'Learn of Me and you shall find rest unto your soul. You shall find rest.' The only way Rose knew how to learn about God was to read the Bible, something she had seen Audrey do many times.

She read it to learn of God. And there Rose stayed, and read from God's word all day and late into the night. Somehow she knew her life would change from that day on and she would never be the same again

"How long 'av we been stranded?" Joseph quietly asked as Audrey and Lanna helped him to sit up. To Audrey, it seemed an eternity, but she didn't really know for sure so she glanced at her ladies maid.

"As best as I can figure, about three weeks," Lanna replied. Audrey turned back to Joseph. She couldn't help but wonder if he knew of his confession of his feelings.

Does he even remember giving his life to you, Lord? she silently asked. Ever since Joseph had said he loved her, it was all she could think about. She tried to push the thoughts aside, but they had a way of lingering in the back of her mind. Now that Joseph was getting better, Audrey wished he would at least bring it up somehow.

I wish there was some way of knowing if Joseph really meant it or if it was just the fever.

"'Av any other ships cum by?"

"No, but Jake Harper is ready when one does. He's got a large pile of wood an' things, and his matches are always in 'is pocket," Lanna replied.

"Did ye ever fend out how he survived the wreckage?" Joseph asked again, but there was a hint of apprehension in his voice.

As Lanna began to tell the sailor all Jake had revealed to them, Audrey got to her feet and slowly walked to the opening of the ravine. Even though the homesickness never left, Audrey barely thought of Primrose any longer. The only thing she often thought of was what she would tell Rose about her father and what questions she would ask.

"Ship! Ship!" Jake Harper shouted and suddenly came tearing into the cave. The adrenaline made him momentarily forget the pain in his leg. When he saw that they heard him, Jake rushed back out to the pile of wood, Audrey and Lanna quickly following his lead. His heart began to beat uncontrollably.

I only have one chance at this, he anxiously pulled a match from his vest pocket. His hands shook violently in the process. After building a fire every night to keep themselves warm, he only found five left.

It shouldn't take more than one, should it? But if the pile is wet, it might take a few! Jake slowly picked up a single match. He was about to light it against a nearby rock, when it slipped from his fingers and landed right in a small puddle. Jake Harper sighed heavily and took another out of the box. Glancing up at the ship, he tried to calm his nerves before lighting it. Thankfully he was finally successful and the pile was beginning to burn.

"It's only a matter of time now," he smiled and gazed back out at the glorious vessel, once the wood began to burn. Though the ship was headed in the opposite direction, Jake Harper was sure they would see the flames once the whole pile was engulfed.

Once Jake Harper helped Joseph walk to shore, they all marveled at how big the flames had become. They must have been nearly twenty feet high and the billowing smoke rose even higher.

"Surely they must see us," Audrey hopefully spoke, but no one answered. Unfortunately, as ten minutes had passed, the ship still hadn't changed its course. The silence was now getting tense, but everyone's gaze never left the ship.

"Why won't they turn around? Do they see us and jist don't care?" Lanna suddenly stood up from the rock she'd nervously been sitting on.

"We're here, turn around!" she started shouting hysterically. Audrey rushed over to her.

"Don't worry Lanna, God is still with us," she comforted in low hushed tones.

It seemed like forever before the ship slowly turned and was now sailing toward the island. Although both sailors tried to hide it, there wasn't a dry eye among the four of them as they watched the wonderful ship anchor about a mile out and two men row toward shore.

As Audrey and Lanna embraced each other, Audrey caught a glimpse of Joseph. He was staring at her with an expression she didn't quite understand. When his gaze didn't move, Audrey smiled at him. However, all confusion quickly left when the small boat slid up into shore. Jake Harper ran up to them and helped pulled the lifeboat up farther.
"Aye, are we glad to see you," he helped one of the men step out. While the men spoke to him, Audrey moved closer to Joseph.
"What a strange accent he has. Where is he from?" she whispered.
"'e's American, to be sure," Joseph replied and continued to eye them suspiciously.
"Do you think it's safe to go with them?"
"I don't nu, but we don't 'av a choice."

"They're going to England!" Jake Harper spun around and shouted, but when he noticed their solemn expressions, his smile quickly faded.
"Come on, what are ya waiting for?" Audrey and Lanna slowly looked up at Joseph in question. After nodding his approval, the young ladies helped him into the boat and they were on their way.
We're going home! Audrey joyfully thought as they slowly rowed out to the beautiful ship, Olivia.

The small boat arrived portside of the ship, then Jake Harper helped Joseph climb up the long ladder to the deck. Audrey swiftly noticed that Joseph was not very pleased to be in need of the older sailor's assistance, even though he could hardly stand. After all Jake had done to help, Joseph still didn't fully trust him.

Audrey took her turn and made it onto the deck. She was surprised to see that the ship's crew was entirely different from the St. Carlin's. They were all clean shaven and wore uniforms. The ship was about the same setting, but it was much grander than the other horrible vessel. The sails and deck were much cleaner, and the whole place seemed to be in order. Peace of mind slowly came over Audrey when the realization hit her. Their venture home would be far different than the previous. They would be safe. While the crew scrambled about deck, one man finally came forward. He was obviously the Captain of the regal ship. He had kind features, but at the moment his expression was suspicious as he stiffly approached.

"I'm Captain Locklear. The administrate of this vessel would like to speak with you," his gaze then moved to Joseph, who had his arm draped over Jake's shoulder for support. In all the excitement, Audrey hadn't noticed the cold sweat that now covered his pale face.

I hope he hasn't overdone it.

"First let me have someone show you to a cabin to lie down," Locklear informed Joseph.

The Captain led the rest of them into a large office. Nearly the entire room consisted of wall to wall bookshelves with a desk sitting in the center. The man sitting at the desk smiled warmly as they entered.

Just by looking at him, Audrey immediately thought he didn't look at all like a seamen. He seemed much too refined and intelligent, as if he'd never worked a day in his life. Unlike the worn, depressed crew from the St. Carlin.

"Sir, these are the three we just picked up from the small island. There's one more, but he appeared to be ill so I showed him to a cabin to rest."

"Thank you, Samuel." With that, Locklear took his leave.

"Please have a seat," the man behind the desk motioned to them. Audrey and Lanna sat down on the chairs that faced the desk, but Jake Harper had to pull up a chair from the wall and placed it beside Lanna.

"I'm Edmond Thomas. And you are?" he kindly extended his hand to each of them until they were all introduced. He was about to speak again when the door suddenly opened and a young lady slowly sauntered into the room.

Audrey guessed that the girl was about fourteen years of age and she wore the most beautiful gown she had ever seen.

"Oh, hello dear," Edmond greeted as he stood and moved to her side. Out of respect, Audrey, Lanna, and Jake also stood.

"This is my daughter, Bridget."

They must be very wealthy, Audrey thought. The richest family she knew were the Gordons. But she had never seen Beatrice, Rupert Gordon's mother, wear a gown that even compared with the one Bridget wore.

And she's on a bloody ship with no one to impress. As Audrey took in every detail of Edmond's daughter, she suddenly became very aware and self-conscious of what she must look and smell like.

"These are the three of the four people that were on the island." Edmond informed Bridget.

"How did you arrive there in the first place?" he then asked as if the thought had just entered his mind.

"The ship we were traveling on hit a reef and went down," Jake Harper simply replied.

"Oh, how terrible! How long have you been stranded?" Bridget asked as she tossed one of her several long golden ringlets behind her back in a very flirtatious manner.

"We've been there for nearly three weeks."

"Oh dear," Bridget replied breathlessly. It was then Edmond gently placed his hand on his daughter's shoulder.

"We'll try not to ask many more questions, for you must be quite hungry and exhausted. Where were you traveling to?" he asked.

"Augustine, England," Audrey and Lanna quickly stated in unison. While Edmond walked over to one of the shelves to retrieve a map, Audrey felt Bridget's eyes on her.

How terrible I must look! She blushed.

"Ah yes," Edmond sighed when he found the map he was looking for, laid it down on his desk, and opened it.

"We were going to port in Lyleton, which is about thirty miles north of where we live in Rolyned. But we could easily port in Scottsford instead. That would put us right between… Augustine and your home." He continued to study the map when Jake Harper's stomach growled loudly without warning.

"That settles it," Edmond smiled, "We'll port in Scottsford. Thankfully we have some empty births you can sleep in. But first, Bridget, would you be so kind and lend these two young ladies a change of clothing or two?" Bridget quickly glanced up at her father, then to Audrey and Lanna. Her nose slightly wrinkled in disgust, but all she said was, "Why of course father."

"Thank you dear," Edmond turned to the three. "We'll get all of you cleaned up and fed in no time."

CHAPTER TWENTY~SIX

*O*udrey briskly stepped out of the elegant dining quarters and shut the door behind her. She then walked over to the rail, took off her hat, and let the cool breeze blow her hair free from the pins that held it. She felt like a new woman. She was clean, her stomach was filled and she was wearing a cream colored day dress that Bridget had loaned her. The ensemble was complete with a pink sash and a hat to match. Truth be told, it was one of the finer gowns Audrey had ever worn. The only downside was, more than once, Bridget mentioned she disliked it and often thought about giving it away to one of her many maids at home. While Audrey was grateful for the Thomas' help and thanked God for them every day, her patience toward Bridget was wearing thin. It had only been three days since they'd been rescued from the island, but Bridget's high pitched voice and so called innocence seemed to never end! And, once the girl met Joseph, who was regaining his strength a little more every day, she scarcely ever left his side. Her flirting and girlish giggle that sounded whenever Joseph was near, made both Lanna and Audrey cringe.

"Wus wonderin' where ya disappeared to," Joseph suddenly stepped up to the rail right beside Audrey. Because he was still a bit shy around her, he kept his gaze looking out over the water. Audrey felt her face redden at his nearness. She never stopped wondering if Joseph knew of what he'd said in the midst of his delirium. How she wanted to ask, to be sure.

"I needed some air," Audrey lamely replied.

"Ye feelin' seaseck?" the sailor made himself turn to her in concern.

"Oh no, I'm fine. I just needed to get away from…it's not that I'm ungrateful…." Joseph then raised his hand.

"No nade to explain. I nu too well," he smiled knowingly.

"Are you feeling better?"

"Aye, thanks to yer an' Lanna, I'd say," Joseph turned around and leaned back against the rail.

"And Jake Harper," Audrey quickly mentioned. Before the sailor could reply, the door they'd just come from quickly opened and Bridget marched over to them.

"Why Joseph, you didn't finish your breakfast! Are you alright?" she cried and took his arm.

Oh bother, Audrey sighed, but decided to make the best of the situation.

"Bridget, we've told you and your father everything about us, but what about you? You're traveling home now, but where are you coming from…if I may ask."

"My father is in the steel industry," she giggled and faced Joseph as if Audrey wasn't even present. "We're returning from America. It's such a marvelous place!"

"Is that why ye went with your da? Because ya love goin' to America?" Joseph now asked.

"Well, yes. But father doesn't like to leave me. I don't know why of course. I'm obviously old enough to be on my own."

She must have plenty of servants to look after her, Audrey smiled, but then swiftly scolded herself for being spiteful.

"You see, my mother died when I was only six years of age. This ship was named after her…Olivia. Ever since then, my father brings me with him everywhere he travels."

"Oh, I'm sorry." Audrey said quietly and felt ashamed for judging the girl so quickly. She then promised herself that she would at least try to befriend her for the remaining of the voyage.

Days later, Audrey, Lanna, Joseph, and Jake Harper were enjoying the beautiful night under the stars with the Thomas'. The weather was wonderful and there was only a small breeze. Because it was Sunday, most of the crewmen were also enjoying themselves on their night off. Bridget of course, sat as close to Joseph as possible. When Audrey was able to get past her vain disposition, she actually began to get along with her, though there were still times when she managed to get under Audrey's skin. It was now Joseph who was having a hard time being polite to the girl.

Being out in the night air felt so good, everyone seemed to forget how late it was getting. Finally, Edmond slowly stood up and stretched.

"Well Bridget dear, I believe it's time we retired." Bridget quickly turned from Joseph and looked like she was about to protest. However, since her sailor was present, she swiftly put on her obedient manner.

"As you wish, father." With that, Edmond and his daughter said their good nights and left.

Joseph let out a heavy sigh of obvious relief, making everyone chuckle.

"Aw, it's alright, laddie. We'll soon be getting off this ship, then you'll be free of her," Jake Harper bellowed and slapped his knee.

"Aye, I don't nu what ye think is so funny," Joseph replied, but another round of laughter sounded at his teasing tone. When they all fell silent again, Joseph suddenly sat forward and rested his elbows on his knees as if he was about to tell them something very important.

"Audrey." Strangely enough, Audrey's heart quickened at the sailor's voice. He had never called her by her first name before. It was always Miss, or Miss Wesley and he would always say it rather nervously as if he wasn't sure what to call her.

"I did what ya said," Joseph said again.

"I beg your pardon?" Audrey blushed and glanced over at Lanna to see if she knew what the sailor was talking about, but all she found was Lanna smiling at her.

"I've given me life to...to the Lord Jesus," Upon hearing this, Audrey's confusion swiftly left, and in its place a joyful excitement washed over her. Her first urge was to jump up and embrace him, but instead she stayed where she was.

"That's wonderful!" Thankfully, her reply sounded much

calmer than she felt.

"When did you do it?" she asked as if she didn't already know.

"Well, I don't really remember much except prayin' an' askin' Him to save me. It wus loike someone wus showin' me the words to say," Joseph sat back in his chair again and looked up at the bright moon, joy and peace radiating on his face.

"Is that all you remember?" Lanna hoped he would say more, for Audrey's sake.

"Aye, the rest is al' a bit confusin'."

"Well, I'm very happy for you. I just wish I still had my Bible to let you read. It has so many answers to the questions I had when I first became saved."

Jake Harper's gaze quickly shot to Audrey.
The Bible has the answers to my questions? That's what I need. I have so many things I need answered, he thought.

"Well, I think I'll retire now," Audrey stood up. "I had such a wonderful time sitting under the stars this fine evening. Congratulations again Joseph."

Lanna knew Audrey was truly thrilled for the sailor, but obvious disappointment showed on her face. At least she noticed it. After everyone said their good nights to the young lady, Lanna also left.

Some minutes had passed, but neither Joseph nor Jake Harper said anything. Joseph couldn't understand why, but something wouldn't let him leave. It wasn't as if he was enjoying Jake's company. The two sailors had barely said five words to each other since Jake arrived on the scene and helped save Joseph's life.

Joseph knew his caution toward the other man was foolish. After all, they had worked side by side for nearly five years. A certain trust usually formed between ship mates when they worked together for so long, but everything had changed when Joseph attempted to protect Irish and Audrey, only to be hit over the head and thrown overboard. He wasn't sure who he could trust any longer.

But Jake Harper did save my life. All our lives! And McNeil is dead... He's the one who ordered his men to do what they did. Not Jake, Joseph told himself. Suddenly, Jake spoke.

"I too have done it...asked Christ to forgive and save me." That was the very last thing Joseph thought he would hear him say.

"Whaen?" With that, Jake Harper told him everything he'd told the young ladies several nights ago. In doing so, a friendship between the sailors started that night, and not merely one out of workmanship, but a brotherhood. A brotherhood in Christ.

They both had been working silently in the ship's kitchen for nearly an hour and a half when a smile formed on Audrey's face as she continued to peel. She couldn't help but recall Bridget's expression when she found out that her and Lanna decided to peel potatoes to keep themselves busy as they awaited their much longed for destination.

"You're going to do what?" Bridget's high voice cracked in surprise as she grasped Joseph's arm tighter.

"You do know we have plenty of servants for that."

"Yes, I'm aware it's the cook's job, but I can't bear to sit around any longer," Audrey stated and caught a glimpse of Joseph smiling at her.

"It's just somethin' to chucker and make the time pass more quickly," Lanna piped up. However, Bridget only stared at them in confusion.

"Well, do what you want then. Joseph and I are going to have tea now." With that, she practically pulled the sailor to the dining quarters.

"Poor lad. He's probably counting the pure hours until we arrive at port," Lanna quietly chuckled as both young ladies made their way to the kitchen.

"Aye, what are you smilin' about?" Lanna interrupted Audrey's thoughts and asked.

"Oh, nothing. I was just thinking about when Bridget found out we wanted to help in the kitchen."

"That was quite funny, but now Joseph has to keep company with her and her da without us," the ladies maid said.

"He could have come with us," Audrey picked up another potato and began peeling it with a little more vigor than was necessary.

"Are you angry with him?"

"No," Audrey suddenly stopped and glanced up, but didn't look at Lanna. "I'm not angry, just a bit frustrated. I want to know for sure...if Joseph knows of his confession or not. Do you think he does?"

"I don't know."

"But if he remembers giving his life to God, then he must." Audrey sighed heavily and went back to work.

"You can't be sure now but God knows. Just keep trustin' Him," Lanna assured her with wisdom beyond her years.

"Well, I'm finished with my pile," Audrey stated and finally moved her gaze to her ladies maid.

When we finally get home, I can't imagine having Lanna serve as my maid and wait on me again. No, I won't do it. Mother will just have to get over it, she thought to herself.

"I'm almost done, but why don't you go on ahead. It sure does get stuffy in 'ere."

"Are you certain? I can help you finish."

"Naw, I insist. I'll be done in no time," Lanna persisted, never looking up from her work.

Once she left, Lanna began to softly hum to herself. Without warning, Joseph came around the corner and purposely cleared his throat. However, he immediately regretted it for Lanna nearly jumped out of her skin from the noise.

"Ah Joseph...you startled me!" Lanna breathed once she saw who it was. "Did you finally decide to peel some grand spuds with us?"

"Sorry, no," Joseph swiftly declined, "But there is somethin' I nade to nu." Lanna's peeling immediately stopped. She then slowly glanced up at the sailor.

"What?" she swallowed.

"I overheard yer an' Audrey talkin'," Joseph took the seat Audrey had sat in, and gazed at Lanna. The ladies maid didn't know what to do. She couldn't possibly tell him anything.

Besides, it's between Joseph and Audrey. I shouldn't say anything, Lanna told herself, but from the look in the sailor's eye, she knew he wasn't about to give up easily. He was indeed a stubborn Irishman.

"What did I confess?" Joseph asked.

"What are you talking about?" she began peeling once again, but knew she wouldn't be able to fool him. Her face already felt flushed. Joseph quickly snatched the potato right out of her hands.

"Don't be playin' dumb with me. I've been raun feigned innocence for quite a while now an' I nu too well av what it looks loike." Lanna couldn't help but smile at his obvious referral to Miss Bridget Thomas.

"I'm sorry...I can't tell ya," Lanna pleaded. She'd never witnessed the sailor's boldness before.

He hardly says anything when Audrey's present. Oh, why did I say she could leave?

"I nade to nu what I said," Joseph's voice lowered as he slowly handed the half peeled vegetable back to the ladies maid.

"Why can't ya ask Audrey yourself?" Lanna sighed defeat.

"Aye, stop stalin' an' get on with it," he nearly smiled in return. She reluctantly took a deep breath and slowly told him everything. When she finished, Lanna desperately wished she knew what the sailor was thinking. His expression was completely mysterious. However, she hadn't the slightest idea how troubled Joseph really was.

While he did have strong feelings for Audrey, he didn't want everyone to know. Especially Audrey!

What have I done? I barely know her. She must think I'm an eijit. Stupid, stupid man! I can never speak to her again. Joseph suddenly stood. He got to his feet so quickly the bench he'd sat on, fell to the floor. He then rushed out of the room. Lanna didn't know what to think; only that she'd made a horrible mistake.

CHAPTER TWENTY~SEVEN

*A*s Audrey and Lanna made their way to the deck to have breakfast, Lanna was unusually quiet. She didn't say anything at first, but once they arrived outside of the dining room, Audrey came to a halt to find out.

"Are you feeling alright?"

"Yes, I feel fine. Why do you ask?" Lanna felt her face grow warm.

"I don't know, you just seem kind of quiet."

"Oh, don't worry about me," With that, the ladies maid opened the door and walked inside, Audrey following close behind.

Edmond and Jake Harper were already seated at each end of the table. Of course Bridget sat at Joseph's right, giggling loudly.

"Good morning." Edmond smiled and stood along with the other two men.

"Top of the morning," Lanna replied and nonchalantly glanced over at Joseph, but his gaze was downward. When the young ladies were seated and the wonderful food was set before them, Audrey glanced up at Joseph and was about to ask if he'd slept well as she did nearly every morning. However, she found him eating his breakfast as fast as he could. At first, she presumed he merely wanted to get away from Bridget quickly. But he'd always felt the same towards the girl and he'd never eaten so fast.

Once he stuffed the last bite of his toast in his mouth, Joseph wiped his face with his napkin, and stood.

"Please excuse me," he announced but only looked at Edmond.

"Are you feeling ill? I set up a game of chess for us, but...I guess it could wait," Bridget piped up in her sweetest voice, reminding everyone of how young she truly was.

"I'm sorry. Maybe I'll fale up to playin' a bit later," Joseph replied as he walked to the door and left.

Edmond and Jake Harper soon continued their conversation about ships and such, leaving the young ladies to their thoughts. Lanna slowly glanced up at Bridget, who appeared to be pouting, then moved her gaze to Audrey. What could she say? Joseph was obviously very troubled towards Audrey.

And it's all my fault, Lanna anxiously thought, *It must be from what I told him. Why else would he act so strangely toward her? Before Joseph learned of his confession, he could hardly keep his eyes from Audrey. I should have just kept my big mouth shut. Lord, please show me what to do!*

The ladies maid's anxiety hadn't lessened nearly ten days later, but had grown far worse. Joseph would hardly acknowledge Audrey's presence any longer. Lanna was so angry at the sailor, but still hadn't the slightest idea of what could be done about it.

It's just a matter of time before she brings it up, she anxiously thought as she turned over in her small birth above Audrey's and listened to her even breathing. Suddenly, she heard Audrey's mattress creak from her sitting up. Although the ladies maid couldn't see much in the dark room, she heard her get out of bed, pull on a shawl, and slip out of their cabin.

I wonder where she's off to? Lanna thought and almost got up to find out, but then decided against it.

As soon as the cool night air hit her face, Audrey immediately felt better. The weather wasn't warm but their cabin often became quite stuffy. She was also having a hard time sleeping for she couldn't get Joseph out of her thoughts.

Why has he been acting so strangely all of a sudden? But then again, no one else seems to notice. Perhaps it's just me, Audrey climbed the steep stairs to the deck and sighed. *Will this voyage ever end? Time seems to have stopped and I'll be on this ship forever.* She sauntered over to the bow, but didn't get very close to the edge. She could never make herself approach the very edge at night, for when she did, an eerie feeling would stir in the pit of her stomach. The darkness of the deep water made her realize just how small the ship really was. How easily a storm could come about and overtake them.

Audrey had just begun to quietly pray, when she heard someone. Bridget's loud giggle nearly echoed, followed by Joseph's shy chuckle. When Audrey glanced down and realized she wasn't properly dressed, she quickly hid behind some crates until there was a chance to leave. She didn't have to wait long for she heard the voices become quieter. She was about to dash back to the hull when she heard Joseph speak. Strangely enough, it made her stay.

"I should probably turn in now."

"Aye, sure is quare that we both 'appened to cum out 'ere at the same time." Bridget giggled again at the sailor's reply.

"And why do you think that is?" she asked as she batted her eye lashes.

"Must be the calm weather...makes everyone want ter be oyt in it. Well, Goodnight." Joseph turned to go, but Bridget grabbed a hold of his arm. She then quickly stood on the tips of her toes and kissed him.

When Audrey didn't hear them any longer, she figured they both had left and it would now be safe for her to return to the hull. But as she slowly peeked around the corner to see of the coast was clear, she saw them. Audrey swiftly covered her mouth to keep from gasping then rushed back to her cabin, knocking over some rigging in the process. Joseph quickly pushed Bridget away as soon as he realized what was happening. In fact, the small crash a few feet away was what made him awake out of his stupor. However, out of the corner of his eye, he saw Audrey fleeing the scene!

"Waaat are ye doin'?" Joseph gasped loudly.

"What do you mean?" Bridget innocently asked.

"Ya nu what I mean. Mind that ya never do tha' again!

Goodnight Miss Thomas," he curtly replied and took his leave before the confused girl could say a word.

Lanna was just finally drifting off to sleep when Audrey burst into the room, crying.

"What's wrong?" the ladies maid jumped down from her berth and quickly lit a nearby lantern. Audrey was now sitting on the edge of her bed.

"Why are you crying? What happened?" She asked again as she approached Audrey and sat down next to her. However, she was fairly certain why she was so upset. Audrey didn't say anything right away for in truth, she was a little embarrassed. It wasn't as if Joseph had asked her to marry him.

Why am I so jealous of Bridget? She completely annoys him. At least I thought she did, Audrey couldn't believe what she was thinking. Along with the embarrassment, she also felt ashamed of herself.

"Audrey, what's wrong? You can tell me."

"I don't know why I'm so upset... it's nothing really. I just found out that Joseph never meant what he said earlier...on the island."

Oh no! Lanna feared. "Why would you think that? You said yourself that if he remembered givin' 'is life to God, he—" the ladies maid began to try to convince Audrey, but was quickly interrupted.

"No, no. I was wrong...all wrong."

"But how can you know for sure?"

"Lanna, I saw Joseph. He was kissing Bridget," Audrey's voice broke as a fresh batch of tears sprung. Lanna couldn't believe her ears. She then stood and she felt her Irish temper quickly rising.

"Well, maybe you didn't see it right. Maybe Bridget threw herself at him. Aye, that's it. Wait! It's dark out, what if it wasn't Joseph at all? It could have been someone else."

"I know what I saw. There's no question. I was foolish to

think that he meant what he said in the midst of his sickness. Besides, we'll be home soon. Then we'll be parting ways," Audrey finally lied back down in her birth and turned towards the wall. The ladies maid was about to blow out the light, when Audrey spoke again.

"Didn't you assume we would go our separate ways once we arrived in England?"

"I don't nu what I thought, but I didn't think it would end loike this."

Nor did I, Audrey wiped away her last tear and tried to go to sleep.

At first light, Joseph finally realized he was not going to fall asleep. In fact, the sailor laid awake all night thinking about Audrey and what she had seen.

What must she think now? First I confess my love right in front of her, then I go and kiss Bridget Thomas of all people! Audrey probably never wants to see me again. There's no way she'll hear me out and give me a chance to explain, Joseph slowly got up and dressed. He was so angry at Bridget for doing what she did, but then again, he'd played a part in it.

I'm such a coward! If I would've just been straight forward with Audrey, instead of avoiding her, this wouldn't have happened. I don't want to lose her. The sailor poured water into the small basin and washed his face as if he could wash away his troubling thoughts. *Well, the least I can do is to try and make her listen.* He then grabbed his jacket and left the cabin to seek Audrey out.

Turn around! She won't want to look at you, much less listen to what you have to say. Turn around. His mind began to scream as he made his way down the narrow hallway toward Audrey and Lanna's cabin, but something made Joseph continue.

No, I won't stop. I messed everything up by being a coward and now I'm going to fix it! He momentarily quickened his pace with determination. That is, until the door of the young ladies cabin suddenly opened and Lanna emerged. Joseph swiftly came to a halt and tried to calm his nerves.

Calm down man! It's not Audrey. I can talk to Lanna. However, when he saw her expression, Joseph's newly found confidence quickly faded.

"Is Audrey awake?"

"Aye, but she's not feeling well," Lanna quickly shut the door behind her but continued to stand in front of it as if she was guarding the entrance.

"Will she be 'avin' breakfast with everyone?"

"Well, if Audrey is feeling shuk, then I dare say we won't be seeing much av her today," she replied much more sarcastically than she intended. She then felt a small pang of guilt as she watched Joseph's shoulders slump when he turned to leave. She was about to apologize and let him see Audrey, but swiftly decided against it.

It surely wouldn't be proper. Suddenly, Joseph stopped and made himself turn back. He couldn't give up that easily.

"I must spake to 'er. I've got to. I nu I've messed everythin' up." Lanna thought she saw tears form in his eyes as he approached.

"Please give me a chance ter explain to 'er," he grasped her hand pleadingly.

"But it wouldn't be right. You can't go into her room." When she saw the disappointed sailor, she quickly tried to think of another way.

"You're right," he sighed, "I don't nu what I wus thinkin'."

"I know, I'll try an' talk Audrey into going up on deck, then you can speak to her there."

"What will ye tell 'er?"

"Now, don't you worry. I'll think av something. You go and wait for her," Lanna smiled warmly, although it would be no easy task.

After sulking all night, Audrey finally made herself get out of bed. However, she'd made up her mind that she wouldn't leave her cabin until they arrived at port. What she hadn't taken into consideration, was how stuffy their cabin got at times. Thankfully, Lanna had offered to bring their breakfast to their room.

Lord, thank you so much for Lanna. She's such a dear. I don't know what I would do without her. As if on cue, Lanna entered the room.

"That was quick," Audrey smiled, but when she noticed Lanna wasn't holding a tray, it faded. "What's happened?"

"Well, uh…nothin' really. I came back to tell you that…." *Hurry, think of something!* Lanna panicked.

"What is it?"

"The Captain needs you," she gulped. *She'll never believe that. Lanna Ryan, what are you thinking?*

"Why does Captain Locklear need to see me?" Audrey asked.

"I'm not sure. He just told me to come an' fetch you."

"But I don't want to leave my room."

"You're bound to see Joseph sometime. Don't you think yer man would try to avoid you at al' costs, after last night?" Lanna continued to lie.

"Does he need to see me straight away?"

"Aye, that he does."

"Well, alright." Audrey quickly dressed and fix her hair, and was finally off.

Whew! I guess that was easier than I thought, Lanna breathed a sigh of relief, *I just hope she won't be too angry at me for lying to her.*

Audrey arrived on deck, but she couldn't find the Captain anywhere.

"Lanna must have been mistaken," she muttered to herself.

"What was that, Miss?" She was startled by a nearby sailor, swabbing the deck.

"Oh, I didn't realize I was talking out loud." Right at that moment, Audrey had a glimpse of Irish, her father, when he had swabbed the St. Carlin's deck and tried to avoid her in order to protect her.

"Are...you alright?" the man asked again as she continued to stare at him. Audrey swiftly came back to the present then.

"Yes," she blushed.

Deciding to return to her cabin, Audrey turned and caught sight of Joseph, nervously pacing back and forth at the bow of the ship.

Oh no, not him. Unfortunately, Joseph also saw her. When their gaze met, Audrey began to panic. All she could think to do was quicken her pace to the hull.

"Miss Wes—Audrey! Please stop," Joseph pleaded and went after her. He soon caught up to her and reached out to touch her shoulder.

"Please, I nade to spake to ya."

Audrey finally gave up trying to avoid the sailor, but her anger and frustration quickly rose as she turned to face him.

"What do you need to say?" Her eyes slightly narrowed. Joseph opened his mouth to speak right when a sailor in the crow's nest above them shouted, "Land Ho!" Both of them quickly looked out and scanned the horizon for the much longed for destination. Everything was forgotten as the deck swiftly grew crowded as the crewmen readied the ship for port.

CHAPTER TWENTY~EIGHT

$\mathcal{N}$o one could keep their gaze from the wonderful land nearly fifteen miles away and slowly getting closer. Audrey couldn't help the tears that streamed down her face at the sight of it. She never thought she would see her home again, and now she was almost there! Everyone was overjoyed, that is, except for Joseph. His thoughts were consumed with trying to get Audrey aside to explain himself. But with all the excitement, it would be nearly impossible.

After all hands were called on deck, Lanna quickly found out about their soon to be arrival as well, and rushed to the deck to see for herself. But when she saw Joseph standing to the side, against the rail, she walked over to him.

"Did you git a chance to speak with her?"

"Naw, I wus jist aboyt to whaen lan' ho wus called." Suddenly Joseph got an idea. *I know, I'll have Lanna tell her for me. Otherwise, I might never get a chance to.*

"Oh, well. I'm sure you can do it later," Lanna replied and was about to leave, when the sailor spoke.

"But there is somethin' ye cud do for me…once again."

Oh no, what will it be this time? The ladies maid anxiously thought as she slowly felt herself nod.

"I nade you to tell Audrey that I'm sorry," he stared at her pleadingly.

"Sorry for what?" As if she didn't already know.

"Well, I've done a lot av things I regret. Jist please tell 'er that I'm sorry…for everythin'."

"Aright, but Audrey's going to ask the same thing I jist did. She needs to know what you're sorry for, don't you think?" He said nothing for several minutes, then finally agreed.

"I'm afraid Audrey saw Bridget an' I together on deck. An'

uh…she saw us…shiftin'. But it's not what she thinks. Bridget thru 'erself at me. After I scolded 'er, we went our separate ways. That's all. Will ya tell 'er that for me?" he sighed and waited for a response. A smile slowly formed on the ladies maid's face.

How wrong I've been. Somehow I knew it couldn't be true. Joseph is a good man.

"Will you tell 'er for me?" Joseph hastily asked again.

"Aye, in fact I'll go to her right now."

She walked up to Audrey and was pleased to find she was alone.

"Lanna, there you are! Isn't it exciting? We're almost there."

"It is indeed! I need to—" Lanna began, but was swiftly interrupted. Right at that moment, Edmond and Jake Harper walked out of the office and both sauntered over to them.

"Isn't England beautiful?" Edmond warmly greeted.

"Yes, I was just talking to Lanna about it. I want to thank you once again. If it weren't for you, we would have…God knows what we would have done without your generosity," Audrey had to stop when her voice suddenly broke with emotion.

"Oh my dear girl, think nothing of it," Edmond comforted. "Jake Harper and I have actually been discussing your means to return to Augustine."

"Jake Harper?" Both women glanced over at the smiling sailor.

"You didn't think I would let the two of you travel the rest of the way without any protection, did you?"

"I guess I never thought of it," Audrey replied and saw Joseph also coming over to join the group. A strange feeling suddenly came over her. While she was still quite angry over the sailor's actions, she also felt sad because their journey together would soon be coming to an end and she would never see Joseph again. As much as she wanted to deny it, Audrey still had feelings for him, even after he kissed Bridget. She was jealous, pure and simple.

Lord, I shouldn't feel this way. I'm sorry.

"What about you Joseph? What will you do once we arrive?" At Jake's question, Audrey listened intently to see what his answer would be. She'd wanted to ask the sailor the same thing ever since they'd been rescued, but couldn't bring herself to do it.

"Aye, I plan to see them safely 'um as well," Joseph glanced over at Audrey, but couldn't tell what she was thinking for in truth, she was trying to conceal her surprise as best as she could. However, he looked away when he remembered his shame.

Who am I fooling? She'll never accept my apology. And if she does, would she ever trust me again? Did she ever trust me? Joseph's troubling thoughts were swiftly interrupted by Edmond.

"Joseph, I was just telling the young ladies that Jake and I have been making plans for travel once we reach the harbor. After the ship is unloaded, I'm going to hire a carriage to take all of you to Augustine." he then turned to face Audrey, "And I know it's not much, but I've also spoken to my daughter and she has graciously given her consent to let you and Lanna keep the clothing that was borrowed to you."

"That's very kind of her," Audrey smiled, but Lanna could tell it was forced. "Where is Bridget anyway?"

"I guess she's not feeling well this morning," Edmond replied.

Aye, I bet she doesn't feel well, Joseph sighed. *Will Edmond ever see through his daughter's feigned personality?*

"I also want to give each of you this," Edmond started with Jake Harper and dropped a small leather bag in each of their hands. When Audrey untied hers, she found twenty shillings inside! She glanced up at Edmond in confusion, as did the other three.

"We can't take this. You've done so much for us already." Jake took the words right out of Audrey's mouth.

"But you must. I can't let you all leave my ship with merely the clothes on your back," Edmond declared.

"My family will surely pay you back for your kindness," Audrey offered.

"Think nothing of it, my dear," Edmond quickly replied.

The group quietly continued to watch England grow larger, although Joseph had an extremely hard time keeping his gaze from Audrey.

When The Olivia finally docked in Scottsford, Jake Harper, Joseph, Lanna, and Audrey got off and immediately smelled the foul odors of the busy town's harbor. It was so crowded at the moment, they couldn't take more than a few steps without being knocked into and even stepped on. The ground was a mixture of mud and horse manure that soiled their shoes and dresses. Needless to say, their welcome was a bit wanting. But none of it bothered Audrey. She was finally home or at least her homeland anyway. The very thought of being only hours away from Primrose made it fairly easy for her to overlook everything else.

While they waited for Edmond's ship to be unloaded, they decided to look around and buy a few things necessary for the remainder of their journey.

"Maybe I'll luk raun a bit," Joseph sighed as he watched Audrey walk down the street with Lanna.

Jake Harper scanned the main street for a general store or mercantile and was delighted to find one only two blocks away. He was on a mission ever since Audrey stated that her Bible had answered all of her questions. Jake knew he had to get his hands on one as soon as possible. As soon as Joseph left, Jake Harper headed to the store.

The sailor's heartbeat quickened as he entered the store.

What if they don't have one? Jake tried to push aside his fears as he approached the counter.

"May I help you?" the short storekeeper asked.

"I need a Holy Bible," Jake Harper held his breath while the man scratched his head.

"Why yes, I believe I have a few," he led Jake to a shelf that had several books neatly organized on it.

"I have some fine family Bibles in."

"Oh, that…would work I guess. But do you have anything a bit smaller?" Without replying, storekeeper continued to scan the book shelf, until his hand stopped and he slowly pulled out a dusty black book.

"It looks like this might be my last—"

"I'll take it!" the sailor interrupted and reached into his vest pocket for his coins.

"That'll be three pence."

Jake Harper hastily left the store so he could find somewhere quiet to begin reading.

But where could I possibly find a quiet place without anyone around? he thought as he sauntered down the street. Fortunately, he found a small alleyway that wasn't busy at all.

What luck! And I'll be close enough so Joseph and the young ladies will be able to find me when it's time to go on with our journey. The sailor smiled to himself as he moved closer to a crate to sit on.

Where should I start reading? Should I start at the beginning? Yes! But wait, what did Irish read to me? It was Ro...romans. I'll begin there. Suddenly a troubling thought crossed Jake's mind. It quickly poisoned his newly found joy. *What if I won't be able to read it?* Reading and writing had never been Jake Harper's strong suit, as was the case with most seamen he knew. As a child, he'd managed to get as much book learning as he could until age ten. After that, his father died and Jake had to help take care of his mother and three younger siblings. His life had not been an easy one.

While he kept walking to the crate, Jake Harper was so consumed in his anxiety, he didn't see the large rock he was about to stumble over. He nearly fell, face first into the ground, but his hands quickly went out to catch himself. Unfortunately, the act sent his Bible flying into the dirt.

Oh no! He scrambled over to his newly prized possession. He carefully picked it up and began wiping the stained pages with the hem of his shirt. He even licked his shirt and continued to rub the page vigorously. When the sailor managed to uncover a few words, he couldn't help but read them, for they seemed to jump out at him.

"Cleanseth us from all sin." Jake Harper seemed mesmerized by

them. Without moving his gaze, he stood to his feet, moved to the crate directly behind him and sat down on it. He had found what he was looking for. The sailor then glanced up to see what book he was reading from. *First John.* He read the words that had gained his attention over and over. Once he finished with that, Jake backed up to the beginning of the sentence and began to read aloud, very slowly.

"'But if we walk in the light, as He is in the light, we have fell...fellow....'" *Oh buggar. What is this word? If only I could read better.* The sailor felt his frustration spark, but something inside him told him to skip the word for now and continue.

"'...one with another...and the blood of Jesus Christ his Son cleanseth us from all sin. If we say that we have no sin, we deceive ourselves, and the truth is not in us. If we confess our sins, he is faithful and just to forgive us our sins, and to cleanse us from all un...unrighteousness.'" Jake Harper had to stop for he couldn't see the words through his tears any longer. He'd never felt so relieved, so free. It was so simple. All he had to do was confess his sin, and God would forgive him. He swiftly fell to his knees and began confessing all that he had done.

Joseph aimlessly roamed around Scottsford. His mind was consumed with Audrey, and if Lanna was telling her of his apology.

What will she think? Will she believe I'm sincere? I probably should have told her myself. Joseph passed a quiet alley and spotted someone kneeling on the ground. His pace slowed a bit. To his surprise, Joseph recognized the man as Jake Harper of all people!

Oh no! Did he get robbed or beaten? "''ey!" Joseph shouted as he ran down the alley. "Are ye alright? What 'appened?" Once Jake glanced up, Joseph immediately saw joy in his eyes. His fear quickly disappeared. He then noticed that he was holding an open Bible.

"Where did ye git that?"

"I just bought it," the sailor got to his feet and bashfully wiped his eyes. He noticed that Joseph couldn't take his gaze from the Book.

"We could go back to the.. oh wait, this was the last one they had. Sorry, mate."

"That's alright," Joseph reached out to help Jake stand up. He didn't say another word about it as they made their way back to the street, but the young man's disappointment was apparent.

"There you two are," Lanna waved from across the busy street just as both men emerged from the alley. Audrey stood behind her, holding some packages.

"Mr. Thomas said they're done unloading the ship an' he wants to see us," Lanna continued after Joseph and Jake Harper approached.

Joseph couldn't help but look at Audrey, as if he could tell if Lanna had been able to speak to her yet. Sadly, she avoided his stare.

They all made their way back to the harbor and finally found Edmond among the crewman.

"I see you've found some things," he greeted.

"Yes, thanks to you." Joseph heard Audrey speak for the first time since they'd gotten off the ship.

"I've hired a carriage, driver, and horses for your journey home. However, it doesn't leave until tomorrow morning. I'm sure you're all tired from the excitement though, and it's probably best to be well rested for the long ride, so I've also reserved two rooms at the inn over there," Edmond pointed to a plain but clean looking hotel across from the busy harbor.

"It looks wonderful. Is Bridget feeling any better?" Audrey asked.

"Yes, a little. She's resting because we'll be leaving tonight. But first, I thought we could all have one last meal together before we go our separate ways," he finished and offered his arm to Audrey, for they happily agreed.

"Lanna," Joseph touched the ladies maid's elbow so she wouldn't leave, then waited until everyone else was out of ear shot.

"Ye git a chance to spake ter her yet?"

"Aye, not yet. But I will just as soon as I can," Lanna smiled reassuringly.

Later that night, just after dark, the four finally walked up the hotel stairs to their rooms after saying their heartfelt goodbyes to Edmond and his men. Bridget never did grace them with her presence. While it was kind of a relief, Audrey wished she could have at least seen the girl one last time and thank her for the apparel.

Once Audrey and Lanna said good night to the sailors, they went to their separate rooms. They could hardly keep their eyes open.

"Tomorrow morning, I plan to visit the lovely bath," Audrey sighed as she climbed into bed.

"And I as well. I hope the carriage ride won't seem too long." Lanna slipped out of her day dress and tried to braid her curly locks.

"Well, I hope it's shorter than the journey aboard The Olivia. It seemed like it would never end. Lanna, can you believe we're going home tomorrow?"

"Hardly...I heard Mr. Thomas say we aren't very far from Primrose," Lanna replied and heard Audrey yawn.

"It's so wonderful. I wonder what Jake Harper and Joseph will do once we arrive?" Audrey said, almost in a whisper. It was as if she wasn't talking to Lanna at all. The ladies maid got into bed and finally spoke.

"Speaking of Joseph, I must tell you something," she glanced over at Audrey. Unfortunately, she found her, already fast asleep.

"Jaykers, will I ever be able to tell her? Hopefully I can speak to her tomorrow at breakfast," she sighed heavily.

"It's too bad this was the only Bible they had," Jake Harper said as he watched Joseph sit down on the edge of his bed and take off his boots.

"Aye," was all he said in return.

"You can borrow mine if ya like." Jake also sat down, but Joseph still didn't say anything.

"You've been awfully quiet today. Somethin' wrong?"

"Nathin'…jist a bit knackered. I wud like to borrow your Bible sometime though. I think I'll turn in nigh if ya don't mind."

"Alright, I'm going downstairs for a while," Jake replied.

"What are ye headin' to do?"

"Get some more reading in." With that, Jake Harper left. And he didn't return until the middle of the night. Once he started reading the glorious Book, he lost all track of time.

CHAPTER TWENTY~NINE

*L*anna still wasn't able to talk to Audrey the next morning. By the time they awoke and realized they'd overslept, both young ladies were in a frenzy trying to ready themselves for the day.

"Hurry Lanna! Jake Harper and Joseph are waiting for us. We're quite late," Audrey grabbed her things and called to her ladies maid, who was just finishing up with her hair.

"Alright, alright I'm done."

"Good morning, did you sleep well?" Jake Harper smiled when they finally joined them in the small lobby.

"Aye, a bit too well, I'd say. We didn't mean to sleep so long," Lanna sighed.

"We better get goin' then. Our carriage is waitin' for us at the livery," Joseph spoke and of course, glanced over at Audrey.

Little did they know, as they quickly walked down the busy cobblestone street, past the harbor and the docks, someone was intently watching their every move.

"I don't believe my eyes! It can't be who I think it is."

"What was that Sir?"

"Uh, please excuse me for a moment. Then we'll continue our business," Rupert Gordon replied. His gaze was fixed on, who he believed to be Audrianna Wesley.

It's impossible! She was killed in that storm. I was at the memorial service her family held for her. It can't be! Then Rupert looked at Lanna. *Wait...is that...that maid? I could never forget her mass of unruly hair. But who are those two men with them?* Rupert scratched his chin and tried to decide whether he should go and find out if it was truly her or not. Instead, he just continued to watch the group.

"You don't think that we're too late, do you? Would they give our carriage to someone else?" Audrey anxiously asked as she quickened her pace to catch up to Jake Harper, who led the way to the livery.

"I should hope not. Mr. Thomas paid dearly for it," Lanna put in.

"We're almost there, so we should be alright," Jake Harper hopefully replied.

Suddenly, Rupert's presumptions were confirmed when Audrey quickly turned and looked back at the busy harbor.

"How long will The Olivia stay docked here?" she asked once again.

"Probably 'til the Thomas's use it again, I'd say," Joseph finally spoke, but when Audrey caught his gaze, they both slightly blushed, all the while marching down the road.

Now I'm certain she's my beloved Audrianna. However, Rupert's pleasure swiftly faded when his gaze moved back to the two men who were with her and Lanna. Even from the distance where Rupert stood, he couldn't help but notice how comfortable both young ladies seemed around the strange men. It was as if they'd known each other forever. The mere thought caused his anger to rise.

No one is going to steal my betrothed! He watched all four of them arrive at the livery and climb into the large carriage.

I need to find out who those men are and what they mean to Audrianna. But first, I must finish my father's business as quickly as I can. "Mr. Hodges, I'm ready to continue our transaction. And we'll need to be quick about it," Rupert called to the man. He continued to watch the carriage until it rounded the corner and disappeared from sight.

After they rode along for about twenty minutes, Audrey realized the carriage ride would undoubtedly be a long one! With Joseph sitting directly across from her, it was nearly impossible to avoid him and his frequent glances.

What does he want me to do? I can't just pretend as if nothing happened. He doesn't care for me anyway. And if he does, it's only because he feels it's his manly duty or something.

"Isn't it wonderful Audrey?" Lanna broke the tense silence. "We're only hours away from Primrose!"

"Oh yes, I can scarcely wait. I'm trying not to think on it so the time will pass more quickly," Audrey grasped Lanna's hand. She then felt Joseph's gaze, which made the walls of the carriage close in, making her feel very warm all of a sudden.

Lanna noticed her discomfort and quickly tried to help the situation. She looked at Jake Harper reading from his Bible once again. The precious book never left his side for more than a few seconds at a time.

"Jake, it would be so grand if you would read to us from your Bible. It would make the ride seem much faster."

"Oh...uh...why sure. I guess I could," the sailor nervously replied. "Where should I read from?"

"Just continue reading from where you are right now." Because the sailor was a bit nervous, he was a little slow at first. He'd never read aloud before since he could barely read to himself. Strangely enough, since he'd made the decision to read it anyway, something changed. It was as if he wasn't alone in doing it.

"'Let love be without dissimulation. Abhor that which is evil; cleave to that which is good. Be kindly affectioned one to another with brotherly love....'" Everyone began listening intently, except for Audrey. She couldn't seem to make herself pay attention. She just wanted to get there quickly, but only thirty minutes had passed and it already felt like an eternity.

"'Do not be overcome by evil; but overcome evil with good....'" Audrey's head jerked up when she heard it. It was the same verse that convinced her that Irish was truly her father. She felt her throat constrict and tears sting her eyes. Thankfully, no one seemed to notice as Jake Harper continued.

Lord, thank you so much for letting me meet my father. It was nearly worth being kidnapped just so I could see him and finally know the truth. She blinked a few times to keep from crying. Suddenly something inside of Audrey spoke to her heart.

"If it hadn't been for you, your father might not have made peace with the Lord before he died." Tears did come then, so she turned to glance out the small carriage window to try and hide them.

"Audrey, are you alright?" Lanna whispered and nudged her.

"Yes, I'm just thinking about some things." she slowly nodded in return.

"Are you going to tell Rose about meeting your father?"

"I don't know," was all Audrey could say as her thoughts swiftly moved to her mother. *I wonder what my family will think when we finally arrive. Are they still out looking for me? It's been nearly three months.* As she began rehearsing what she would tell her, Audrey drifted off to sleep.

"We're here. We're finally home!" Lanna excitedly shook Audrey's shoulder until she awoke. Once she saw that the carriage was parked in front of Primrose, Audrey immediately sat up and realized the time had come at last. Her heart quickened and she suddenly felt butterflies in her stomach as the hired driver come to the door and opened it. She slowly grasped his hand and stepped down, all the while gazing at her home. Lanna got out next and moved to her side. She wondered how Audrey planned to present herself to her family.

"Are you gonna knock?"

"I'm just…a little nervous all of a sudden," Audrey breathlessly replied.

"I'll go to the door if ya like," Lanna took charge and walked up to the large door, but before she knocked, she glanced back to wait until everyone was behind her and ready. After rapping the door several times, it was opened by Claire. As soon as she saw the young ladies, her hand immediately went to her mouth in sheer disbelief.

"Lord of mercy...my eyes must be failing me!" she gasped and, forgetting all formality, clasped both young ladies in a firm hug, nearly knocking them down in the process.

"Oh my! What am I thinking?" the maid suddenly ran back inside and began shouting frantically. "Miss Rose, Miss Rose! Come quickly," she screeched. It wasn't long before Audrey heard her mother's voice.

"Claire, what are you...." Rose stopped at the top of the grand staircase when she saw two young women standing in the doorway. But when she noticed tears in Claire's eyes, she felt her knees buckle. Claire gazed steadily at Rose as she very slowly walked down the stairs, one by one so she could get a closer look.

Silly maid, why won't she tell me who they are? She was about half way down, when a crying young woman, finally came into full view. Rose had to blink a few times to be certain she wasn't seeing things, for the girl looked exactly like her daughter.

Impossible. I'm just seeing things. It can't be!

As Audrey watched her mother's expression turn from curious to complete bewilderment, her voice left. How badly she wanted to call out to her mother and tell her she loved her, but try as she might, nothing came out.

"My—" Rose breathed and grabbed onto the banister, as her legs gave out from under her. Everyone gasped when she fell down several stairs.

"Mother!" Audrey was finally able to cry. Both Joseph and Jake Harper rushed to Rose's aid. While Claire and Lanna began fanning her flushed face, Audrey supported her mother's head.

"I should have known better than to spring this on her, without any warning," Claire whispered.

"What do you mean?" Audrey glanced up at the maid.

"We all thought you and Lanna...were dead."

"What? But how?"

"We thought you had drowned." Before Audrey could question Claire further, Rose's eyes fluttered open.

"Mother." At the sound of her daughter's voice, she immediately came to.

"How? I never thought I would see you again!" she started to weep as she slowly sat up and held Audrey's face in her hands to look at her.

"I love you so much," Rose cried. Audrey could only choke as they embraced. She had never heard her mother say that, nor had she experienced such love other than her Heavenly Father.

"I thought I'd lost you. How is it that you're alive?" Rose asked when she released Audrey.

"It's such a long story, but I'll tell you…I'll tell you everything." Audrey's father came to mind. She was about to reveal the news when she noticed her mother's gaze quickly move to the two strange men. "But first you must meet the men who helped us get home safely. In fact, if it weren't for them…well, I don't even want to think about it," Audrey glanced at the sailors, who helped Rose, then shyly stood to the side.

"Let me introduce Jake Harper and Joseph Brionny. This is my mother, Rose Wesley." Without warning Rose surprised everyone especially her daughter, by quickly embracing both men.

"Thank you for bringing her back to me," Rose then glanced over at the ladies maid. "And you, Lanna, I'm so happy to see you're alright." When she hugged her, Audrey was certain that her mother had indeed changed somehow.

"Please excuse my ill manners. Let's all go into the drawing room. You must all be famished," Rose turned and caught Claire's gaze. "Have cook prepare something, will you?"

"Yes ma'am," she happily replied and bustled out of the room.

Rose grasped Audrey's hand and was about to lead them through the foyer, when Audrey suddenly remembered something.

"Oh wait, we have some things in the carriage that the driver's probably waiting to unload."

"Don't worry, we'll get it," Jake Harper kindly offered.

Once they were seated in the drawing room, Audrey wanted to immediately tell Rose about who she met. But strangely enough, something told her to wait.

I have to wait until we can be alone for a while, she tried to calm herself. It was then that she noticed her mother staring at her. It was as if she was trying to take in everything that had just taken place.

I can't believe everyone thought we were dead. At the thought, Audrey recalled something else.

"Where are grandfather and grandmother?"

"Oh, father had some business in town, and mother insisted on accompanying him. They should be back shortly. They'll be so shocked when they find you're home. Oh Audrey, thank God you're alright!" Rose hugged her.

Thank God? What has happened since I've been away?

As the carriage moved closer to Primrose, Audrey's grandfather noticed a carriage sitting right outside the front entrance, but he didn't recognize it.

"Do you know whose carriage that belongs to?" Harold slightly leaned out of the window to get a closer look.

"What? What carriage?" Victoria looked out. Once she saw it, she sighed. "Oh, isn't that the Foster's carriage? I already told her I didn't want to join the sewing project. Why must she keep bothering me about it?"

"Well, I don't know. It doesn't look like the Foster's," Harold replied.

When they stopped behind the mysterious carriage, they saw two men unloading some things from it.

What's going on here? A strange feeling came over Harold as he slowly stepped out of his carriage before his wife and approached them.

"May I help you?" he called to the driver, who was sitting up on the seat, holding the reigns.

"I...uh...." the man stuttered then looked down at one of the men who was unloading.

"You there, what are you doing?" Harold moved closer.

"We're unloading our things," Jake Harper nervously replied as Joseph came out of the house to get another load to bring inside. Victoria walked up and took the words right out of her husband's mouth.

"Who's things? Who are you?" However, once Joseph saw Mr. Wesley's stern expression, he froze.

"I'm Jake Harper and that's Joseph. We've come with Miss Wesley and Miss Ryan," Upon hearing this, Harold felt like the wind had been knocked out of him.

"What did you say?"

"Audrey and Lanna...they've returned," Jake said again.

Before running inside to see for himself, Harold wondered exactly who the men were and why Jake would refer to his granddaughter in such an informal manner. When Harold and Victoria rushed into the room and saw Audrey, tears swiftly came to their eyes.

"Audrey, your alive!" Victoria cried as Audrey jumped up and embraced her warmly. She then turned to Harold.

"It can't be true," he whispered as Audrey fell into his arms.

CHAPTER THIRTY

S everal hours had passed and Audrey had only begun telling her family all that had happened, when Claire suddenly entered the room.

"Mrs. Gordon and her son are here."

"How strange, and right before dinner. Oh well, the more the merrier I suppose. I'm sure they'll be pleased to find that Audrey has come back to us," Victoria said from her place on a mahogany armchair.

"Claire, show them in then go and tell cook to plan for two more."

Oh bother, what do they want? I have so much I need to tell my family, especially about mother. Rupert Gordon is the last person I wanted to see today. Or any day for that matter! Audrey then caught a glimpse of Lanna, who wore a wry smile from across the room.

"Lanna Ryan, would you care to tell me why you're smiling at me like that?" Audrey asked, but couldn't help smiling herself. The ladies maid was about to answer when Beatrice and Rupert made their appearance and everyone got to their feet to greet them.

"Is it really true? You've given everyone quite a scare! Wherever have you been, child?" Beatrice asked when she greeted Audrey, but didn't pay any attention to Lanna or the two sailors.

Audrey could barely stand to look at Beatrice's son, who was standing behind her, trying to look as sweet and innocent as possible.

"Hello Mrs. Gordon, Rupert," she made herself greet Rupert so he might stop staring at her, but it was no use. "It's quite a long story. I'll have to tell you all about it some other time perhaps," she politely hinted and thought she heard a quiet chuckle escape her ladies maid.

"Let me introduce you to the two men who brought Audrey and Lanna home to us," Rose spoke up and bid the sailors to come closer.

"This is Jake Harper and Joseph Brionny."

"Why don't we all sit down until dinner is served," Victoria suggested when all of the introductions had been made.

Those were the men I saw with Audrey in Scottsford! Rupert recalled as he moved to a chair. *So all they did was bring her home?* However, right when he started to feel the least bit relieved, he caught Joseph and Audrey's gaze meet. Rupert thought he had been so clever rushing home and persuading his mother to stop in for a visit at Primrose. When in truth, he only wanted to find out who the mysterious men were. But now he was certain there was something more.

I will not lose Audrianna to some mere commoner!

"I have a splendid idea," Beatrice broke into her son's musings. "You should put on a ball, celebrating your return."

"I don't—" Audrey was about to protest, when her mother spoke up.

"Well, that might be a good idea, but she's just come back. Maybe in a few months."

Lord, thank you for the change in my mother. I pray we'll get a chance to speak soon and find out what's happened, Audrey smiled and decided to make the best of the Gordon's company and keep thanking God that she was home.

"That was a wonderful meal. What a feast," Beatrice wiped her mouth with her napkin.

"Well, it's not very often that my granddaughter, who was believed to be dead, comes home to us," Victoria smiled at Audrey, tears brimming in her eyes.

"It's so good to be home," Audrey replied. She momentarily looked at the very silent sailors. *It will be a bit hard to see them leave.*

"It's such a beautiful day. Perhaps we should go and sit in the garden for a while. We set up several chairs and a small table. It's where we've been having our tea of late," Rose suggested.

What? I thought mother disliked the garden?

"That sounds marvelous," Beatrice stood.

"Why don't you go ahead while the men and I retire to the library for a while," Harold spoke up.

"So if I understood correctly, you both worked for the same Captain who kidnapped my granddaughter?" Harold asked, once they all sat down and had been offered a cigar and something to drink.

"Yes, until the ship went down, that is," Jake Harper shyly replied.

"And you were the only survivor?"

"Aye, except for some who had been thrown overboard earlier."

"Amazing story. What do you plan to do now?" Rupert spoke up. Since Joseph didn't seem to be in much of a talking mood, Jake Harper kept answering.

"I haven't really thought about it. I worked on the St. Carlin so long that I thought I would do that forever. But the man who owns the vessel that brought us to England offered me a job...so I guess I'll do that," Jake then looked Joseph.

What? Jake never told me that, nor did Edmond offer me a job. Although, I could never work on the ship as long as Bridget travels with her father.

"And what of you?" Rupert interrupted the sailor's thoughts.

"Aye, what wus that?" Joseph blushed, for he couldn't remember what they were talking about.

"What are you planning to do now?"

"Well, I'll probably chucker something' aboyt the same as Jake. I'm a sailor...salt water flows through me veins."

Nearly half an hour had passed before the men finally decided to join the ladies outside, to watch the sun set. It couldn't have happened sooner for Joseph. He didn't know how much longer he could have been polite to the insolent Mr. Gordon.

As they walked down the hall to the back door, Rupert purposely slowed his pace so he could pull Joseph aside. He waited until Harold and the other sailor were far enough away before he spoke.

"Mr. Brionny," he called and waited for him to stop.

"Aye?" Joseph reluctantly turned to face him.

"Before we join the others, I just wanted to thank you," his voice lowered, "Thank you for returning my bride to be safely." Joseph didn't know what to say. He felt as if he'd been punched in the stomach.

"What?" he finally managed to ask for he didn't think he heard right.

"Right before Audrianna was captured, I asked her for her hand…and she happily accepted." Rupert tried his very best to hide the smirk on his face.

"She probably never mentioned it. One could hardly expect her to speak of such things with someone who was associated with her capture."

It all makes sense now. Audrey's been engaged to Rupert this entire time. She knew that once she returned, they'd be married. I've been such a fool…such a fool. How could she ever fall in love with someone like me, when she has Rupert?

"Oh, there you are. I must say you've missed some lovely weather, but there might be a little left for you after all," Beatrice greeted the men as they entered the beautiful garden. Everyone began talking when Audrey unconsciously felt her mother staring at her again. It swiftly reminded her of all the things she had to tell her. But how could they get away from everyone long enough?

I wish the Gordon's would leave soon. I can't bear to wait much longer.

"What is it?" Audrey asked when Rose's gaze remained.

"I just can't believe you're here...alive and well! I fear you might disappear if I look away for too long," Rose smiled warmly. It was then Audrey sighed heavily.

"Is something wrong?"

"Well," Audrey hesitated and glanced at both Beatrice and Rupert. Thankfully, they were too busy listening to Harold.

"I must speak with you, alone." Rose suddenly stood, gaining everyone's attention.

"If you would all excuse us, Audrey and I are going to take a walk. Thank you for coming Mrs. Gordon, Mr. Gordon. It was nice visiting with you."

My mother would rather talk with me then entertain? And not just anyone, but the Gordons for that matter! Audrey could barely contain her shock.

They finally left the group, but Audrey couldn't help noticing that her grandmother was not pleased with them for leaving so abruptly. As they strolled through the garden with their arms linked, Audrey still hadn't said anything, for she was silently rehearsing how to tell Rose. She just couldn't make herself start. Before Audrey knew it, they had already made their way past the garden and were now in the shaded woods that her grandparents owned. The same woods she'd been taken through atop the old wagon.

"I guess...I hardly know where to start," she finally broke the silence as they came to a halt. Rose turned to her daughter, her expression serious.

"What's wrong dear? Did they hurt you in any way? Did any of those men—"

"No, nothing like that," Audrey quickly spoke up.

"What is it?" Apprehension was beginning to rise up in Rose. *What could she possibly have to tell me that's making her so nervous?*

"I've told you all that has happened to me...except one thing," Audrey put her hand in her pocket and grasped the scarf that had been with her ever since Irish had given it to her. She then pulled it out very slowly.

"I met someone…." The moment she laid eyes on it, Rose covered her mouth with her trembling hand. She was suddenly back on the horrible ship, being dragged to a lifeboat. But she hardly noticed what was happening. Her eyes were fixed on her husband. He was helpless to save her and he held her scarf. He'd taken the same scarlet scarf Audrey now held.

She didn't say a word as she watched her mother fall to her knees and begin to cry loudly. Audrey immediately lowered herself to her side and cried with her while they clung to each other.

"How did he know you were his?" Rose managed to choke.

"He was a sailor on the ship I was taken to. Somehow he knew," Audrey replied as she handed the scarf to its rightful owner. Rose clutched the cloth and wiped away several tears, although it didn't do any good. They just kept coming. Rose was about to ask how he was, but she quickly found out.

"But he didn't make it," Audrey could barely continue through her cries. "He was on the ship when it went down. But before we were taken from each other, he said that he loved you and me…and always would. He told me everything would be alright," She had to stop, for her voice failed her. Several minutes passed before she could continue.

"I met my father, only to lose him."

"At least you were able to meet him. Evan was a wonderful man," Rose embraced her again. Audrey wanted to ask her more about him, but last time she tried, they ended up having a horrible argument. Unbeknown to her was that Rose was thinking the same thing.

I have to tell her, but yet, it's so painful to speak of.

"You've been set free from your past. You no longer have to be afraid, for I am with you." Something spoke to her heart.

Rose took a deep breath and slowly began.

"Evan Fintan, your father, was a gardener on an estate. Bettsthorne was only five miles from here, but was burned to the ground in a fire nearly sixteen years ago. One day I decided to go for a ride. I used to love to ride…for hours and hours. I never tired of it. When I was a several miles from home, something spooked my horse and I lost control. I didn't know what to do. When your father saw me, he quickly got one of the many Bettsthorne horses and rode after me. I don't know how he did it, but Evan caught up to me and grabbed the reins of my horse. He saved me. It wasn't long until we fell in love. I would ride over to see him nearly every day. However, when my parents found out, they forbid me from ever seeing him again because they didn't approve."

"Why didn't they approve?" Audrey in surprise.

"Well, he was poor, and an Irishman. So instead of getting my parents blessing, we ran away and were married in secret. Evan even quit his job so we wouldn't be found. My parents were furious. They searched everywhere for me, but they couldn't find us."

"Where were you?" Audrey asked again.

"We went to live in the part of town where more of the Irish lived. Our house was more like a shack, but I didn't mind, for we loved each other. A few months later, I found out I was in the family way. So, we decided to sell the little we had to gain passage to America." Rose continued. "But when we were about to board the ship, someone robbed us of all our money! It was everything we had. In desperation, we stowed away on the St. Carlin." Upon hearing this, Audrey gasped.

"We were so foolish to think we could get away with sneaking on board. We were quickly found of course and were brought to the Captain. That's when he found out about the shell."

"Jake Harper said that Captain McNeil had been trying to find the shell ever since he'd first laid eyes on it." Audrey finished.

"To think that Evan was alive all this time…and I never even cared to find out," Rose choked as tears came to her eyes again. But she was swiftly reminded that even though her husband was gone, Audrey was still there.

Audrey had gotten to her feet, then helped Rose.

"Audrey I'm sorry. I feel like I've lost so much time with you as well."

"That only means we'll have to make up for it," Audrey replied.

They started walking again before Rose continued her story.

"We heard the Captain order his men to throw us both overboard, but he never did...I don't know why. Instead, I was put on a small boat. I was never more frightened, not only for my sake, but for yours. He must have kept Evan on board."

"How did you ever make it?" Audrey asked.

"It's all a blur really. I can remember a big wave overtaking the boat and tipping me over. I couldn't swim, so I hung onto the side with everything in me. After what seemed like an eternity, another ship threw me a rope. They rescued me, but all I could think about was where the other ship had gone with my husband. When they brought me to land, I had nowhere to go but home. Needless to say, my parents weren't pleased to see that I was carrying a child, but they took me in and eventually forgave me. However, they did make me take Wesley for our names instead of Fintan. They thought it would somehow help the gossip. I have yet to understand how." At that, Rose fell silent. They walked for several minutes before Audrey finally spoke.

"Why did you think Lanna and I had drowned?" Rose then told Audrey all about David's letter, and giving Jesus her life as they made their way back to house.

Audrey couldn't believe her ears. Her mother went from saying there wasn't a God, to actually confessing Him as her Lord!

I never thought...I mean, I've prayed for so long!" Audrey stopped and had to embrace her mother once again. It was as if they reunited all over again.

"I'm so happy for you,"

"I've still said so many things...things that I regret—" Rose began, but was suddenly stopped.

"Mother, you're forgiven of all your past mistakes. God has promised that He won't remember them, and I won't either."

"Thank God for that," Rose sighed, "I was so consumed with the past. It seemed to choke the very life out of me. I couldn't get free. That is, until I found the Lord, or rather until I finally let Him in."

"Before we go inside, I must ask you something. It's about Lanna."

"Yes? What is it?"

"Lanna and I have always been close, but after everything we both have gone through, we've grown closer than sisters. So I've been thinking, could we hire another ladies maid to take her place and make Lanna my true sister? I couldn't stand to see her return to waiting on me when she saved my life numerous times."

"I couldn't agree more," was all Rose said in return. Audrey was overjoyed. Lanna wouldn't have to wait on anyone ever again!

Rose never did tell Audrey about almost ending her life the day she thought her only daughter had died, nor the mysterious voice that had stopped her. Somehow, she couldn't bring herself to say it, as if it was too sacred to speak of.

Audrey could hardly wait to tell Lanna the wonderful news as they joined everyone in the drawing room, She sighed with relief when she found that the Gordons had finally left. She then happily took a seat beside her ladies maid and was about to speak, when Rose beat her to it.

"Lanna, could I speak to you for a minute?" Everyone's gaze moved to the ladies maid, who suddenly looked nervous.

"Alright," Lanna stood and slowly walked out of the room behind Rose.

"Is something wrong?" she asked, waiting to be scolded. *I knew I should have immediately returned to my room to change back into a maid uniform. What did I expect? We're back now and everything will go back to the way it was.* She tried to think of a way to explain why she hadn't returned to her duties straight away, but in truth, Lanna promised Audrey on the long carriage ride over that she wouldn't.

But Rose will never believe that.

"No, everything is wonderful," Rose replied, "I've talked with Audrey and we've decided that you will no longer be required to fulfill the duties of a ladies maid."

"What?" Lanna blurted before she could stop herself. This was far worse than what she feared would happen.

I will not just leave! I can't.

"I'm sorry, but I don't think I could bear leavin' Audrey. We're cronies," she boldly stood up to Rose Wesley for the first time in her life.

"No, that's not what—I'm sorry. What I meant to say was we want you to stay on with us, not as a maid, but as Audrey's sister," Rose grasped the shorter woman's hand. Upon hearing this, tears came to Lanna's eyes.

"Are you certain? Jaykers!"

Everyone stayed up talking late into the night for no one seemed to remember to retire.

"Well, I suppose," Harold yawned and finally stood up after looking at his pocket watch and realized the time.

"I've had Claire ready your room for you," Victoria also got to her feet and informed the sailors.

"I'm sure you'll be most comfortable, although you'll have to share it because Rose has informed me that Lanna will be staying in the other one," she continued, but said the last part almost under her breath. She was quite perturbed about the entire situation.

"Thank you for your kindness," Jake Harper replied, but Joseph was too busy looking at Audrey, who had just fallen asleep. How he wanted to go to her and hold her. He'd had to fight the urge countless times in the past few weeks.

When Rose noticed Joseph's steady gaze, she followed it and also saw her sleeping daughter.

"The day has been too much for her, I see," she moved closer to her and touched Audrey's cheek to wake her up before Joseph had a chance to offer to carry her upstairs himself.

"Dear, it's time to retire."

"Oh, I'm sorry," Audrey stirred, but had a hard time opening her eyes.

"Goodnight everyone," Rose said as she led her daughter out of the room and up the stairs, with Lanna following behind.

Will I ever be able to speak to Audrey about Joseph's apology? The former ladies maid asked herself.

CHAPTER THIRTY-ONE

$\mathcal{J}$ ake Harper awoke when he heard a strange noise, but immediately relaxed when he saw Joseph washing in the basin. He then realized it was morning.

"Where are you off too?" Jake yawned.

"Nowhere," the sailor lied once he'd finished drying his face. Joseph was actually planning to find Lanna as quickly as he could, to stop her from speaking to Audrey about his apology. It no longer mattered.

And even if she did forgive me, Audrey would never pick me over Rupert. He's rich, and a true gentleman. I don't even stand a chance.

"Would ya like to borrow my Bible today?" Jake Harper asked. Joseph had nearly forgotten.

"Aye, that I wud. Thank ya." Joseph took the black book from Jake and left.

Although he really didn't know where Lanna might be, Joseph thought he would start his search in the dining room. Unfortunately, the only person sitting at the large table, was Harold.

"Well, good morning, son. Come and have a bite to eat with me. Other than Jake Harper, I'm afraid everyone else has already eaten."

Uh, no thank ya. I'm not pure starval jist yet. I wus actually wonderin' where…." Joseph hesitated because he wasn't sure what to call Audrey and Lanna, especially in front of her grandfather.

"You're wondering where Audrey and Lanna went?" Harold finished and smiled at the sailor. Joseph's face grew red as he nodded in return.

"They went with Rose and my wife into town, although I haven't the slightest idea what they're doing there. Women are mysterious creatures, you know," Harold chuckled and poured himself another cup of tea.

"Aye, I think I'll go for a walk," Joseph sighed and made his way down the hall toward the back door.

He began to walk down the road when he decided to visit the inviting garden. Once there, he sat down in a shady spot, and leaned against a large tree. Unbeknown to the sailor, was that he was now sitting in the exact spot Audrey loved. He held up Jake Harper's Bible and looked at it, but he couldn't make himself open it. All he could do was flip through the pages, over and over.

I don't know where to start. If I could only ask Audrey...she would know.

Several hours later, Joseph hadn't started reading the precious book, nor did he see Audrey until dinner was served. But now, he couldn't make himself ask her in front of everyone. However, he probably wouldn't have been able to ask if he wanted to, for the women were quite busy discussing what they had done all day. He barely heard Lanna, excitedly describe all the dresses they were going to have made.

I'll just ask her after we're done eating. Then I'll go to Lanna, the sailor told himself.

When everyone was finished nearly an hour later, Audrey suggested they all go to the garden to enjoy another sunset. Everyone happily agreed and began to get up and make their way out of the dining room, leaving Joseph with the feeling that he'd lost yet another opportunity to speak to her. That is, until he noticed Audrey's pace was slower than the others. This was his chance! He finally stopped fighting with himself when he watched her come to a halt and turn to look at him.

What is he doing? Audrey thought. He was standing there, with his hands in his pockets. She finally decided to put aside her feelings.

I'm being impossible by not speaking to him. After all, he did help me get home.

"Aren't you going to come?"

"Aye," Joseph slowly approached.

"I wonder if I might 'av a ward with ya?"

"Yes?" she felt her face grow warm. Was he going to finally explain his actions?

"I wus aboyt ter start readin' from Jake's Bible today, but I don't nu where to begin. I thought maybe you wud." Audrey tried not to appear disappointed.

"I would probably start in the book of John. It's wonderful, but then again, the whole book is life changing." Joseph desperately wanted to ask her about Rupert, but he held his tongue.

It would only make matters worse...and it wouldn't be proper. The sailor repeatedly told himself.

"Audrey, are you coming?" Lanna called from the doorway, but when she saw that they were finally speaking to each other, she scolded herself for interrupting.

I'm such a doss! The one time Audrey and Joseph are talking, and what do I do? I ruin the whole thing.

"I'm coming," Audrey quickly replied. As Joseph watched her leave, he didn't follow. Instead, he decided to go to his room to do some long awaited reading.

The next morning, Joseph finally decided what had to be done. It was still fairly early, but he couldn't lay there, trying to fall asleep any longer. He nearly jumped out of bed and made his way to the stable to see if he could borrow a horse to go into town.

The sailor still hadn't returned as everyone finished eating a late breakfast. They were going to wait for his return, but by ten o'clock, it was apparent that he wasn't going to appear, at least not for a while.

"Are you certain you don't know where Joseph went?" Audrey asked Jake Harper once again, but she immediately blushed when everyone glanced at her.

"He was gone before I awoke," Jake replied.

Audrey didn't know why, but it actually bothered her that Joseph would leave without telling anyone, especially her.

What do I expect? I haven't exactly treated him well. I haven't given him any reason to stay. Surely he'll be back, she told herself. *He wouldn't leave without saying goodbye… would he?* Then as if on cue, Joseph walked through the front door.

"Joseph, there you—" Audrey shouted, but stopped herself in mid-sentence. Thankfully no one noticed her sudden outburst, for Jake Harper asked the very same thing.

"There you are. Where have you been, mate?" Jake went over to him and roughly patted him on the back. However, he only smiled in return.

Audrey couldn't believe how happy she was to see the man again.

What's wrong with me? One minute I can't stand him, and then I'm overjoyed to see him, the next! She swiftly pushed aside her musings when she realized that Joseph wasn't answering Jake's questions.

"Is everything alright?"

"Aye, I'm sorry that I lef withoyt tellin' anyone. I went into town. I 'ope it wus alright that I borrowed a horse."

"Quite alright," Harold quickly answered.

"I stopped at the wee 'arbor and foun' a ship that's sailin' at dawn. I plan ter be on it," Joseph quietly stated and glanced at Audrey, who was so surprised she couldn't speak.

He's leaving? He's really leaving us? I guess I knew he would sometime…but so soon?

"Where will you go, son?" Harold was the first one to break the silence.

"Wherever the wind takes me I guess. I thanks ye for al' your kindness."

"I suppose this 'ill be the last time we see you, Joseph." Lanna spoke up as everyone sauntered out into the hall, about to retire.

"She's right," Jake Harper put in. Everyone suddenly stopped, including Audrey, who still couldn't speak for fear of breaking down.

Victoria, Harold, and Rose took their turns shaking the sailor's hand and again thanking him for bringing Audrey home. Lanna was next. After stepping up to him, she gave him a quick hug, then took his hand.

"Thank you for everything," the former ladies maid said, tears in her eyes.

"You'll alwus be a corker," Joseph chuckled.

"I'm sorry I never got a chance to do what you asked," she continued, but only in a whisper.

"That's alright. Mind yerself," Joseph replied.

While she waited for her turn, Audrey told herself several times to remain calm and not to cry, but now knew it would be impossible. She felt herself trembling as she slowly stepped forward.

Lanna wished her dear friend could've said goodbye to the sailor a few moments alone, but it was not to be.

"Thank you," Audrey began and thought she sounded much calmer than she truly felt. Everyone's eyes were fixed on her.

"If it hadn't been for you…." Suddenly her voice failed her. *Oh no, not now!*

"It's gran' so. I wus glad to 'elp. I'm jist sorry for everythin' ye 'ad ter go through," Joseph tried to avoid eye contact as best he could so he wouldn't show any emotion. *Don't make this harder than it already is!* He told himself. It was easier said than done. The sailor was about to turn away, but then Audrey spoke.

"Right before…we arrived at England, you said you wanted to tell me something. What was it?" Joseph couldn't believe she remembered or even cared. However, now that Audrey finally asked, Joseph couldn't make himself say it in front of her entire family.

"Oh, it doesn't matter anymore," was all he managed to say.

"Alright," Audrey slowly backed away, but the sailor seemed like he wanted to say more.

"I'll have a carriage ready for you in the morning," Harold stated.

Joseph and Audrey never did fall asleep. The sailor couldn't stop trying to come up with a reason to stay. All night he fought with himself. But how could he stay? He had nothing; nothing to build a life on.

And even if I had the means to make Audrey my wife, she's promised to another. She would never pick me over Rupert, Joseph tossed and turned in frustration. *Lord, can't You show me a way? Can't You make a way? I love Audrey, but I fear that's not enough,* Suddenly a thought came to him. *What if I could get the means...working on The Olivia!* For a few wonderful moments, he thought he'd found the answer. But he swiftly came back to reality.

Rupert...she's to marry Rupert. She's loves him and my staying would only ruin things. And I don't want to do anything to interfere with her happiness. Besides, I'd never be accepted being Irish and furthermore, Edmond Thomas never offered me a job...only Jake Harper. And that was it. Joseph made up his mind then and there. But it did little to calm his mind enough to sleep.

CHAPTER THIRTY-TWO

" ake, Jake Harper," Joseph whispered and nudged the
sailor's shoulder until he stirred.

"What is it?"

"I jist wanted ter say goodbye before I left," Joseph said,
his voice still a bit groggy.

"Are you sure you want to leave so soon?" Jake sat up and
rubbed his eyes.

"Aye, it's time. Ya can cum with me if ye loike," Joseph
suggested and hoped he would consider it.

"I think I'll stay a few more days. Hey, when you go into
town, will you take this letter for me and send it?" Jake opened the
small drawer of the bed stand and took out an envelope. "It's to
Edmond Thomas, telling him to send for me when they sail again.
You could stay until then and go with me?" It was now Jake's turn
to ask.

"Thank ya, but I've made up me mind," Suddenly Joseph
smiled. Strangely enough, the simple act made Jake blush.

"What are you smilen' for?"

"The same reason your bake is turnin' red...same color as a
certain *rose*," Joseph chuckled when Jake Harper quit hiding it,
and grinned sheepishly.

"I think you'd better go before the ship leaves without you,"
Jake teased.

"Alright, but you're not foolin' me," With that, the sailors
shook hands then Joseph finally took his leave.

"You're making a mistake in leaving," Jake Harper whispered
to himself once Joseph was gone. If truth be told, the sailor had no
idea how much his job offer tempted Joseph.

Audrey suddenly awoke. She was surprised she'd finally fallen asleep. When she slowly glanced up at the grandfather clock that read eight o'clock, Audrey jumped out of bed. She grabbed her robe and rushed down the hall toward one of the spare bedrooms. After she found that the door was wide open and the bed was empty, she walked back to her own room and quickly dressed.

Once she looked presentable, Audrey made her way downstairs. However, before she entered the dining room, she breathed in and out to calm herself.

"Good morning, dear," Rose greeted as Audrey entered and looked at everyone.

"Has Joseph left already?" she asked as nonchalantly as she could and took a seat at the end of the table near her grandfather.

"Well yes…he did say he would be gone before sun up. Don't you remember?" Rose asked.

"Oh, yes of course." Audrey sighed and suddenly felt very foolish.

As breakfast was served, Audrey felt Harold's gaze, so she looked up at him.

"Anna, I wonder if I might speak with you in the library for a moment." He simply stood, pulled Audrey's chair back for her, and followed her out.

Harold closed the door behind them and motioned for Audrey to take a seat. He sat on the edge of his desk located in the middle of the room.

"May I ask what is going on between you and Joseph?" he quickly began.

"What…are you talking about? There's nothing between us, and never will be. He's gone," Audrey replied much faster than she intended.

"Anna, you're not fooling anyone." Audrey recalled what her mother had said earlier about her parents not approving of Evan because he was Irish.

"I've seen...we've all witnessed how Joseph looked at you. And you at him, I might add," Harold stated and crossed his arms over his chest. Audrey didn't know what to say. She was completely taken back.

"Do you love him?" Several silent moments followed the bold inquiry. Audrey desperately tried to come up with a truthful answer.

It doesn't matter anyway. He's gone! "Yes grandfather...yes I do," she slowly stated. Embarrassment washed over her so quickly that she buried her face in her hands, waiting to be chastised.

"And you let him leave without telling him so?"

"What?" she couldn't believe her ears!

"Why did you let him leave?" Harold asked again and smiled. He'd never seen his granddaughter so flustered. It only confirmed how much she truly loved the sailor.

"Joseph left because he doesn't love me. He didn't want me," tears stung her eyes.

"How do you know?"

"Because he loves...someone else."

"No he doesn't." Harold argued, "Not from what I've seen in only three days!"

"Why would he leave then? I'll never see him again. What would you have me do?" Audrey stood and walked over to the window for her tears flowed freely now.

"We could go after him." Audrey quickly spun around at his preposterous suggestion. But when she saw that he was serious, she didn't know what to think, only that it would be impossible.

"He left before dawn. He's long gone by now."

"No, ships are almost always delayed," Harold reassured and moved closer to her.

"Alright...if you're certain," she finally agreed.

As they walked down the hall, Audrey suddenly stopped.

"Shouldn't we tell someone where we're going?"

"We don't have time for that," he replied and kept walking to the front door.

"Why do you approve?" Audrey finally made herself ask once they were seated in the carriage.

"What do you mean?" he asked as they rode down their driveway and passed the white washed fence that lined the entrance of Primrose. She took a deep breath then continued.

"Well, Joseph has no means…and he's obviously Irish. Mother told me how she met father."

"I've made mistakes that I terribly regret. If it hadn't been for my stubbornness, your mother's life would have been far different. Evan might still be alive. I loathe what I've done…and I will not ruin your life as well," Harold's gazed moved to the window for quite some time.

When they finally drove into town, it began to rain. Audrey first thought the ride home was long, but this was far worse than the mere hour it took to get to Augustine. She began to silently pray as the carriage made its way through town and to the small harbor. It was the same place where Audrey had been taken aboard the St. Carlin. However, it seemed so much closer when she'd been taken through the woods.

Audrey was much too nervous to look out the window, once the carriage came to a halt. So instead, she watched her grandfather glance out. Unfortunately, his expression instantly turned from hopeful to solemn.

"That's alright grandfather. It was kind of you to accompany me all this way," she tried to hide the disappointment in her voice, but to no avail.

"I'm so sorry my dear," Harold managed to reply.

Suddenly, she couldn't take it anymore. She quickly opened the door and climbed out into the rain.

"Anna, come back inside! You'll catch your death out there," he shouted after her. The guilt was more than he could bear.

"I have to be certain he's gone," Audrey shouted in return. But there wasn't a single ship in the harbor.

Harold finally got out and made her return to the carriage. As they made their way back home, the silence grew more and more, tense every mile that passed, but the rain had stopped and the sun came out again.

"I'm going to the garden for a while," Audrey climbed out of the carriage after her grandfather, and spoke for the first time since they left the empty harbor.

"Are you sure you're alright?" Harold turned and asked.

"You mustn't worry about me," Audrey forced a smile. She moved to the pathway that led to the back of the house before her tears had a chance to fall. She didn't want her grandfather to see how upset she truly was.

Audrey made her way to her favorite spot and immediately fell to her knees. She felt the still wet grass seep through her skirts. She could finally let her tears flow freely.

When Harold walked in the door, he was surprised when Claire wasn't there to meet him. He then took off his coat, and went in search for everyone. However, when he heard laughing coming from the parlor, his pace quickened.

He found everyone seated and facing none other than Joseph Brionny!

"Oh, there you are. Where did you and Audrey disappear too?" Victoria asked.

"Look who's come back," Rose stated before Harold could reply.

"What a lovely surprise," he finally said and tried not to appear overly excited. Fortunately, there was a seat right beside the sailor on the settee. He quickly took it and tried to get Joseph's attention without gaining anyone else's. The conversation continued then, and Harold decided that now was his chance.

"Joseph," he whispered as the sailor turned to face him. "Audrey...she—"

"I noticed that she didn't cum in with ya," Joseph finished.

"She's in the garden and wants to speak to you," Harold smiled.

"I'll go to her then," the sailor calmly replied, but inside, he wanted to run out of the room as fast as he could. "Excuse me everyone. I'll be back in a bit," he immediately stood and left.

"Is he alright?" Victoria glanced over at Harold in question.

"Oh yes, quite alright."

Joseph had to continually make himself slow his pace on his way to the garden. Suddenly, he heard someone. A woman's crying. Fear quickly washed over him as he moved closer. Then he found her. Audrey was kneeling inside the garden. Joseph's first urge was to run to her side to see if she was alright, but something stopped him. Audrey wasn't only crying, she was also talking to someone. The sailor took a few more steps until he hid behind a nearby tree and listened intently.

She's talking to God, he finally realized, although it was hard to understand her plight through her cries.

"Lord, when I was on the St. Carlin, I made the decision to trust you no matter what. It was only then You gave me the peace and hope that saw me home safely. But...I don't understand what's happening. Did I do something wrong? Did I make a mess of things?" Audrey prayed as her cries momentarily grew louder.

Joseph's heart went out to her, even though he didn't really know what she was talking about. But his confusion soon faded as Audrey continued.

"I love him...I love him and now he's gone."

She loves me? Audrey loves me! Tears stung the sailor's eyes. However, now the question was, when should he declare himself and tell her that he'd overheard her confession?

Please show me what to do. Now it was Joseph's turn to pray.

"Help me to move on. I know that with Your help, Father. I can move on...and somehow forget him. Help me to continue to put my trust in You. I give You everything. My future and all of my hopes are Yours." Audrey grew silent then and began to wipe her tears.

Alright, it's now or never, Joseph took a deep breath and came out from behind the tree. Her back was still turned towards him, so he cleared his throat. Although he didn't want to frighten her, she jumped anyway.

"I'm sorry," he said as she quickly got to her feet, but tripped over her wet skirts. When she finally met his gaze, Joseph felt embarrassed for her. Her face grew quite red.

"Joseph, I thought I would never see you again," she choked, trying to regain her composure.

Joseph could see that she immediately became nervous, wondering if he had heard her prayer or not.

"I a…accidentally overheard ye. I'm sorry."

Audrey didn't say anything, but her mind was reeling.
What must he think of me? Probably that I'm an immature child, with a silly infatuation. Blast this horrible blushing!
"I couldn't make meself git on the ship."

Audrey quickly raised her hand to her face and found that it was very warm indeed.
I can't let him see me like this. She then glanced down.
"I know you're promised to another, but I couldn't leave without telling you…."
Promised to another? Audrey was completely confused. *Rupert!* The thought suddenly came to her.
"I want to ask you to forgive me…for everything." Joseph moved closer.
Father, let this be true, Audrey silently prayed. Her heart pounded loudly, but she still couldn't make herself look up at him. She was about to tell the sailor that she'd already forgiven him, when he stepped closer. He grasped Audrey's hand and felt it tremble in his own.
Lord, help me tell her, Joseph gently drew her even closer, but she still wouldn't meet his gaze.
"Audrey, I…." Revealing his true feelings was the hardest thing Joseph had ever done. But regardless, he couldn't lose her.

She could barely take it in. First she feared she'd lost him forever and now he was not only back, but standing before her, very near. Joseph slowly reached out, tenderly touched her chin, and raised it so she would look at him. When she finally gazed into his eyes, they enraptured her heart. His lips brushed against her cheek as he whispered, "I love you."

Audrey could hardly breathe. Everything she'd hoped and dreamed was swiftly coming to pass, but she couldn't say a word.

When Joseph heard her sigh, confirming that she heartily felt the same, they embraced.

"Audrey, will you wait for me?"

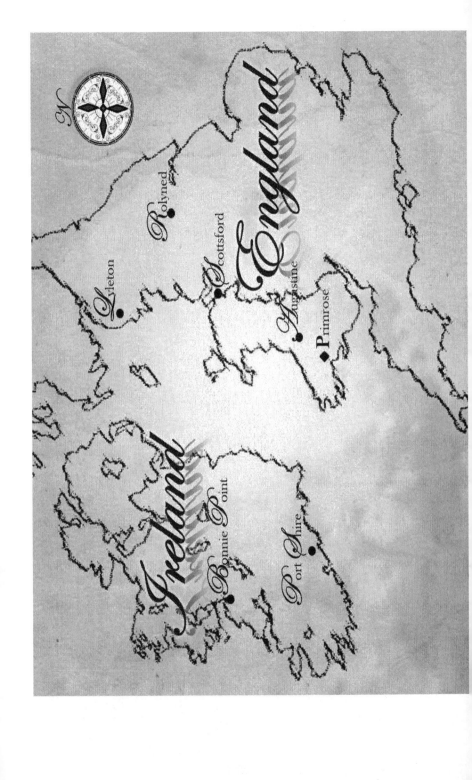

Sneak Peek of Book 2
(Coming Soon!)

"We're leaving now, so get your brother and wake up Benjamin." William started to move toward the door, but Theodore stiffly stood in the way. It was only when William met his gaze that Theodore spoke, "Wait…a moment. I just have to say…I don't have words to express how sorry I am and how much I regret what I've done," his voice was hoarse and filled with emotion. William was completely taken aback by it. It was the last thing he ever thought he would hear. However, the refreshing, yet at the same time sorrowful confession quickly became distasteful as he continued, "As much as it's difficult to hear what Loren and Elizabeth speak of," Theodore gulped, "I agree with them." William grimaced and quickly looked away in disgust. His father never looked him in the eye, and now that he finally had, although for a brief moment, Theodore began to doubt the plan. He knew fully well that what he was planning to say next would not bode well. But he had to. This was his only chance to spare himself and his brothers from searching all over England for someone who was most likely deceased.

"Well, it doesn't matter who or what you agree with, now does it? No one is asking for your opinion," William then approached and strangely enough touched his son's arm, but it wasn't an act of affection. He was merely pushing Theodore aside so he could pass by and leave.

"Come along, we're leaving straight away." He began to walk away, so in a desperate act to stop him, Theodore swiftly spoke, "I won't be going with you in the morning." William came to a halt just as he had hoped.

"What?" At his cold tone, Theodore almost wished his father wouldn't have stopped and turned to face him.

"I say, what was that?"

"Seeing as I'm…" Theodore wavered, but forced himself to continue, "of age, I would like to remain here and finish my education." He was doing a horrible job of standing up for himself, but he couldn't back down now.

"And what if I was to disown you and have you thrown out of Kenwood?" By William's furious tone of voice, it was obvious that he was seething. Theodore was glad he hadn't revealed more of the plan that Edwin wasn't to accompany him either. At least he wouldn't mention it just yet.

"Loren has offered to let me stay with him and Elizabeth." Theodore braced himself, but William didn't move. However, he began to shake with rage. Theodore looked down for but a second, when he glanced back up, he didn't have time to think for his father charged towards him and didn't stop until he roughly pinned Theodore against the wall.

"How dare you speak to me with such insolence!" It wasn't until the pain in his back momentarily subsided, that Theodore realized William was only inches from his face and his hand around his neck.

"It's because of you we're in this unspeakable mess, so you are going to do everything in your power to get her back!" William's grip was slowly getting tighter. It took everything in him to finally release Theodore and walk away, leaving his son gasping for air and feeling like a hopeless coward.

The morning came bright and clear. The calm winds promised that the sailing would be easy. The crew had been working long before dawn, loading the necessary cargo to make sure they'd be ready to leave as soon as possible.

William and the boys were just finishing up directing the crew as to where to put the rest of their belongings when they saw a carriage approach. William immediately recognized it and was surprised to see Loren and Elizabeth emerge from it when it came to a halt.

"We had to come to see you off." Elizabeth forced a smile as she walked over to embrace the somber Theodore, Edwin, and Benjamin as Loren slowly moved to William's side.

"I didn't think you would come," William stiffly spoke but didn't turn to shake his brother-in-law's outstretched hand. Instead, he continued to stare at the busy ship before them.

"I'm fully aware that you think I'm heartless, but I'm not entirely unfeeling. You're like a brother to me." When Loren placed his hand on William's shoulder, he finally glanced over at him, his gaze still guarded.

"I think of you dearly as well. I only wish you weren't trying to continually change my mind when I'm immovable. Why couldn't you have supported my decision? Our last moments together could have been far different."

"But can't you see that you're making a mistake?" Loren tried to interrupt him, but William swiftly cut him off.

"Instead, you go behind my back which you had no right to do." Loren was dumbfounded. As much as he knew William spoke the truth, he hated the feeling of being caught in his own scheme.

"I would have embraced you and thanked you for your help, but now I don't know what to say other than, never make plans with my son behind my back." With that, he walked away from Loren and made his way to his sister.

"Goodbye, dear."

"Goodbye," Elizabeth replied and quickly kissed his cheek. Tears streamed down her face. This was the scene that Captain Vincent Pearce came upon. He didn't want to intrude on this solemn family gathering, but he had to. William made it very clear that he wanted to leave as quickly as they could.

"Sir, the ship is completely readied and waiting for you to say the word."

"We'll leave straight away." William quickly replied. "Edwin, Theodore, come along." He then took Benjamin, who was crying, by the hand and followed the Captain up the gangplank, never looking back to Loren or his sister. Benjamin on the other hand waved goodbye to them.

Edwin and Theodore shook their uncle's hand while he tried to offer them one last word of encouragement.

"I'm sorry we couldn't change your father's mind, but I'm sure everything will be alright. It will all work out in the end as soon as he realizes his decision to be foolish." Unfortunately, as they slowly made their way to the ship, Theodore knew it would be a long time before William would ever admit to being wrong. It was then that Edwin spoke to him for the first time in days.

"I've never hated anyone more than I loathe you at this moment," he said through clenched teeth. Theodore would have preferred his brother's silence rather than this, especially when he was helpless to change anything.

Kelly Aul lives in a small, rural town in Minnesota with her parents and two younger siblings. They were homeschooled which made their family very close. Growing up, Kelly had a very vivid imagination. She was always pretending, making up games with her siblings, and finding adventure around her home on a small lake. Kelly is enthralled with European history, especially the 19th century, writing, and most importantly the things of God. She is in full time ministry, along with her family, studying to be a pastor. She also works part time as a pharmacy technician.

Some people might be thinking, "Why do you have to mention God throughout this whole book? Dedication and everything?"

"Whatsoever ye do in word or deed, do all in the name of the Lord Jesus." (Colossians 3:17)

I can't stop talking about Him because He *is* my everything. And because He's my everything, God is in everything I do.

I've read some Christian novels, and it seems almost as if they try to go as close to the edge as they can and still call it a Christian book, but the question shouldn't be how close can I get before crossing the line. It should be, how close can I get to God? How much can I talk about Him? How can I give more glory to Him?

I don't ever want my readers to have to ask themselves, "Should I be reading this? Would God read this book? Could I read this book in front of my pastor or parents without guilt?

Thank you for reading. I hope you enjoyed yourself and were inspired. And I have to say again, I give God all the glory for every part of this book. Without Him, I can do nothing.

— God bless, Kelly

Jesus said, except a man be born again, he cannot see the kingdom of God. (John 3:3) Being born again or the New Birth is not: confirmation, church membership, water baptism, being moral, doing good deeds.

Ephesians 2:8-9 "For by grace are ye saved through faith; and that not of yourselves: it is the gift of God: not of works, lest any man should boast."

You have to simply admit you are just what the Bible says — a lost sinner. Then you come and accept what Christ has purchased for you — a gift! (Romans 10:9-10)

Please pray this prayer to receive Jesus as your Savior.

Dear Heavenly Father, I believe in my heart that Jesus Christ is the son of God, that He was crucified, died, and rose from the dead.

I ask you, Lord Jesus, to be Lord of my life. Thank you for saving me and coming into my heart, for forgiving me and redeeming me from all sin.

It's important to find a church where they teach the Word of God by studying right from the Bible, and to renew your mind by reading the Bible every day.

— Maggie Aul, Senior Pastor
Love of God Family Church
www.LoveofGodFamilyChurch.com

❖ Please visit the Official Author Site

   www.kellyaul.com

❖ Like on Facebook

   facebook.com/AudreysSunrise

❖ Follow on Twitter

   twitter.com/AudreysSunrise

❖ Watch Audrey's Sunrise Book Preview Video

   http://youtu.be/mrgABZLImjc

Also available for Kindle on Amazon.com!

Made in the USA
Charleston, SC
25 November 2013